ROBIN MARR

Blood Hunt

First published by Metaphoric Media 2021

Cover Design by Melody Simmons

First edition

This book was professionally typeset on Reedsy.
Find out more at reedsy.com

To Dawn

Well, you said you expected something special...

Contents

A Messenger

The hairs on the back of my neck bristled as I foamed up a full jug of milk on the steamer. Nothing too dramatic, so I didn't spin around and scan the shop for trouble. When the milk was hot enough, I banged the jug on the worktop—for effect as much as to get the foam to rise—then poured it into the mixing bowl-sized cup I had already thrown eight shots into. Then I got the J-shaped template and sprinkled chocolate flakes over the top of the foam. No cheap cocoa dust at Jimmy's.

The cup was a two-handed carry, and the recipient was about an inch taller and five pounds heavier than me. Or that's how he looked. In Jimmy's, appearances could be deceptive.

Only once Ollie, if that was his name, had scuttled off to swim in his coffee, did I sweep my eyes across the room. It looked quiet enough, but I still felt edgy. Grabbing a towel and a tray, I meandered through the customers, retrieving the occasional empty cup and wiping down tables whether they were dirty or not, so long as they got me closer to the disturbance.

The room seemed normal. Israfil was on the sound stage, blowing some muted blues through his trumpet, and the babble of noise sounded like it always did. Still, an angry buzz hung in the air. Not something I could hear, but more like an itch in my mind. And not just angry, but bitter and vengeful. Each time I crossed the room, I got closer to nailing it down.

And there it was. Just as I found the specific head the anger was coming from, the body it was connected to jumped from its chair and spun around. A long knife glittered in the air, raised to stab into the back of someone sitting at the next table. Nobody could move fast enough to intervene. Except me. I gripped his wrist in an imaginary hand, and shouted "*Stasis!*"

"VI-O-*LATION!*"

The roar from the bar filled the room and everybody stopped, glancing towards the back wall. Jimmy, displeased, came out from behind the bar like a destroyer leaving port. Everybody looked to see where he was heading, and found me.

"Oh, come on," I yelled.

"Violation," Jimmy repeated, and I was left wondering how he knew so quickly. Unless he had been looking right at me when I used my magic.

The individual holding the knife was squirming, trying to get his arm out of my grip, or to at least let go of the knife. The creature underneath the blade realized it had been the target and slid its chair sideways until it could rise to its feet. Unhappy at the attention it was drawing, it bolted for the door.

Jimmy arrived and plucked the knife from the would-be assassin's grip, his oversize hand moving with unexpected delicacy. The bad guy tried to run when I let go. He didn't make a second step before Jimmy's other hand grabbed the back of his shirt and held him in place. Two of the door staff arrived seconds later and took over.

"First rule?" Jimmy's enormous voice boomed out around

the room like he had a radio mic to the PA.

"No fighting," came the congregational response.

"Take him out, and add him to the ward's no entry list," Jimmy told the bouncers. "One year ban."

He turned around, looking at his flock. "*Second* rule?"

"No *magic*," came the ritual response.

"Penalty?"

"One year."

I thumped him on the arm. "I work here, you jerk. And for free."

"Insubordination," he bellowed, his face a mask of astonished outrage, and the room roared with laughter. He patted down the noise and held up the knife. "I grant extenuating circumstances. Do we accept a lesser punishment?"

Another roar, with whistles, that morphed into a slow handclap with accompanying foot stomps.

"The people have spoken." Jimmy raised his hands above his head. The house quieted in expectation.

"Humiliation!" He cried, and the room erupted.

Face blazing, I slouched over to the sound stage. Jimmy would die for this later, if I could catch him with his back to me. Israfil – tall, unblemished mahogany skin, with his snow-white wings tucked neatly behind him – bowed me extravagantly to the mic. The room fell silent as Jimmy handed me a battered sheet of paper, and there were a few chuckles as I groaned. Taking a deep breath, I stood straight, and began.

"On the gooooood ship..."

He made me sing through to the end, but the crowd gave me a standing ovation. Jimmy escorted me back to the bar.

"Bastard," I muttered.

"You know the rules, even for you," he rumbled back.

"Besides, wait until you see the size of the tip jar when we close up."

The room settled back down. If anything, the mood was lighter and there was more laughing. The bar certainly got busier and yes, the tip jar was very generous.

Jimmy said I was mad when I asked him if I could come work as a barista on Friday nights. Tasha told me I was nuts too. But I work my ass off all week. I want to graduate high school, finally, and to do that I have to study. No, not *in* high school. I would turn half of them into frogs or snails in the first semester. And no, I don't know how to do that. Yet. But if I don't graduate, and then pass the exit exam, the State will never license me as a Private Investigator. For now, I can get away with it, because I'm technically a student studying under Tasha. They'll only let me do that for so long.

On top of that, I have single-stick classes, which is more like fencing than Akido, firearms classes, studying magic with Mr. Peterson, and doing any scut work Tasha needs—plus manning the office for her most mornings.

Tasha still doesn't do mornings.

And I get it. Pulling a six-hour shift on a Friday night will seem to some like I'm self-harming, but I love it. At one point, it was everything I had ever done, the only thing I knew, so maybe there's a bit of comfort there, too. But Jimmy is a hoot, the other guys are fun, and I love the place. It's less like work and more like being out with my buddies—just my buddies aren't all necessarily human.

That was my reasoning, at first. Jimmy's place is in the Shadows, and the Shadows is home to a lot of things that are best left in your nightmares, as well as some creatures that live in the light with us. Working in the bar was a great way to meet as many as I could in relative safety.

So that's why I was working my butt raw on a Friday night and loving it.

I knew the evening was about to take a turn for the weird—no, the attempted stabbing was not that unusual—when I felt the wards howl in anger at something. Wards are magical protections you can put around a home. You don't get them around public places so much because it takes way too much effort to get them to stay where things are so busy. Jimmy's was an exception. Maybe it was because he lived there, maybe it was because he treated everybody like family.

Hey, I've only been a mage for a year. This time. It's complicated. I can't know everything yet. Especially when I'm still trying to figure which of my stolen memories I got back.

To get to the point, Jimmy's wards were as friendly as he was, mumbling away to themselves most of the time, getting smug when they could block someone on the no-entry list. But I'd never heard them this mad at anything. So far as I could make out, they just had to let someone in they didn't want to but had no good reason to keep out.

Jimmy had strict rules, and everybody was welcome so long as they stuck to them. Everyone.

A pool of empty grew around the doors, the inside ones at the end of the corridor. People were moving out of the way even before they opened. I expected some ghoul dripping slime to step through, but he wore a dark suit, black shirt, and a black tie with a subtle glitter. Over the distance, he looked about six foot, slim, maybe a hundred eighty pounds and trim. Clean shaven, dark hair, with a sprinkle of gray at the temples.

So why was everybody getting out of his way like he was made of anti-matter? Even those sitting down leaned away from him like he repelled them.

And he walked straight towards me. His eyes had been on me since the door opened, like he knew exactly where I would be standing. I felt Jimmy's reassuring bulk arrive next to me. "Want me to handle this, Janie?"

He was the only person I let get away with calling me that. "Why?"

"He may be out of your league. That's the Emissary."

Discord

"The who?"

"Personal representative of Duke Ladislav, the most senior vampire noble for two hundred miles, maybe more."

"Let's see what he wants."

Jimmy moved away, but not far, and I put on my best smile.

"How are you this evening? What can I get for you?"

He smiled back. It was a nice smile, and I would have sworn everything I knew he was human. I was getting pretty good at sensing when magic was about. Some could disguise it, but the only thing coming off him was *Sauvage*.

"I have no doubt that the proprietor just advised you who I am, but for the sake of formality, my name is Simon Miller, and I am the personal representative of Duke Ladislav. Please confirm I am speaking to Miss Jane Doe?"

The smile I kept glued in place was supposed to hide how impressed I was. I knew I shouldn't be, but he was cute, and he carried his authority lightly, but with total confidence.

"That's me."

"Wonderful." His hand slipped inside his jacked. I felt Jimmy tense up even though he was six feet away, and my automatics readied a shield and a wind spell. He froze, smiled an apology, and moved more slowly. When his hand came out, it held a business card between his first and second fingers.

"Quite impressive, Miss Doe. It seems my intelligence about you is accurate." He placed the card on the bar top. "I would not dream of taking up any more of your time while you are working, but this seemed the safest and most open place to introduce myself. When you have time, please call the number on this card, day or night, so we might set up a more convenient meeting."

He gave me another smile, then offered a respectful half-bow to Jimmy, before turning on his heel and retracing his steps to the exit. When he left, I felt the wards flip him the finger.

"What the hells was that about?" Jimmy asked, but I had no answer. I shrugged, tucked the card into the back pocket of my jeans, and served the next customer as the background rumble of the bar eased back to normal.

It didn't seem that important, so I didn't show the card to Tasha until Monday afternoon. *Late* Monday afternoon. I didn't know if she was working on something, but for the past couple of weeks she had been coming into the office around three, and even that late was grumpier than usual.

Perhaps it wasn't helping that I was a little edgy too. Life was getting a bit all work and no play, and I was starting to feel like a secretary.

"What do you think?"

"Did he say anything?"

"Just that he wanted to set up a meeting. Should I call?"

Tasha shook her head. She wasn't looking at me, she had her eyes on something on her desk. My heart sank, but I felt a spark of anger flicker into life too. I sat on it. Bad things can happen if you know magic and get angry.

"Why?"

She glanced up from whatever was so fascinating on her desk. A brief flash of irritation lingered on her face, and the spark of anger in my chest fanned a little brighter.

"You don't mess with blood suckers. Nothing good ever comes out of working with them." The bitterness in her words surprised me, but I pressed the point.

"Is that what he is?"

"Miller? No, he's human." Her brow wrinkled. "Nobody knows what his deal is. I've never heard he has any arcane abilities, and there's never been a hint he's a pledge. And there's no tattoo. But nobody messes with him because they'll be dead by sunrise the day after. Or worse. He has contacts. Everywhere. He can make things happen."

"Then why shouldn't I meet with him?"

"Don't you have anything better to do?"

"I certainly don't have anything more interesting. Let's see what I do have, shall we? I have just about caught up on the reports you never filed with the City. Your accounts and expenses are now in a form an accountant would understand. In the last month I have tracked down one lost dog and tailed two adulterous partners, one male, one female."

Tasha stared into the air behind me, face blank, eyebrows raised. An '*are you finished yet?*' look. Infuriating.

"Welcome to the world of private investigation. What were you expecting?"

"Something a little more interesting."

"You're a trainee," snapped Tasha. "An apprentice. You have to learn the basics."

"I'm learning to be a secretary and to do your scut while you go out. You're supposed to be my teacher too." I took a breath and lowered my voice when I realized what the actual issue was. "We haven't worked on anything together for months."

"Like I said, welcome to the world of etcetera."

"Why I shouldn't at least find out what he wants."

"Didn't I just explain that?"

My inner teen stamped her foot. "I'm going." Then again, all my memories of teen tantrums got ripped away by Victor Corvax, so maybe I was entitled to make some new ones.

"What?"

"He wants to meet, so I'm going to. We should at least find out what he wants."

"No."

The spark inside me kindled into a flame. "No?"

"I'm the licensed operator here. I decide what work we undertake. And it's my responsibility. You do something stupid and it could cost me my badge."

"So, you're the boss of me and I'm just your bitch?"

"As far as working for this agency goes, damned right."

"Well screw you and screw this agency, if that's the way things are going to be." I grabbed my satchel and my jacket from the back of my chair and stomped towards the door at the top of the stairs.

"Jane." Tasha's voice cracked like a whip and I turned despite myself. "I should report you for this. They could throw you off the program."

Grabbing my crash helmet off the coat stand, I yanked the office door open. "Do what you've got to, *boss*."

An Old Friend Reaches Out

Tasha sat in a quiet corner of her favorite diner. The place wasn't glamorous or trendy. It didn't have a retro Fifties vibe. No high-tech replicas of dime jukebox selectors at each table, nor waitresses in short, frilly skirts trying to serve on rollerblades. But it was clean, and it served the best coffee in the state, perhaps in continental North America.

And it was open twenty-four hours a day.

With Jane covering more of the day shift minutiae, Tasha slipped back towards being an owl, or maybe a bat. Even before she was twisted—she refused to use the word 'turned'—she had preferred to work at night. Which was why she was eating breakfast an hour away from midnight.

But tonight, she was working her way through a full stack, dripping with maple syrup while a double scoop of vanilla ice cream melted over the top. Tasha never shied away from a fight, but she hated conflict. And she had no idea how to react to Jane walking out on her that afternoon.

Tasha knew she was right, but also wrong. You never, ever trusted a bloodsucker or anything to do with them, and Miller was one of them in every way except actually *being* one. You didn't even speak to a bloodsucker, if you could avoid it. If she had her way, she would kill them on sight.

But she could never tell Jane why. And at was where the *wrong* came in. Jane wasn't a child. To use 'because I told you' wasn't good parenting and was no way to win an argument. Jane deserved better, but Tasha had nothing better to offer.

As she lifted another fork-full to her mouth, the bell above the door jangled. Tasha glanced towards the sound before groaning around her waffle.

He saw her, but he stopped just inside the door and flicked his gaze into the other corners of the diner. Tasha remembered he was always cautious. He took a hesitant step toward her, and she saw his jaw clench as he considered the wisdom of ruining her breakfast. She watched the reluctant decision solidify in his eyes, and he walked toward her table.

As his backside hit the plastic of the seat, the waitress appeared, cup and saucer in one hand, coffeepot in the other. Angelic soul that she was, she topped off Tasha's cup before filling his with the bitter dregs of the jug. The woman was an expert judge of character.

"Hi."

As an opening, it was less than original, but about what she expected from him. Tasha looked into his eyes, which always made him squirm, and raised her eyebrows for a second before turning her attention to her replenished coffee. It would annoy him, put him off balance. That was the point.

The lines around his eyes were deeper than the last time she had seen him. Had it been almost a year? His beard was three days old, and he looked like he had slept in his suit. The evening drizzle had beaded on his expanding forehead like sweat. One lapel had a stain that hadn't washed out. Could be food, but equally likely to be blood. His hair was gray at his temples, too. But when he took his jacket off, his stomach was still flat, and his eyes were sharp, even angry. She was cheating time, but it wasn't being too unkind to him.

"Figured I might find you here. I remembered you liked the late breakfast back when you made us pull all those night shifts."

She could feel him stretching for comforting memories he could share, and wondered if he thought he could undo what had happened between them by skipping over it to a happier time? Maybe. He had never been a particularly deep thinker.

"Eddie Weston, you were never one for small talk unless you were trying to tell me something you knew I wouldn't want to hear."

He shifted in his chair and procrastinated by taking a mouthful of his coffee. His face screwed up in disapproval and he set the cup down again.

"Nat, I need help."

Though she expected him to call her nothing else, hearing the name jarred her. Nobody had called her Nat, or Natasha, for a long, long time.

"On a case." He added the qualifier quickly, and Tasha bit back the snide jab she had ready about finding an analyst on Yelp.

"No."

He leaned back against the bench seat, doleful eyes like a scolded puppy. "You haven't even heard why."

"And I'm not particularly interested. Unless you are seeking to hire me in a professional capacity on behalf of the department, in which case the answer is still no."

"Why?"

Tasha was cutting herself another morsel of syrup-laden

pancake, but the plate split in two under the fork, and the blade of the knife bent and twisted. She stared at the ruins of her breakfast, then slid it to the side. She would apologize to the waitress later and stick an extra ten on the tip.

"Do you need it laid out for you, Eddie? And how far back do you want me to go? The way you treated my associate last year when her house caught fire? Or the way you spoke to us when we called in the murder of my client? About which, I should add, I haven't heard one damn thing from the department. Or shall I go back farther, to my so-called partner standing by and not doing a damned thing while they drummed me out of my job on a technicality?"

She forced herself to stop and took a breath.

"We were partners, Nat. We made a great team."

"The key word here is *were*, Eddie. I can't forgive what you did to me, and I don't like who you've become."

Weston leaned forward, finger stabbing toward her. "You cannot blame me for a department wide change of policy. I went along with your crazy need to work permanent nights for five years, even though it put both our careers in the slow lane. What was I supposed to do, quit my job too? Would it have hurt you to go out on a day shift? You looked like a ghost then too."

Not a ghost, thought Tasha, a vampire. And then she hit the same wall she had walked into ten years ago; how could she tell him? He would never believe her. It had been easier to tell some nobody she had only just met—Jane, a year ago—than it was to even think about telling Eddie. Still.

Perhaps he had a point. Perhaps if she had been able to find a way to tell him, all those years ago, he would have quit with her, or fought harder to find a way for her to keep her job. And the fault was not all his. She could tolerate sunlight most days. She had not fully turned, had not taken a life to sate her hunger. Factor 50 with bronzer might have made her look a little less pale, too.

The waitress wandered past the table with coffee jug in hand, saw the carnage, and gave Tasha a look. She returned an embarrassed smile. "My fault. And could my friend have a fresh cup? I think something might have fallen in there."

They waited in silence while the waitress repaired the damage. When she finally bustled away, Weston leaned forward and put his elbows on the table.

"Nat, hear me out. I can't undo what's past. Like I said, the department's changed. Not much I can do about that either. But what you said last year is true; I don't have to go along with it, and I don't have to be like them. I'm trying, but I can't do any good if I rock the boat so hard they throw me overboard. There's something about this case. It's like those wacky ones you used to push me to take back in the day, the ones that nobody else wanted. And I can't get any traction in the department. Narco have everything all buttoned up and won't let anybody else in."

"Narco? You're homicide."

"They might be junkies, but if somebody kills one, I still call it homicide."

"That's a blurred line, Eddie." Tasha slouched back against her seat and threw her hands in the air. "What the hell. It's a quiet week, and I'm making no promises. What do you have?"

Drive into the Dark

Nobody touched my motorcycle. Nobody would dare, even though I left her parked on the street. She radiates a low-level threat, which gets stronger the closer you stand. If you're stupid enough to ignore that, the grips feel electrified if you touch them, even wearing gloves. I won't go into what happens if anybody got stubborn enough to try to sit on her. Magic has many uses.

After I stuffed my arms into my jacket, I slung my satchel over my shoulders. Then I had to stop to wipe tears from my eyes before I could put the helmet on. Why was she being such a bitch? Or should that be extra bitch?

And my beautiful red motorcycle just made me feel worse. Tasha bought her for me, when we started the agency. Where the hell had things gone so wrong?

I threw my leg over the saddle, flipped out the kick-start and put my weight behind it as I pushed down. I was heavy enough—just—and my girl was well behaved. She always caught on the first try unless it was miserably wet, and she never kicked back at me. I knew a guy in the Shadows ... Well, not quite sure what he or she was, but he or she was a damn fine mechanic and kept my girl running sweet.

She rumbled into life. I pulled my helmet over my head,

rolled her forward off the stand, and pulled into traffic.

It was quite a bit later that I called Simon Miller. I had taken a two-hour side trip on my way home. Tasha had really upset me, and I took the bike out along the mountain roads to calm myself down.

"Hello?"

"Mr. Miller?"

"Miss Doe? I was beginning to wonder if I had said something to offend you."

"I wanted to talk things through with my partner first."

"So you aren't willing to meet with us?"

First I had heard of an 'us', but then I heard what he said.

"Wait, no. Why would you say that?"

"Miss Campbell's position regarding those I represent is well known and a very hard line. I assumed she would veto any further contact."

"I'm my own person, Mr. Miller."

"Indeed you are." I heard a hint of approval and felt clever, then realized he could be playing me to think that. "Pardon me for the inappropriate assumption. Does this mean that you are willing to attend a meeting?"

"I'd like to know who with first."

"That is not for discussion over a public circuit. Nor is the agenda for the meeting."

I could see the sense in that. Hacking cellphone calls was almost impossible since things went digital, but there were plenty of places in the network someone could intercept the call. See. I learn things from all these courses.

"OK, but just because I attend the meeting doesn't mean I commit to anything. I'll sign an NDA if it's specific."

"Doesn't client confidentiality apply?"

"You aren't technically a client. And, fair warning, I am still a trainee. I'm not sure any agreement you make with me is binding. Or even legal." I sighed. "Perhaps this isn't such a good idea."

Damn. I wanted some excitement. I wanted *this*. And to hell with Tasha; I didn't need to abide by her prejudices. Still, it might not be a good idea. Certainly not if I wanted my PI badge.

"Come to the meeting anyway. As you say, it commits you to nothing. And the people I represent will respect you more for waiting until you have all the information before making your decision."

Damn, but it was tempting.

"When?"

"I can have a car at your home address in fifteen minutes, but might I suggest an hour. Business formal would be an appropriate dress code, if you don't object."

My *I'll wear what I want* high horse was saddled up and ready to mount, but then I remembered; Tasha had made me buy exactly that outfit, and I hadn't had a chance to wear it yet. In fact, I hadn't had a chance to dress up in ages. Might help if I worked on growing my social life.

"An hour, then." I agreed.

"If you don't mind, I'll text you when the car arrives. You house wards are formidable and I would prefer to avoid any misunderstandings."

The line went dead and left me with another pat-on-the-head glow. And over a comment on the house's magical force shield that I hadn't even built. This guy was clever, and I was going to have to be on my A-game. I hurried toward the shower.

My cell pinged exactly an hour later. I was ready fifteen minutes ago, and spent the time pacing up and down the living room. My mouth wanted a drink, but I knew I would have to put my lip gloss back on if I did—and that I would need to pee halfway through the meeting.

Outside was the promised limo—Mercedes, I think—and the driver had the door open for me. I glanced over my shoulder and saw a curtain twitch in the floor above mine. Amanda, one of my tenants, obviously couldn't resist snooping to see who the limo was for.

My first surprise came when I bent to slide into the seat. Simon Miller was sitting in the other side of the car. I don't know why that unsettled me, and I don't know why I was expecting to get a solo ride to wherever this meeting was.

"Good evening, Miss Doe. I hope you don't mind sharing. I needed a ride."

The driver closed the door and walked around to his side of the car while I settled into the seat and fastened my belt.

"No problem." I replied, horrified that I was going to have to find small talk for however long the drive took. He tapped a folder on his lap.

"Forgive me, but I need to attend to some other business while we drive. Rude, I know, but…"

"It's fine." I smiled and tried not to look too relieved.

The car pulled away and I wondered if I should have taken my jacket off. My suit was dark blue, so it ought to hide most of the creases in back – I hoped. I had matched the suit with a pale blue blouse and black flats. Heels I refuse to wear unless I have to.

Right from the moment we pulled away, I knew the driver wasn't taking us where I expected. I kept watch on where we were going but tried to make it look like I wasn't. My phone—new and able to do things without me nursing it—was already running a mapping app and tracking our route. Knowing who Miller was now, it was a safe bet we would be going into the Shadows. I knew one entrance, and I knew there were others. Looked like I was going to find a new one tonight.

We drove out of town, not deeper in. Way out, into farming land, and onto an actual farm. Then, as if he was deliberately trying to mess with my head, the driver headed straight towards an enormous barn.

The doors split open just in time for us to pass through. There was the usual sensation of dropping in an express elevator, and in a blink, we were driving along a stone tunnel. Two minutes later we drove out the side of a hill, and we were in the Dark.

Let me explain. The Dark is where the true night-dwellers live, where there are no lights. The Shadows is the name for the little hub of civilization where most of my kind—us —interact with the night-dwellers. And when they called it The Dark, they weren't kidding.

Except I could see.

Almost perfectly, and way better than night vision. None of that uncomfortable sparkling green. The world was cast in shades of blue, like moonlight. Except no moon hung in the sky.

Miller closed his folder. "I apologize for the darkness, but we mustn't use any internal lights. It interferes with Stephan's night vision."

For a second or two, my eyes met the driver's in the rear-view mirror. He had taken off his shades and his eyes shone green like a cat's. He smiled. Just a flicker of the lips, as if to share with me that he knew. He knew I could see. I wondered if my eyes looked the same to him.

"Is it always like this?" I asked nobody in particular, but Miller answered.

"It is. I find it unsettling to be in such utter dark, featureless all the time. I'm told others can see quite clearly in it, such as those we are about to visit." He settled back in his seat and closed his eyes, hands clasped over the folder in his lap. "If I am honest, the effect can make me car sick."

Turning a little, I stared through the window beside me. I could see fields, split up by low walls of stone. Something ambled around in the fields, about the size of pigs or sheep, but I couldn't make out more than that and didn't want to. Mountains broke the horizon in the far distance, but the ground between them and me lay flat as a pan. My neck started to ache, so I sat straight.

Ahead, a shape lumped up from the horizon. Too quickly, at least to my eye, it resolved into a structure. I couldn't make my mind up if it looked more like a castle, or a half dozen British Buckingham Palaces all piled up, over, and around each other. In any case, it was huge, and I knew it was where we were headed.

Ruby

"It's called Ruby, sometimes Ruby Meth."

"I've heard the name," Tasha frowned. "It hasn't crossed my path in any professional sense, and I've had no cause to look into it yet."

"All the usual fun of methamphetamine, but with a few quirks. Users can get strong, like Batman strong, and fast. Rumors of people tearing their muscles and breaking their own bones."

"Rumors?"

"Like I said, Narco has it sewn up tight. Nothing comes out of them, not even warnings of how to deal with users, nor hotspots and notspots in rollcall."

"Who runs Narco now?"

"Creep by the name of Greg Palmer."

"I don't know him. Is he one of ours?"

Weston shook his head. "Outsider. Transferred in from New York a couple of years ago."

"And he's already running Narcotics?"

"He headed up a big outfit back east. Headhunted, if you believe his own brag."

Tasha grimaced and waved a finger to move the story on.

"It's sold in capsules, taken orally as far as I know. It's rare and expensive."

"How expensive?"

"Hundred bucks a cap."

Tasha pursed her lips. "Must be quite a high for that kind of money."

Weston scowled. "This is what makes things so damned difficult. We don't know. I get rumors from my snitches, but none of them have the sort of money you need to get this stuff and most of it they heard from somebody who knows somebody who has a friend who uses this shit." His hands, until then resting on the table, clenched into fists. She saw him look at them, surprised, then force them to relax.

"What does it offer that meth doesn't?"

"Not sure. Could just be the exclusivity, the way coke used to be back in the early eighties, champagne drug for the rich and famous? I hear the effects are different. Sure, they get pretty much everything they get from meth, but there's the strength thing, and a massive confidence boost that makes them believe they can do anything. Not flying out windows, but business stuff, like cramming for exams. Others have said it's more like self-belief."

"So what's in it?"

Weston growled. "Narco says nobody knows."

"Preposterous. Forensics could analyze it, and if they couldn't isolate the added compound, a specialist lab would."

He shook his head. "Narco claim they tried all that and they still can't figure it out."

Tasha snorted and Weston raised his hands. "I know, but that's the official line."

"What are the distribution and sales paths?" She shook her head before he could answer. "Don't tell me, I can guess."

"Nothing official, but it's not normal. No schools, no street corner market that I can find."

"Then I don't see why you would need my help. It hardly seems like a contagion."

"I don't like what I hear."

"Then tell me."

"Junkies brought in dead with puncture marks, but only in their arms and no signs of overdose. Hearts bursting inside their chests."

She felt her eyebrows rise. "Unusual."

"That one is just a rumor. But there are all kinds of crazy stories, and I can't get a handle on it."

"I still don't understand why this is vexing you. It's not your case. Move on."

"I can't." He stopped, but she knew he had more that needed saying. Why he couldn't ought to be worth hearing. She had never known Eddie to be backwards in offering an opinion.

"Go on."

"There's this girl." He scowled at her as soon as she raised her eyebrows again, and before she had finished raising the corner of her lips. "No, not like that. She has a friend who lives in my apartment block. Somehow she found out I was a cop and came to see me. Her boyfriend has gone missing, and he fits the profile."

"And you told her to report it."

"She already had. Desk Officer took the details but told her they don't bother looking for junkies."

"Honest, if lacking in compassion."

Weston's lips tightened into a thin line. "There's something not right about this, and the girl and her boyfriend are the only lead I have. Narco have locked the rest of the precinct out, and the captain doesn't give the furry crack of a rat's ass. Will you help?"

Tasha raised her cup to her lips, buying time to think. The coffee was tepid, disgusting, but she took a sip anyway.

"Eddie, is this some bourbon-inspired plan to get back with me?"

"What? No!"

"You tried before."

"Well …" He raked his hand through his hair. "Back then I missed working with you."

"Back then?"

He scowled. "Fine. I still miss working with you. We never divorced; they broke us up. You were still my partner. We did outstanding work. But no, I am not trying to get back with you, or angling for a partnership in this agency you set up."

He sighed and some of the fire left his eyes. "I just need your help. If you have the time. I can't pay you—not much, anyway. I know I don't hold any stock with you, but as a favor? For the old times?"

Tasha sighed. Eddie had been closer than a lover; they had been more like siblings, each the other's ideal complement. After she had been twisted, Eddie had rationalized away all the little mistakes and reveals she had committed that exposed her true nature. But even though they hadn't formally divorced—as partners—it was difficult to look past a grudge she had been holding for ten years.

"Departmental policy is that detectives don't work with private investigators unless sanctioned by a Captain or above. That's the rule, isn't it? It's reviewed and republished every six months in the policy newsletter the City circulates to PI's. Working together could get us both in trouble." She dug into her purse and slipped a couple of twenties under her saucer. "I'm not sure I'm the one to help you, Eddie."

She rose from the table, and as she reached back to pick up her purse and her coat, she caught a glimpse of his face even though she had been trying not to look at him. Then she turned away from the table and walked out of the diner, waving goodbye to the waitress.

The drizzle was stained yellow by the streetlights and she took the umbrella from her purse and fiddled to get it up. Her car was parked a hundred yards back down the block, and for the entire walk the look of shock and hurt on Eddie's face haunted her. Too much water had passed under the bridge for her to turn round, to change her mind and go back. And if things in the department were as bad as she had heard, as bad as she had seen last year when she and Jane had fallen foul of them, then getting involved with Eddie Weston could be a catastrophe.

So why did she feel so bad about it?

The Citadel

I t was the sort of door where you expected to have your ID checked, but they didn't even look in the window. The guards leapt out of the way and so did everybody else. We swept through courtyards and up ramps to ever higher levels, and I realized the place was the size of a small city. I counted six levels, though I might have missed one, and each time we went up, the structure that continued up and back was more ornate, and better defended.

The place was lit, too. Not in the streets, but we passed cracks and chinks of lights from windows. That made no sense to me. We were in the middle of the least illuminated place I had ever seen, in a castle full of monsters that can see in the dark. Why did they need light?

We swept into a courtyard through the only way in or out, and I figured we had arrived. I thought the fountain in the middle of the plaza looked romantic and elegant—until I realized it was a vampire biting the throat out of a young woman. The car swung around the fountain and pulled up at the foot of some steps with old fashioned lamps shining over them. The driver got out, opening Miller's door for him as he passed, then holding my door open and offering me a hand to help me out. He even gave me the tiniest of bows when I thanked him. I couldn't shake the feeling he knew more about me than I knew about him.

Huge doors of leaded glass opened at the top of the steps, and Miller gestured that I should go first. Given the ride up, I think he was showing me some special honor to impress me, but it didn't work. I tried not to stomp up the stairs and forced myself to remember I was wearing a suit. Maybe I should have worn the heels after all.

At the top, a woman stepped through the doors to greet us. Miller bowed to her, but there was something more than just formality in the way he moved. I was wondering if I should bow or curtsey, but she saved me from guessing wrong by stepping towards me with her hand outstretched. I shook it. Nice shake, firm but not pushy. And none of this limp sausage grip like she expected me to turn her hand over and kiss the back.

"Miss Doe. A pleasure to meet you. My name is Andrea. Allow me to show you to my uncle's study."

She pronounced it 'Anne-DRAY-ah', with a rolling R, summing up who she was and our relative importance with just a few words. Neat. Model-beautiful, but with that little bit of extra padding in the right places making her truly remarkable. She towered over me—she *was* wearing heels—and a silver net, that looked like it cost more than my condo, caught her hair and molded it around her head before it cascaded over her shoulders in strictly sculpted 'random' curls.

But her dress made me want to frown. It was too revealing. Silver-white, ankle length, but split up the front so far you weren't sure if you were seeing panties or shadow. The bodice was snug, which was fine, but the fabric was so revealing over her bust she might as well not have worn it. Then again, if my boobs looked that good—and that natural—maybe I would show them off more too.

Miller walked two paces behind, but Andrea made it clear I was to walk with her. I tried to focus on what she was saying, and not on the sumptuous decor around me. It made Jessander's place look like the Home Economy range from an out-of-town outlet store.

"How was the journey?" she threw out as an opener.

Ah, small talk. I settled on "Informative." That earned me a raised eyebrow.

"How so? I never knew our Emissary could be such a gossip." She tossed an arch look over her shoulder and he rewarded her with an uncomfortable cough. I got an even stronger feeling that we were all putting on a show. I played along.

"He was the soul of discretion," I said. "Buried his face in a report and ignored me the entire trip. No, I was meaning this is the deepest I have ever travelled into the Dark. And the limo was very nice too."

"How can staring out into all that darkness have been so informative?"

My turn. I turned my head, so we looked right at each other, raised my eyebrows and smiled. A flicker of surprise crossed her face. Score one for me.

"A woman of many surprises," she murmured, so softly I doubted Miller heard it.

I turned away, but looking so closely into her eyes left me rattled. Her body might look in its early twenties, but her face had that ageless thing going on, and her eyes were chillingly cold.

We stopped outside another set of pointlessly massive doors. They had to be thirty feet tall, and each door was ten feet across.

29

There were even two guards outside. It made me feel like we were standing outside a throne room, or the dining hall at Hogwarts.

"I shall leave you here," said Andrea. "My uncle is expecting you."

"It was a pleasure to meet you," I said, and I wasn't lying. Quite. It had certainly been another education. She turned to face the Emissary.

"Miller, please stop at my apartment on your way out." Her eyes flicked towards me. "And bring Miss Doe, if she has the time."

"My lady." Miller bowed and Andrea swept away as if she was floating half an inch off the ground. Miller nodded to the door guards. One rapped on a knocker, then each took a handle and hauled the doors open.

His presence swept over me like a breaker on the beach. My heart pounded and I felt he had stolen the air from my lungs. Gods above and below save me, I *wanted* him. Yes, sexually. I closed my eyes for a couple of seconds, took a long breath, and used it to center my thoughts. If I let him do this to me at the doorway, then I might as well hand in my wand and my Glock and get his tattoo on my neck.

I opened my eyes. It was still there. I could still feel everything, but it didn't *own* me. Miller wasn't giving me any cues, so I bowed.

"Well done," he muttered then, louder, so his master could hear him at the far end of the room. "My lord, may I present Miss Jane Doe. You expressed an interest in meeting her."

He was sitting in an armchair, next to a roaring fire and reading a book that, from a distance, looked like a crime thriller. He looked up at us and I felt the power of his presence again. Damn, he had nearly knocked me off my feet and he hadn't even been looking at me. He waved, and Miller gestured that I should go in ahead of him.

The duke looked about fifty, full head of gray hair, craggy-handsome face, solid but not overweight. He wore chinos and a burgundy red smoking jacket, and turned his attention back to his book while we walked the forty or fifty feet from the doors to the other end of the room. When we were standing in front of him, he lifted the hand not holding the book, a single finger raised.

"Inexcusable," he said as he finally put the book down. "But I hate stopping in the middle of a scene. My apologies." He rose to his feet and held out a hand. "A pleasure, Miss Doe. I have heard a great deal about you."

From the corner of my eye, I saw Miller's eyebrows crawling up his forehead. Either the duke liked me, or he wanted me to do something significant. He waved me to the chair opposite his, while Miller took up position behind and to the side of his master's chair. He still looked rattled. I waited until I saw the duke start to sit and did the same. I was sure I remembered some rule about waiting until royalty planted their butts before you did. Then I waited to be spoken to. See, more learning.

"A situation has arisen which I feel would suit your unique talents," said the duke. He was sitting forward in his chair, his expression serious and intense. Whatever it was, it worried him a great deal.

"Thank you, sir, but I must advise you I am not a full Private Investigator yet. I'm still probationary."

The duke's face soured like he had sucked the lime ready to down the shot, and I saw some tension around Miller's eyes. Seriously? That counted as an interruption? "It might be better if I understand the nature of the task, then take it back to my supervisor, at least at first."

The duke waved a dismissive hand. "Sadly, Miss Campbell does not hold my people in good standing. We expect any approach to her will be vigorously rebuffed."

Which left a huge 'why' floating around in my mind. It also opened the possibility of a decent case I could work myself.

"I see. Forgive me for interrupting. I just wanted to make you aware that I might not be able to help you before you disclosed any sensitive information."

"Very professional of you, I'm sure." He sounded disinterested and paused for a moment to brush imaginary fluff from his smoking jacket. "You are aware that my kind propagate our species by selecting certain members of yours, and exchanging certain body fluids?"

I decided it was safer to just nod.

"The process creates a bond between parent and offspring. It is not a sophisticated thing. We cannot, for example, communicate through it, or use it to determine another's location. But we can tell if one we are connected to is in great distress, or dies.

"A death, these days, is uncommon. For one of our people in such distress the Dam or Sire can feel it is unheard of. The mob is our primary predator, or a lone hunter with a passion for slaying my kind. Both are rarities now."

Fire started to smolder in his eyes. I wanted to hide behind the chair or run from the room. Miller didn't look worried, so I clamped my hands together in my lap and rode it out.

"So you can imagine my outrage, Miss Doe, to feel such distress from not one, but two of my children. And to feel one die, not in the glorious fire of combat, but fading away, whimpering into the void."

He leapt to his feet and slammed his fist down on the back of his chair. I got to my feet too, but he wasn't paying me any mind.

"Those I deigned to make my own were carefully chosen, nurtured. That someone would dare to do this to them is intolerable."

He turned to face me, and I couldn't stop myself. I flinched. Just a little, but enough to annoy me and make me stand straight again.

"You." He stabbed a finger at me. "You have the abilities. You and that Campbell creature have the resources. I cannot use my own tools. I cannot reveal there are some who fear me so little. There would be chaos. Find who is doing this to my children. Find them and give me their name, and I shall... I shall..."

He was losing it and I didn't want to be around when he did. Besides, I figured I could get more out of Miller than I was getting out of the duke right now. I bowed.

"It will be my honor to look into the situation and advise you, through the Emissary, how best I feel I can be of assistance to you."

When I glanced over his shoulder at Miller, I got a nod before his eyes flicked towards the door. I bowed again, then backed away from the duke for half a dozen paces before turning and walking towards the door. Miller joined me before I got halfway there.

"Do not look back," he muttered, and picked up the pace a little. Once we were outside and the doors were closed, I saw his cheeks puff out and his shoulders droop. Just for a moment. Then he glanced at the guards and everything was back to business as normal. Appearances must be maintained, it seemed. Or some such nonsense.

"Not here," he said in a low voice. "Follow me."

Peering through Death's Door

Tasha's finger hovered over the red button when she saw the caller. It was Eddie Weston. She left the phone on the desk but answered on speaker.

"What is it, Eddie?"

"Something new. The girl I told you about—"

"We discussed this. I said I wasn't interested."

The silence stretched until it got uncomfortable. "And you're sticking to that?"

"Why would I change my mind, Eddie?"

"Maybe you reconsidered? Had a change of heart?"

"Based on what? A good day's sleep? The facts are still the facts; this wouldn't be good for either of us. Nothing has changed."

"Except that I have the boyfriend." He sounded smug, like he always did when he got something she hadn't. Most of the time he was wrong, and she had figured it out before him, but she let him keep the odd win. She almost smiled at the memory.

"And how long do you think you have until Narco come and sweep him up?"

"They don't even know about him, unless that Desk Officer actually processed the paperwork, and my money says she didn't."

"Well, I hope it works out for you, Eddie." Tasha reached out to disconnect her phone.

"Wait. I need you to come down here."

For a split second she considered killing the call, pretending she hadn't heard him.

"Why? And where is *here*?"

"Hospital. I need you to talk to the girlfriend."

"You mean boyfriend? You said you had the boyfriend."

"Yeah, but he ain't talking to nobody. His girl is here too."

"She's your client."

"I'm a cop, I don't have clients."

"Whatever you want to call her, she's your problem."

"Please, Nat. She's in pieces. You we always better than me with the emotional stuff."

Gender profiling in the workplace, Tasha thought to herself, but he was right. Eddie had the sensitivity of a brick. The best the poor girl would get from him would be *there, there* and a pat on the shoulder at arm's length. If the love of her life was in a hospital, languishing at death's door, she deserved better than that.

"Which hospital is he in?"

"Mercy Memorial. Fourth floor. The patient's name is Ryan Ellis. I'll meet you at the nurses' station."

"And who am I?"

"Damn. Hadn't thought of that."

"Exactly. I don't carry the right badge anymore, and if they're any good at their job, they won't just let me wander around the floor poking my nose into patient rooms."

Another silence, longer.

"Come on, Nat. Don't make me ask."

Which was as close as he could get. From the ambient noise, he was either using a payphone or had borrowed a line at the nurses' station. Either way, someone might overhear him, or the line could even be on a call logger.

"Eddie, I'll see if I can get someone to help you. I know a trauma councilor. Her name is Betsy Fornham. I'll call her and see if she can join you."

"Thanks, Nat."

"This is the end of it, Eddie. The last time, the last favor. Don't try to drag me into this again."

Tasha hung up before she heard his reply.

She had to change. Tasha strode into her bedroom and slid open the door of the walk-in. One side was lined with her clothes, the other with what she thought of as costumes. Time to start putting herself in character.

Fornham wore an off-the-shelf suit and blouse from a chain store, with comfortable shoes and opaque tights. She was around the pay grade of a public employee. Her makeup was unimaginative, with lip gloss a few shades too bright and mascara that clumped.

She had used Fornham before. Claiming to be a councilor was generic and flexible. She even had an ID card that identified her as working for Central Counselling Services. If anybody was curious enough to check out the number on the back, the call would route to an agency that would take a message.

Tasha worked quickly and precisely, and was ready when the Uber arrived thirty minutes later.

Mercy Memorial looked like the people it served. The hospital lived up to its name and turned nobody away, but it paid the price. The overflow from the leaking gutters left black tears down the dark red bricks, and most of the ambulances were transferring patients that had no insurance from the ERs of State University and Ellen J Fenway.

Inside was better. Tasha adjusted her preconceptions, as she always needed to here. Mercy was many things, but it was clean. Desperately in need of maintenance and decor, yes, but clean. She walked around the unmanned information booth in the entrance foyer and joined the crowd waiting for elevators. Things seemed unusually busy, until she peered through the taller heads and saw red 'Out of Service' signs on two of the cars. She headed for the stairs.

On the fourth floor she made her way to the nurses' station and waited for someone to have a moment to speak to her. Three nurses crowded into the undersized space, one on the phone and two trying to keep notes up to date. A bell on the wall over the station clamored, forcing them to pay attention to it, and two red lights lit up on a board full of numbers. Two of the nurses hurried off in different directions, and Tasha wondered if the smart thing might be to ring Eddie and listen for the sound of his cell.

"Whaddaya need, lady?" The nurse on the phone had cupped her hand over the mouthpiece and was looking up at her.

Tasha waved her badge and tucked it away before the nurse could pay it too much attention. "I'm from Counseling. I was told to meet a Detective Wilson here?"

The nurse pointed up the hall with her pen. "There's a Weston up at 415, but be quiet. Poor guy's circling the drain."

"Oh?"

The nurse nodded. "Sepsis, anemia. Not—" Her attention

was yanked back to the handset. "Yeah, Raul, still holding. No, Mrs. Atkinson, not Mr. Hutchinson. Not unless he has a cervix, and in this place who knows."

Tasha gave the nurse a wave she didn't see and walked toward 415.

Eddie was standing outside, propped against the wall opposite the door and looking in. He didn't notice her until she was on top of him. Tasha peered through the door, then leaned against the wall beside him.

The shape on the bed was unidentifiable. Tubes in his mouth obscured his face and tape held his eyes shut. The body under the blankets was long, but too thin, an elongated child. A weave of multi-colored wires led left, into the vitals monitor, while on the right a drip hung from a stand and fed into a machine that measured the fluid into his body through a central line coming out of his neck. The monitor beeped softly, a red 'TACH' flashing above a heart rate of 140 and a blood pressure of sixty over 'your guess is as good as mine'. The nurse hadn't exaggerated; the kid was in a bad way.

Halfway down the bed, sitting on a hard plastic chair, hunched a child-size figure that Tasha guessed was the girlfriend. She was leaning against the side of the bed, arm outstretched, holding his hand in hers.

"Does he have any chance?" Tasha asked, voice soft so the girl couldn't hear her.

Weston shook his head. "Excluding divine intervention, not a hope. Doctors say he's falling apart from the inside out."

"What's her name?"

"Constance." Tasha flicked her eyes up to his and raised her eyebrows. "Prefers Connie."

Tasha held out her coat and purse. Weston looked at them

for a moment, then sighed and took them from her.

"Wait here."

"Yes, ma'am."

Side Job

I t was a hike. He should have called the car back to take us to a closer courtyard, but at least all the stairs we took were down. Each level the decor changed, becoming less ostentatious, but still reeking of money. We ended up at another flashy double door, but unguarded and not twenty feet tall. To the left was an out of character entry phone. Miller pushed the button, announced us, and the door clicked open.

We walked into an apartment that wouldn't have looked out of place in one of the exclusive blocks downtown. Everything was a blend of modern convenience and traditional fixtures, and it worked surprisingly well, right down to the 60-inch flat screen mounted in a gilt frame above a fireplace.

Andrea waved us to chairs in a living space, then rang a silver bell she picked up from a side table. A moment later, a girl I hoped was older than she looked walked into the room, her uniform both traditional and flirtatious. Andrea ordered coffee and the maid sashayed off. I stared after her. I was sure she was human, because she was pretty, but she didn't look as perfect as everybody else.

"Attracted or curious?"

It took a second to realize Andrea was talking to me. I turned to her and saw she was trying to hide a smile. "Curious. Was she human?"

The smile faded and I'll swear she pouted a hint of disap-
pointment. "Human? Of course. You think we would use our
own kind as servants?" She turned her attention to Miller.
"How was my uncle?"

"The duke became very agitated at the end. Miss Doe
handled the situation well."

Andrea sighed. "He is getting worse, and the more of these
deaths he feels, the more it troubles him."

"Is the duke unwell," I asked.

"He is *old*, Miss Doe." She looked sad. "People think that our
line goes back to the Middle Ages, but the oldest of us predate
that by millennia. My uncle is over 1500 years old."

"He has a very powerful presence."

The maid walked in with the coffee, putting it on the table
between us and curtsying to Andrea before she left. I made a
point of not looking at her. Miller poured.

"The aura you felt deepens as we age," said Andrea, "but
we normally contain it, only allowing others to feel its effects
when we choose to. Losing the ability to control it, losing the
awareness that others can feel it, is a sign that my uncle's
health is deteriorating. Mention that outside this room and I
will have you killed."

Wrong thing to say. I put my coffee back on the table and
mentally shook out my mojo. "You can try." I kept my voice
calm, matter of fact. Andrea's face came up and we locked
eyes.

"Ladies, please." Miller tried to break the tension, but
neither of us looked away. "This posturing is all very male.
Miss Doe, may I point out you are alone in the middle of one
of the largest concentrations of vampires in the United States?

And Andrea, your uncle invited Miss Doe to the Citadel. She has ambassadorial privileges until she leaves, continuing if she takes employment with him. Death threats are highly inappropriate. Please remember, I work for him, not you."

"My apologies." Andrea still held my eyes with hers. "A sensitive subject, to which I may have over-reacted." She looked away.

"My partner and I work on the basis that information divulged by potential as well as actual clients is held in equal confidence."

"Very professional," said Miller, and we collectively brushed the moment under the rug.

"What did my uncle say?" Andrea asked.

"He requested that Miss Doe investigate the missing," said Miller. "Though the exact remit was a little vague on actual objectives and very clear on what the duke will do if he finds out who is responsible."

"I said I would look into it," added Jane. "And that I would report back if I thought it was something we, I, can help with. I never discuss rates until I know if I can take the job."

"Why would you not accept the contract?"

I explained again.

"Refreshingly honest. However, I can see why my uncle would have chosen you, and it's why I would also like to employ you."

My whole world felt like I was standing on ice about as thick as a human hair. I said "Oh?"

"My uncle is not aware of this issue." She glanced at Miller. "I would prefer to spare him this unless it becomes necessary."

"That will, of course, depend on the subject," he replied, his face neutral. But I had the feeling that Miller would keep her confidence, at least for anything short of rebellion or assassination.

"Somebody is marketing unsanctioned food into the family."

Miller looked shocked. I raised my hand.

"Forgive me for sounding like a rube, but I have no idea what that meant."

Andrea gave me another long look. "Time to talk terms, Miss Doe. Whilst I am comforted by your claims of professional confidentiality, I need something more. My uncle did not discuss payment with you, did he?"

"I was going to explain the charges to Mr. Miller."

"Your normal charges do not apply here."

"Then what—?"

She held up a finger, and I wasn't sure if she was counting or if it was to shush me.

"You will be working with us in a way that will expose truths about our world and our way of life that few outsiders even know."

A second finger rose. Counting it was.

"Because of that, I will personally guarantee, and on behalf of my uncle and by his name, that any inconveniences that occur in your life as part of this contract will be resolved in your favor. Specifically, but not exclusively, we will protect your status as an Investigator in training."

Third finger. "The sum of fifty thousand dollars will be paid for each task completed." She looked at Miller. "So witnessed?"

He nodded. "So witnessed."

They both looked at me, and I felt like a rabbit between two snakes. Part of me wanted to scream for contracts and lawyers, but at the same time I felt something older in play here. Honor, not lawyers. And the terms were absurdly generous.

It *felt* reasonable, safe. It also felt exciting. But I was sitting opposite a woman who could mess with my emotions, if not my mind. I would be nuts to go along with any of it. But I did.

"I agree."

Tension drained from the room and Miller actually smiled. "So witnessed."

Andrea re-arranged herself on the couch before she continued. "A vampire's principal food is blood."

How disappointing. I already knew that. I had expected something new, something explosive.

"Human blood is our natural food, but that is only available to us in controlled quantities."

That much I didn't, and it must have shown in my face.

"From the beginning of the twentieth century, humans have become less–" she hunted for a word. "Malleable. Science overcame superstition, and the masses were in danger of becoming aware of us. Various governments around the world already had. We signed a number of accords. In return, we were given certain supplies, in exchange for our kind limiting their activities in your world."

Now I had my 'explosive'. I knew my mouth was gaping, and I couldn't help but repeat the point to help it soak into my brain. "The US government knows about vampires?"

"Parts of it," Andrea confirmed. "Perhaps less the government itself, and more the people who actually run the government." She sighed. "We subsist now on the blood beasts, and the best of us are granted the surplus or outdated stock from your blood banks."

"Blood beasts?"

45

"Mindless creatures," said Miller. "You don't need to know more about them."

"I thought this was going to be full and frank?"

"And I assumed it would be relevant." He had a point, and I gave him a grin to let him know he had scored.

"So what changed?" I asked.

"We became aware that someone is selling unlicensed blood, true human and fresh. Specialist, perhaps even drawn to order."

"What, different flavors?"

I didn't like Andrea's grin. "Blood is as complex as wine—or gourmet dining, if you will. The sustenance we get from the beasts is akin to eating nothing but instant noodles, and without the flavor packet."

I wondered how she knew. The idea of Andrea slurping rehydrated ramen from a cardboard pot was intriguing.

"Age, sex, and lifestyle all affect the quality of human blood," Andrea's expression was dreamy now, like she was relishing a memory. "It results in flavors from burger bars to haute cuisine. And all of it better than beast blood."

"How long ago did this start?" I felt myself frown as I asked. Something wasn't making sense.

"About six months ago," said Andrea.

"And who is providing this stuff?"

"We have no idea. We believe we know who is bringing it into the Citadel, but nothing of the organization beyond that."

"Why don't you go find them yourselves, or hand it over to the authorities?"

"Either could evolve into consequences we wish to avoid. Also, this trade is insignificant at the moment, and unknown to the general population. If we investigate it ourselves..."

Andrea gave a graceful shrug.

"Word gets out to the masses and everybody wants some?" Now it was starting to make sense to me.

Andrea nodded.

"But I thought you all got your blood from pledges and the like."

"We allow only a small percentage of the populace that privilege." Andrea slouched against the back of the couch and put her arm along the back. "Do you have any idea how many of my kin live in this Hall?"

"Several hundred?" I guessed.

"Several *thousand*," she replied. "Of which barely two hundred are senior enough to have permission to interact with your world."

I pursed my lips, and a thought came to me. "Is there already a problem? With the blood, I mean. Are there some unhappy about the restrictions?"

An approving lift of the perfect eyebrows and a nod. Score another point for me. I pushed the answer a little harder. "If your people find out someone is cheating the system for blood, or that someone out there is hunting you folk, your people might get restless?"

Andrea looked uncomfortable but nodded.

"I do like a challenge." I grinned. "Only one more question." They both looked at me with polite interest.

"What if I can't deliver?"

Andrea and Miller shared a look, and it was Miller who answered. "Provided you act in a professional and reasonable manner throughout, we will cover your expenses and guarantee the protections as discussed. Legitimate expenses will be covered, but the fifty thousand will only be paid on the successful completion of each investigation." He looked at Andrea. "Agreed?"

She nodded and Miller carried on. "Then so−"

I held up my hand and cut him off. "And no repercussions."

Andrea looked offended. "Of course not, unless you betray us."

"And who decides if I worked hard enough?"

Everybody paused, each looking at the other.

"I expect that would be me," said Miller.

"The duke is your master," I objected.

"The duke is my *employer*," Miller countered, and his lips tightened into a thin line. "And I have no official connection to his niece; I am simply acting as arbiter."

And that, I knew, was a lie. Something was going on between those two, but I couldn't to put a label on it − yet. But I felt it was an arrangement I could work with. I had no idea why, but I felt Miller would cut me a fair deal.

"OK," I said. "I accept."

"We are all in agreement?" Miller asked. I nodded and, after a moment, so did Andrea.

"Then so witnessed."

An Ending

Tasha walked into the room, around the opposite side of the bed from where the girl sat. She found another plastic chair hiding against the wall, but she stood until the girl noticed her. Tasha could see her profile, now. She was gaunt, her cheeks pinched in while dark shadows circled her eyes. She wore no makeup, and had dry, chapped lips. Hair that reached half-way down her back was lifeless and tangled, and Tasha wondered how long this boy had been ripping Connie's life apart.

The girl glanced across at her. Tasha smiled, but the girl looked away so quickly Tasha wasn't sure if she saw it. "Connie? Can I speak with you for a moment?"

"You the lady Detective Eddie said was coming?" She never took her eyes off the boy's face. Tasha wondered if he had been a good enough man to deserve this level of devotion, or if he had been a rat manipulating someone who had never felt loved before.

"I am."

"You a cop too?"

"No, but I've worked with them before. Detective Weston and I know each other. May I sit with you?"

Connie shrugged. Tasha pulled the plastic chair closer to

the bed and sat down, and as she did so, her eyes fell on the crook of the boy's elbow. Needle marks: a dozen or more and several of them inflamed and oozing. Angry red lines tracked up toward his shoulder, but something about the holes looked odd. It took her a minute, but she realized they were too big. Drug users normally injected through much narrower needles. These would have hurt.

"What's your friends name?"

"Ryan, and he ain't my friend. We was gonna get married. He's my fiancé.

"Had you set a date?"

Connie flicked a glance at Tasha, the question catching her off guard. Tasha suspected everybody else had only been interested in what drugs he had taken and was he allergic to anything.

"We was still saving up, but I was hoping for next year, maybe in the fall."

"It's pretty around then. Have you been together long?"

"Since high school." Connie said it with pride, as though making a relationship work that long was something to be proud of. Perhaps it was.

"That's nice. How were things going for you two?"

"Great. I mean, real good."

"When did things start to go wrong?"

Connie's head turned and she glared at Tasha. "You mean when did he start using? Wondered how long it would take you to get there, with all your soft and caring. When did he start, what was he taking, where did he get it, who were his dealers, his friends?"

Tasha sat back slowly, trying not to spook the girl. "I didn't mean—"

"Everybody treats him like dirt. Like his mom, when I tried to tell her there was something wrong. Like the cop that wouldn't give me her time when I tried to report him missing. Do you know where he was when they eventually found him? No, they didn't *find* him. Somebody reported him for being in their way. Do you know where he was?"

The girls voice was rising, and if she went on much longer, some overworked and unhappy orderly would be in to hustle her outside. Tasha shook her head. Tears tracked down Connie's cheeks now, and her face was collapsing like a heartbroken child.

"He was in a dumpster, out back of a fast-food restaurant. They say he must have got sick and passed out while he was diving for food, but he would never have done that. Never." Her eyes fell away from Tasha's and she turned her face back toward that of her beau. The fire went out of her, and her voice dropped to little more than a whisper. "Somebody tossed him in there, like they were throwing out trash."

The vitals monitor started to scream. The top line of the display was a jagged scribble and the red 'TACH' had upgraded to a block of flashing red around the word 'VFIB'. Tasha reached over the boy's head and stabbed a finger at a button on the wall. His heart was failing.

A recorded announcement echoed along the hall outside. "Code Blue... 415. Code Blue...415."

Connie looked up at her in horror. "What did you do?"

Tasha hurried to the other side of the bed. She could already hear a cart rattling towards the room. "The medics need to help him. We have to get out of their way."

She tried to pull Connie to her feet, but the girl had a death grip on her man's hand. "Connie, if we want them to help him,

51

we have to leave. We can wait right outside."

But Connie was frozen between mistrust and fear. Tasha sighed, then braced herself as she slid her hand down Connie's arm to her bare wrist. Raw emotion flooded through the tattered remains of Tasha soul, and she flinched.

The beast inside her fed on the feelings of others, but for that part of her to do what she needed it to do, the emotions had to flow through her. The still human part of her. Once she had taken the emotions into her dark center, they echoed back and forth for hours until they faded away. She had to feel everything that Connie felt.

It took her a moment, but she absorbed just enough of the turmoil in the girl's heart to help her to let go of her fiancé's hand and get out of the chair. Tasha flattened them both against the wall as the crash cart barreled into the room, then she eased Connie into the hallway. Eddie raised his eyebrows at her, just a flicker, and she returned an almost invisible shake of the head—old signals they had used so many years ago.

In the room, the defibrillator whined and cracked while the nurses argued over who called the code. Whine and crack. Calls for epi, atropine, amiodarone. The rhythmic thump of CPR. Whine and crack. Whine and crack.

"Call it."

Tasha stopped listening. She had heard it too many times before and wished she could spare Connie from what was coming.

A weary voice, too used to saying the words. "Time of death, fifteen twenty-seven."

The room began to empty. A harassed senior resident stopped in front of them. "Sorry for your loss. We did everything we could." She hesitated, face blank as if searching for something more she should say than the formula pounded into her since she was an intern, then she walked away.

Connie stepped towards the room, but Tasha held her back. "Give them another moment to tidy up."

The last nurse came out. "You can go in now. Come down to the station when you're ready."

"Ready for what?" Connie asked as Tasha eased her into the room.

"Forms and things. Don't worry about it for now."

The nurses had straightened the sheets and the body. At least they had put pillows back under Ryan's head, not left it flat. Tasha had seen both, and the head flat made the body look like it was already on a mortuary slab.

Connie went back to her chair and took his hand. "Still warm," she muttered, then Tasha saw her shoulders straighten. "I think I'd like you both to leave now."

"We're here to help, Connie." Eddie spoke before Tasha could stop him and she shot him a disappointed look.

"No, you're not," the girl snapped as she glared at him. "You're here because you want something, and you thought he might give it to you. Or I would. But he's dead and nobody cares about him, now or before. Except me. So I want you both to go. Now."

Tasha took one of her cards and put it on the bed, not too close to Connie's hand, but where she could see it. She didn't say anything, didn't pat the girl reassuringly on the shoulder. She just turned, grabbed Eddie by the arm, and dragged him out into the corridor.

"Are you crazy?" He hissed. "She's our only lead."

"*Your* only lead," Tasha corrected. "And right now, if you bother her, she will just build a wall around herself and shut everybody out. Give her time."

"How long?"

"As long as she needs. As long as you can. A week, at least?"

"A week?" Eddie exploded, and Tasha slapped his arm.

"Quiet. Yes, a week. Promise me, Eddie, or I walk away from this."

Divisions and Dinners

"Hey, Tasha." I aimed for bright and cheerful.

"Jane." Flat. Neutral. It felt like she would rather be doing just about anything rather than speak to me on the phone.

"Bad time?"

"Not at all."

Real encouraging. I almost killed the call, but we were partners. Or supposed to be. "Remember I told you about that guy who contacted me at Jimmy's?"

"You went, didn't you." It wasn't a question.

"You mad at me?"

"I'm not pleased."

The line went quiet for a moment. To me the blame was half and half, and I'd have been in my rights to make her apologize. Except it wouldn't happen. Tasha wasn't like that. She would rather let something fester than admit she might have been wrong.

"Look, I'm sorry we had words. Can you please try to see things from where I stand? Not asking you to agree with them, but maybe understand a little?" I waited but she said nothing. "They want me to look into two things. We're supposed to be a team, to work together."

"We *are* a team and, until you get your license, I have to be boss."

Again? It was beginning to feel like she was trying to break us up, and I went cold all over.

"They said they'll fix it if anything goes wrong." My gut lurched like an elevator that went down too fast. What if they'd lied to me? "Can they do that?"

"They can, but do you want Bloodsuckers pulling your strings for the rest of your life? Once you owe them a favor, they have you."

"What if *they* owe *you* a favor?"

The line went silent again. I thought I heard a sigh.

"I can learn so much from this, so much more than sitting behind the desk and chasing lost cats. And if you work with me, you can stop me from doing anything stupid."

Oops. As soon as I spoke the words, I wished I hadn't.

"That's what I'm trying to do right now, and I have my own work."

"What? Maybe I should drop the vamps and help you with that." Made sense to me. It kept us both happy and me out of trouble.

"No. It's private."

It felt like she slapped me. "Oh."

"It's nothing interesting." Now it was Tasha's turn to sound like she wished she thought more about her words. "It's a favor. For a friend. I'm not even getting paid."

Neither was I, not by our agency, but that was part of the understanding. I had money from elsewhere. I had even paid the occasional bill Tasha didn't know about, and my inner teen wanted to rub her nose in that too. "Then perhaps one of us should follow the paying work?"

"I'm not going to talk you out of this, am I?"

"Nor help me from the sound of it." I answered in a sulky, bratty voice I hated when I heard it.

"Then I don't think we have anything more to say here."

She didn't sound bitchy, more resigned, but as I took the phone away by from my ear to disconnect the call, I heard a tinny, tiny "...but Jane?"

I put the phone back to my ear and tried not to sound sullen. "Yes."

"Be careful. Very careful. Please?"

This time, she killed the call before I could.

Emotion soup. Dash of excitement that I was working something big on my own. Maybe sprinkle some fear on that, too. Hurt, that Tasha had something more important to do than back me up on my first major case.

Probably a good idea I didn't tell her I had agreed to dinner with the Emissary.

I wasn't quite sure how that had happened, either. We were almost home—my home, that is. I had tried to talk about the case, but Miller had hidden his face in that report until I was almost home.

"You're right, we should set time aside to discuss the work and devise strategy." The words came out of the air cold, with no warning.

"My office?" It seemed the best place. Neutral and professional.

"Awkward, if Miss Campbell should arrive. Also, I am rather busy tomorrow." He tapped the folder. "But I should be able to resolve this issue then. Do you enjoy oriental cuisine?"

I nodded, expecting a chain downtown.

"Hidden Garden at nine? Tonight? Should I send a car?"

"I'll Uber." Always annoyed me when TV shows had influential people getting reservations at impenetrable venues by clicking their fingers, but in real life it was surprisingly impressive. The Garden had a three month wait and a price list that would ruin most people's appetite.

The car pulled up outside the house and the driver opened the door for me. Miller mumbled an automatic farewell; his face was already in the folder again. I turned back to the house and the curtain on the second floor twitched.

I *had* to have a word with Amanda about that.

"So, do you call yourself a witch? Wizard?"

I turned up a fashionable five minutes late, resplendent in my LBD and heels. Miller was already there, sipping from a glass of water. A server sat me, handed me a menu with no prices and rattled the specials off so fast I barely heard a word.

The menu annoyed me. I thought we were beyond that sort of crap. I ordered, and the server disappeared. That was when Miller dropped the 'naming of things' on me.

"Gee, you like to go straight for the throat, don't you? Couldn't you have started with if I liked cats, or what music I listened to?"

He raised an eyebrow and I scowled inwardly. I was seriously considering Botox so I could do that. I really was.

"*Do* you like cats?"

"Never had one." I took a sip of the water and wished it was something stronger. "I don't know what to call myself," I admitted. "Wizard and warlock are too caught up with men for most of eternity, but I'm not sure I see myself as a witch. The Grumpy Old Man–"

"Sorry, who?"

And now I was trying to switch from how I thought of myself to how far into my private life I would allowed him.

"Think of him as my magical sensei. Anyhow, he says I'm listed in the rolls as a Combat Mage. Only most people don't know what a Mage is, and if you throw the word combat around people get the wrong idea. And, to be honest, I have no idea what 'The Rolls' are either."

"Is that how you see yourself?"

"Can't deny I have a talent for it. I'm hoping to be more than that, though." It was time for this to switch. "What about you? Are you pledged to the duke?"

I wasn't sure if the thought amused or offended him, but the appetizers arrived, and he used them to avoid answering. So I waited until the servers had left the table and asked again.

"I am a simple human, Miss Doe, and my allegiance to the duke relies solely on the significant retainer he pays me to look after his affairs in our realm."

"So somebody with enough cash could buy you off?" I made it a tease, but I was interested how he would deal with it.

"If anybody else had that much money, I suppose yes."

"You're that loyal?"

"He pays me that well."

He earned a smile, and I stopped needling him until dessert.

"Shouldn't we spend at least part of this business dinner talking about the cases?"

"I didn't realize this was a business dinner, but if you wish. What do you want to know?"

That caught me out. What did he think we were doing? If he thought he was hitting on me, he needed to check the definition. I decided to ignore it.

59

"Do we have any leads? Information?"

"In the case of—" he flicked his eyes from side to side, and I'll pat myself on the back for doing the same over his shoulder. Paranoid, maybe, but if the wrong person was paying too much attention, it might make things awkward. "Regards the inappropriate supplies, we know of at least one consumer in head office."

"Why didn't we call on him while we were there?"

"Management suggested a separation between the two projects."

I tilted my head from side to side to show I didn't agree but didn't care.

"Want to share where we can find him? Or her?"

"Do you have your phone with you?"

A moment later we were phone buddies and he had sent me an address in the Citadel.

"And how do I get in? Without getting drained, I mean."

"Merciful stars, I almost forgot." Miller looked shocked by his memory lapse, and he patted around his pockets unto he found what he was looking for. He handed me a slim, flat case. I opened it, and inside was an elegant, if chunky, necklace.

"I don't know if I can accept this, Mr. Miller."

"Why not?"

"I'd prefer to keep things professional while we're working together."

Where had the second half of that sentence come from? I certainly hadn't meant to say it. Miller looked panicked, and I realized I'd misread the situation so badly I wanted the chair to drop through the floor. I gave him a wicked, and bogus, grin. "Gotcha."

So many emotions flickered across his face that I may have

misinterpreted one or two, but the icy anger at being made a fool of came through real clear. Only for a second, but unmistakable. Killed the moment.

"Sorry. What is this?"

"The Duke's Tongue." He winced as he named it. "While you show it, you speak with the duke's voice. Once you put it on, it cannot be taken from you while you live, and its authority cannot be revoked by any except the duke or his successor." He looked thoughtful for a moment. "I can think of three people in the Citadel who would kill you for it, one openly. But as I'll be with you at all times, it probably won't be necessary to have it in sight. I would wear it, though. Can't tell when you might need it."

"You're shadowing me?"

"We are working together."

"But not joined at the hip?"

He didn't answer, but his face was setting like concrete and I didn't want to bring this down to a battle of wills when I wasn't sure who would win.

"What about the other project?"

"We know the location, and we have contacts and acquaintances nearby."

"At head office?"

"No, the branch office."

He threw me for a second, then I realized he meant up in my world.

"How come?"

"It's something of a rite of passage, I believe. Once a customer reaches a certain level of maturity, they tend to fly the nest—if only for a time. Think of it as leaving home to go to college."

"Or a perpetual spring break?"

He smiled. "That may be more appropriate."

I thought about what we had and couldn't see a clear winner for where to start.

"Which is more important?"

"To whom?"

"Miller, you are not making this easy."

Soft frown. "I am simply answering questions."

"But with another question. Straight answer: where do you think we should start?"

"I rather through you would make that decision." The frown dug in a little deeper and he paused while the busboy cleared the table and the server fetched in the coffee. And a little plate of chocolate mints. Mine.

"Both situations are explosive," Miller said. "Or will be if word of what we are doing gets out. The contact in the Citadel will be most difficult to keep contained once we have … discussed things with him. On the other hand, that we are looking for the CEO's protégé is sensitive, as well as being the higher priority. That task must be concealed or disguised. There are those who could use the information to hurt the CEO. We could employ the ruse that there is some minor misdemeanor he needs to account for?"

"So we have better reasons to start at the branch office than the Citadel. Tomorrow?"

Miller nodded. "I can pick you up at three?"

"No. If something happens to you, or I need to get some place and you aren't available, I have my own way in. I'll need the GPS coordinates of the, um," I struggled for another way to say suspect. My phone chirped again. A contact record with a phone number and address. I had been going to ask, but our quarry was using the name Charles Hawke.

"You make a good point." Miller folded his napkin and dropped it on the table. "Shall we meet there at three instead?"

The evening was over. I nodded. "Thank you. I enjoyed the meal. And the company."

And where the hells had that come from, or was my auto-polite over-reacting? It got me a nice smile. The most genuine smile I had seen on his face. He lost an edge of wary alertness I hadn't noticed before.

"It was my pleasure. And I insist on driving you home. Getting an Uber at this time is a nightmare."

He wasn't wrong and I agreed. The cloak room rang through to the valet while we retrieved our coats, and a car was waiting by the time we ambled outside. I expected something exotic, but it was an ordinary—if top of the range—BMW. Still nice, though.

Neither of us spoke much as he drove. Maybe he was one of those who liked to concentrate on what they were doing, but he could have run out of small talk, like I had. He pulled up outside my house and was out and had walked round to my side before I could figure out how the handle worked.

He opened the door for me and held out his hand. I appreciated that. The BMW was a little low, and my LBD was maybe a little high. He let go as soon as I was standing, and it got awkward. Part of me was expecting a kiss, at least on the cheek, which horrified me. It had been a nice evening, and somewhere during it I decided he was OK, but it was a business dinner, not a date. Thing was, he looked like the same thoughts were going through his mind.

Inviting him in for coffee flickered across my mind until I remembered what he said about my house wards, and I was still trying to decide what to do when he held out his hand.

"A very productive evening, Miss Doe, and most enjoyable. I look forward to working with you. Until tomorrow?"

"Three o'clock," I agreed, shaking the hand. He walked around the car, got in, and I took a step back before it purred expensively into the night. Had I just watched him go? Crap. What if he saw me?

I turned back toward the house. A curtain flipped in a second-floor window. Late or not, it was time to have that conversation. I stomped up the stairs and knocked on Amanda's door. There were no lights on inside, but I knocked again, louder. I had seen something moving inside, through the door glass.

Amanda came to the door, tousled hair, PJs, and dressing gown. I pushed past her the closed the door behind me.

"Jane, I don't think-"

"My house, my rules. New rule number one. No peeping through the windows at Miss Doe every time she goes in or out."

"I wouldn't-" but her face was bright red.

"You just did, and three days ago. And I've noticed more than once before that." I let the angry in my voice ease away. "I like you, Amanda. You're a good tenant and I want us all to get along. But you can't spy on me."

"Aren't we being a little paranoid?" Amanda tried for arch and superior and pushed my button instead. My voice went back to hard.

"I'm not. Maybe you should be. I won't stand for it."

I let myself out and closed the door firmly behind me. What on earth could she be finding so interesting about the back and forth of my life?

Evidence, At Last

"Is this the lady from the hospital? I'm sorry. I forgot your name and it's not on the card."

Tasha had just answered an 'unknown number' call.

"Yes, there was a mix-up at the printer. This is Tasha. Is this Connie?" It didn't matter that she used her real name here, the girl had never known it, and the Betsy persona had been for the benefit of the hospital.

"Yes."

"How are you?"

The girl paused. "I feel kinda empty."

"Understandable. Anything I can do to help?"

"You said if I needed to talk …"

"Would you like me to come see you?"

A pause.

"Would you prefer to come to my office?" Tasha suggested. "Wherever you feel most comfortable."

"Maybe there's too many memories of Ryan in here. Might feel like I was talking behind his back."

"Then come down to my office. Neutral territory."

"Can you tell me what bus line is closest? Ryan did the driving, and I don't trust–"

"I'll send an Uber for you. Don't worry, I'll expense it.

An address was given. Tasha made the arrangements then tracked the Uber so she could meet it when it arrived. They shook hands after Connie climbed out of the car, then Tasha stood aside to let her go in first. Connie put her hand against the door, ready to push, but stopped still as a statue.

"You an investigator?"

"I'm many things. But yes, I'm the Campbell half."

The was no point denying it. The lettering on the door was very clear. *Campbell and Doe: Investigations.*

"Does it bother you?" Tasha asked.

"Nobody said you were a private snoop."

Tasha chuckled. "Haven't heard it called that in a while, but it fits. Who did Detective Eddie say I was?"

"He said you was a friend who was good at listening to people."

"So nobody told any lies. Can't I be a PI and a good listener? Actually, it's part of the job."

Tasha put her hand on Connie's shoulder and eased her away from staring at the door. "I have a better idea." They kept a sign just inside the door for when neither of them were in the office, asking people to call the message service. She fixed it into the hook on the glass, then locked the door.

"I know a place, just around the corner."

The little Irish bar was in the mid-afternoon doldrums. A pair of old soaks had settled in for a long lunch at one end of the bar, and a couple of tables were taken near the windows. Even the music was at a sensible level. Tasha dropped Connie into a deep booth at the back, private and cozy, while she fetched drinks. The tension around Connie's eyes and mouth had eased some by the time Tasha got back.

"Better?"

Connie, with a pale moustache from the creamy head of the Irish ale she had asked for, nodded. The office would have been a cold and hostile place to the girl, and Tasha would have fought to get anything out of her. Now all she needed was a push to get her started.

"How are things?"

Connie shrugged and wiped away the moustache with a finger. "Hard. The hospital wants to ship Ryan out, but nowhere will take him. I don't have the money for a grave or cremation, and his folks are being funny. I'm trying to get help from the City, but there's so many forms and permits ..."

Tasha felt for the girl. Part of her wanted to throw money at her until she felt better, but that wasn't her place, nor why they were here.

"Was there something you wanted to talk about, Connie?"

To Tasha's surprise, the girl looked her hard in the eye. "You folks seem mighty interested in Ryan's doings. You gonna pay me?"

Tasha leaned against the back of the bench, distancing herself, shifting thing from friendly and cozy to business. "No, Connie." Eddie would be furious if he ever found out she had turned down a lead for the sake of a few bucks, but Tasha had never trusted information that came with a price. "We are trying to help others like Ryan, others like you, and we need information to do that. But I won't pay you for it, not money. I know it's hard, and I know people are pushing you to make decisions to spend what you don't have."

She paused, waiting to see if Connie got mad. She didn't. Her shoulders sloped, and her eyes stared into the top of her glass. Connie had been bluffing.

"What I will do," said Tasha, "is speak to the hospital and tell them to back off. I will look into whether there is anything I can do to expedite your applications to the City, and I will ask around to see if I can find a sympathetic mortician with reasonable rates. Would that help?"

"You'd really do that?"

"Of course."

"I didn't want to shake you down for the money. My friend said the police did it all the time, and she made me promise to try."

Tasha smiled. "I think your friend may watch too many cop shows on TV. Forget it. I'm happy to help."

"What did you want to know about Ryan?"

"Tell when he started to change?"

"Good change or bad change?"

Interesting, thought Tasha. "Whichever came first."

Connie took a deep drink from her beer before she began.

"About six months ago, I guess. Ryan wasn't too smart, but he worked hard. He had a job tossing boxes at a delivery company on the edge of town, moving stuff from the big rigs to the city trucks. He liked a beer most Fridays, but he never come home too drunk, and he never hit me."

"What changed?"

"These guys started coming to the bar he used and took a liking to him. I never met them, but I didn't trust them. They sounded like college boys keeping him around to poke fun at. He started going out Saturday nights, too, and coming home smashed." She sighed. "But it changed again. He was still going out with them two nights, but he wasn't drunk. He was full of himself, all confident and smart and coming up with these grand ideas how he was going to make a fortune and we

68

was going to live in a grand house with fancy cars."

"Did anything else change?"

Connie blushed. "In the bedroom."

"How so?"

Connie couldn't meet her eyes. "We had always been good together, but those nights he would change. He would want it for hours, and he was more ... powerful. Didn't hurt me, but it was kind of awesome."

"And in the morning?"

Connie scowled. "Oh, by morning he was like a bear with a mouthful of sore teeth. I didn't dare speak to him until two coffees after breakfast."

"And what did you think was going on?"

"I knew he was taking something, but he wouldn't talk about it. Told me I was imagining things. Then after a couple of weeks, he changed again. Spent most of the week acting worried."

"Do you know why."

"Because the rat bastard was spending all our savings on whatever shit he was putting into his body." Connie's eyes sparked with fury. "And he'd run the account dry."

"Couldn't you stop him?"

"By the time I found out it was too late. And that was when he changed again." She sighed. "He changed so much. That poison tore him apart."

"How?"

"When we had no money left, he got real desperate about it. Couldn't sleep nights. Twitching and fidgeting all evening. They even gave him a final warning at work because he wasn't concentrating on what he was doing. Then he got all happy for a while, and it was back to grand plans and ... stuff."

"But it didn't last?"

Connie shook her head. "He started to look pale, sickly, and then I noticed those marks on his arm. I asked him right out if he was injecting something, and he promised me it wasn't anything like that. But he got weaker, and then his arm got infected. He was still taking the damned poison, but he wasn't stealing from me to do it. I couldn't figure out where he was getting the money, but I couldn't believe he would hurt anybody. The highs got sharper somehow. Edgy. They didn't last as long, and when he came down, he couldn't move for a day. Just lay there staring at the TV, no matter what was on."

She stopped, then sighed.

"And then he went missing. You saw the end of that."

Connie picked up her glass and Tasha said nothing while she drained it.

"Thank you," said Tasha. "That must have been hard for you."

Connie shook her head. "More I said the easier it got. Any of it help you?"

Tasha nodded. "There is very little information about this drug or how it affects users. At the moment, everything helps."

Connie dug into her bag. "Almost forgot. They let me have his things from the hospital." She held out a plastic zip lock bag. "You may as well have these. I think they burned his clothes. They smelled pretty bad."

Which the hospital wouldn't have done if the police hadn't told them they had no interest in the victim. Tasha tried to keep the anger from her face. Eddie hadn't been exaggerating. Things were even worse than she thought. She took the bag. Through the plastic she could see a phone, a wallet, and a few cards.

"We'll check these out. Does he have a PIN for his phone?"

Connie nodded. "Think so, but I don't know what it is. It won't be clever. Maybe his birthday or mine."

Tasha took a note of both, and those of his parents, plus any other ideas Connie had.

"Are we done?" Connie fidgeted, and looked over Tasha's shoulder towards the door.

"Unless there's anything else you want to tell me. Did he mention the names of any of his friends? Did he take you to meet them?"

Connie shook her head. "I didn't meet none of them, and he wouldn't talk to me about what they got up to."

Tasha could think of a dozen more questions, but Connie had lost interest. She had something she needed to tell. Now she had got it off her chest, and got something back for it, she was done. Tasha could respect that. The girl gave them much more than they knew that morning.

"And you'll speak to those people?"

Tasha nodded. "I will. I'll text you with anything I find out from them, or about Ryan."

They rose from the booth and walked to the door. Rain spattered against the window. Connie sighed and put on a mock-tragic expression. "Don't suppose I'm due another of those Ubers?"

Tasha smiled as she shook her head at the girl's poor-me act and reached for her phone.

Door...

There is an area on the edge of downtown called Petit Paris. That's not its official name. It was christened back in the 30s, when the area got overrun by artists and poets trying to turn it into the left bank of the Seine or something. Might have worked better if there had been a river there.

But it still had a bohemian rep. Loose, but no red-light district. Arty. I had been meaning to visit, but somewhere like that is better with company.

It wasn't all hippies and beat poets in skinny black jeans and berets. Nothing proven, but a persistent rumor claimed that the deeper in you went in, the darker it got. Sounded fun.

Douglas comes off 7th, and I rode west until I saw Aspen Drive. Miller had parked the BMW outside a three-story apartment block, styled to look like a row of New York brownstones. I pulled up behind, got off, and rested my helmet on the headlight. Then I glued it there with a quick spell. Peterson wouldn't have approved; he didn't like me using magic for frivolous stuff. My argument was the best way to feel comfortable with it was to use it. And he wasn't here to complain.

Miller got out his car and came back to stare at my beautiful girl.

"Wouldn't something more—modern?—suit your stature better?"

I covered the turn signals with my hands, like I was covering her ears. "Shhh. You'll hurt her feelings."

"Her? Miss Doe, there is nothing feminine about that machine."

Now he'd hurt both our feelings.

"Never judge a girl until you've ridden her."

As the words left my mouth, my face burned bright red and my hand flew up to cover my mouth. Miller's eyes widened, then he laughed; it was a proper gut-level, ugly laugh, and I laughed too.

"Miss Doe, no offence to your motorcycle, but I can't think of a situation where I wouldn't rather walk than ride. Shall we? His apartment is in the loft."

Face still burning, I followed him up the steps.

Money, again, and it triggered me a little. The outside of the brownstone was smart, clean, as was the street, and the house was *big*. Then you got inside and realized that there were two apartments on each level. Hell, the building even had an elevator. It was just big enough for four people or a couch on its end, but still. And it wasn't enclosed; it was out of the thirties with open grilles on each side, and a folding one at the front. If you were feeling energetic, a stone staircase, maybe marble, wound up around the lift gear. It would take major cash to rent here. Certainly more than I had to spare, and I wasn't hurting.

We took the elevator. It hissed a lot, which explained the absence of cables, and it bounced as we started and stopped.

Miller looked at the door numbers when we got out and turned us left. He pressed the buzzer and we waited.

"Were we expecting anybody to be home?" I asked.

"I have no information on how he lives his life, Miss Doe, only that this is where he lives it. Do you have a means of opening the door that would be more subtle than shooting the lock out or kicking it down?"

"Perhaps." This was the sort of stuff I was still working on, detailed magics with fine control and delicate sensing. The flash-bang stuff is second nature to me, though. I put my hand to the door and let my focus slide down my arm and radiate from my fingers.

It looked like a keyhole, but it wasn't. It was electronic. Something in the keyhole sent a signal into the lock, and the lock sent the information elsewhere for approval.

Magic and tech don't like each other. I keep my phone in a case impregnated with lodestone and obsidian dust. Doesn't do wonders for the reception, but it stops it self-destructing every time I touch it.

That was an option here. A tiny spark of magic could fry the device in the lock, but I didn't think that would get the door open. I reached in further, found the thing that *did* open the door and traced the wires back to a unit on the wall, like the button pad for an alarm. Great, but blowing that up wasn't an option either.

The technology was almost visible, the circuits and connections glowing electrically in my mind, but I didn't understand any of it. So sue me. I can't study everything at the same time. But I did get a wacky idea. I sent it good vibes; positive thoughts and happy magic. Gentle and friendly and unthreatening and *click*.

Pushing the door open before it changed its mind, I looked up at Miller with a grin I couldn't wipe off my face.

"You have never done that before, have you?"

I shook my head, still grinning. Miller rolled his eyes, but I could see he was trying not to smile too. He walked into the apartment and I followed.

It seems visiting vampire cribs gets old real fast. Admittedly, this one was more modern, more tech, than others I had seen, but it still reeked of unearned money, indulgence and entitlement. It was a look I was getting bored with. I checked out the bedroom and decided I really didn't want to search there in any depth. The bed was oversized and there were way too many mirrors, especially on the ceiling. Which stank of narcissism until I remembered vamps had no reflection. So he and his lovers could watch themselves being screwed by an invisible man? It was getting too weird for my taste, so I went back to dig around the living room.

The first thing that caught my eye were the windows. Along one wall they rose from floor to ceiling, and even slid open to give access to a balcony just wide enough for a table for two. I didn't know Ancaster could look so good. The view would have set the rent at twice that of any other apartment. On one side rose the towers of the financial district and the downtown apartment blocks, then the view swept dramatically across the city to the river, but only as far as the ferry terminals. Beyond them, the dreary industrialism of the docks hid behind a couple of fancy office towers.

Don't go trying to find Ancaster. It's not the one in Ontario, and you'll never find it on any map of the US.

A low table sat in the center of the windows. At one end were a pair of high-power binoculars, but at the other was a well-thumbed leather notebook, twice the size of a credit card. I pick it up, flicked it open, and groaned. Seriously? He actually had a 'little black book'?"

Miller came out of the second bedroom, his face expressionless. "There is nothing of interest in there, Miss Doe, and I suggest that you do not waste your time with it."

I didn't buy him. He was hiding something. Then I remembered the master bedroom and decided he might be right. I held the book up, then tossed it over to him. He examined it.

"How traditional." He read a few of the entries. "Frank and detailed, too. There must be dozens of women in here. Will we need to speak to all of them?"

The door opened before I could answer. A girl walked in; tall, leggy, blonde, generically attractive and with a bratty face. Preoccupied with wrangling a half-dozen high-end shopping bags through the door, she had taken three steps into the room before she even noticed we were there.

"Who the hell are you?" She had dropped the bags and was digging in her purse for her phone. "You'd better get out or I'll call the police. Hawke will rip you apart if he finds you here."

I tossed a little ball of magic towards her head and popped it, frying her cell phone. Then I flicked my finger at the door, and it slammed shut behind her. She leapt out of her skin, then gave me a terrified look.

"How did you do that?"

"Sit." I pointed at the couch. She shuffled at first, then hurried to where I had pointed.

"Hardly subtle, Miss Doe," Miller muttered, but I was more interested in her sleeveless cashmere top in flawless white. It had a turtleneck.

"Show me your neck." I tried to make it sound like a

command, not a request. The girl looked like she was about to burst into tears, but I guessed she had used that trick so many times she did it without thinking. In fact, I was betting the whole blonde thing was BS.

"Save it and show me, or shall I come over there and look for myself?"

Her hand crept up under her chin, her fingers tucked into the turtleneck, and she pulled it down a fraction.

"Mess with me once more and I'll make the whole thing disappear."

"Miss Doe!"

I ignored Miller. The girl's arms folded over her chest and I guessed she was commando under there, but Miller was annoying me. I stormed across the room until I was between him and the girl, with my back to her and my face very much in his.

"He is feeding from her," I said, somewhere between a mutter and a snarl. "Or why else would she be hiding her neck? She's aware of the arcane world. She's being screwed by a vampire and knows it. Stop treading on my style."

His eyes widened and I think I surprised him with some part of the outburst. After a heartbeat he nodded and I stepped back, turning to face the girl again. She still hid her neck. "Last chance." I raised my fingers in a fake magical gesture and she flinched. The collar came down and I could see the scar where Hawke had sucked blood from her.

I glanced over my shoulder. "Can you tell how long ago he last used her?"

Miller gave me a nod, crossed to the girl and peered at her neck. He raised his fingers. She flinched away at first, but he lightly brushed them across the scars over her jugular.

77

"My guess would be ten days, maybe twelve." He put his hand on the top of her head and tilted it forward, then pulled the collar down at the back and tutted.

"And he hasn't even pledged her."

He let go of her head, but only long enough to put a finger under her chin to tip her face up to his.

"Does he make you allow others feed from you?"

She nodded, and the hurt in her eyes made my heart ache for a moment, and I decided Hawke better hope Miller got to him before I did.

"Was he the last one to feed from you?"

She nodded again. Miller stepped back and I saw her take a breath like she had forgotten how until that moment. I sat in a chair opposite her, and Miller stood behind me. Knowing he was there, how it must have looked, made me feel incredibly powerful in that moment. I pushed the notion away. I wasn't, and he was just an employer.

"When did you see him last?" I asked.

"I'm not telling you anything."

"We aren't here for you," I explained. I still hadn't sized her up. Was she love struck, or trying to milk Hawke for every penny she could get out of him? "People in his family have concerns for his safety and we are looking into his whereabouts. Did he talk about his family much?"

The sneer hinted at my second option. "He said he hated his family. All his vamp friends tried to find out who sired him, but he wouldn't tell. Just went on and on about how his elders were such a drag and always trying to cramp his style."

"Sounds like an emotionally stunted high school jock," I muttered, more to Miller than the girl.

"Closer than you could know," he mumbled back, but the

girl was nodding as well.

"That was him. Rich boy trying to pretend he hated his folks while he lives off their money."

"And that's why you went with him?"

The girl nodded. "He wanted an innocent little blonde to corrupt. I gave him exactly that."

"While he bought you everything you wanted and showered you with spending money?"

She gave me a twisted grin, loaded with sadness. "That was the plan. Worked fine for a while. I was even OK with him feeding on me. It made the sex ..." She blushed. "I was banking his cash good, and we were great together."

"Then he started sharing you around?" Miller asked. She looked even more miserable and nodded. "Did he offer to pledge you?"

"What's that?"

So that was a 'no'.

Miller answered, as much to me as her.

"Pledging is a commitment, and a protection. To feed from one who has been pledged is unheard of, and usually results in a duel. It simply isn't done. At the same time, the one pledged promises not to willingly allow another to feed from them, thus making sure that the sire always has ..." He coughed, uncomfortable. "An adequately stocked larder."

The girl looked stricken. "No, he never said anything like that to me."

And I understood. "You fell for him."

She glared at me for a moment, trying to look hardened and self-sufficient, but I saw the tears pool in the bottom of her eyes. Eventually, she nodded. "Hard. There's something about him. I'd do anything to make him happy. Have done."

Miller sighed so hard I felt his breath on the back of my neck, and it sent goosebumps down my spine. He got up from the chair and moved to sit next to the girl, then he opened Hawke's little black book and tore a blank page from the back. He wrote a phone number, and a word beneath it.

"Miss." He frowned. "I'm sorry, I don't recall asking your name."

"Amber. Amber Harding."

"Miss Harding, Hawke has abused you. I think you know this even through the infatuation you feel for him. There is no way that you will be able to free yourself from this situation while he lives. Sadly, it is my mission to see that he does." He handed her the slip of paper. "Please, call this number, if you can. They will ask you for an authorization. I have written it below the number. They will help you, if you wish it. Now, let's begin again. When was the last time you saw Mr. Hawke?"

"Ten days ago," said Amber. "He took me to the Green Cat." She swallowed. "They were having a taster night."

"Taster night?" I asked.

"They each bought someone, and they shared us around. 'Sips and licks' they called it. There were five of them. There used to be six, until Selene stopped coming."

"Can you recall their names?"

Amber closed her eyes. "Selene, Diana, Hawke, Cougar, Serpent, and—" she screwed up her eyes. "I always forget this one. He got so mad when I forgot his name, he used to slap me. Scorpio. It was Scorpio."

"All trying to hide their true identity?" I asked.

"All in the book," Miller raised it to eye height and waggled it. "So if they were trying to stay secret, he wasn't doing a good job."

"They used the names to be cool." Amber's voice was bitter. "They sounded and acted like rock gods, or something."

"So what happened at these gatherings?"

"The usual. They shared us around. The boys tried to grope me when Hawke wasn't watching. Diana, too. They knew it would make him flip if he caught them. Then they started talking about Selene, and Serpent started this ghost story thing that she'd gone missing in the Garden."

"Where?" I kept my voice low. I didn't want to startle her or distract her from her story.

"Cherry Tree Garden. It's deep in the heart of Petite Paris. There's a rumor that people go missing if they hang around the bars there. Serpent was pushing that Selene had said she was going there a day or two before she went missing."

"Did they tell anybody when she disappeared?"

She glanced at me and shook her head. "Who would they tell? Hawke was saying it was all crap, but Serpent was going on and on about it, claiming that a vamp had gone missing every month for the last six months."

"Was that true?" Miller looked horrified.

"Hawke didn't think so. He and Serpent got into a fight about it and Serpent dared him to go there every night for a week. Hawke agreed. He went the next day, and I haven't seen him since."

I snuck a glance toward Miller. He looked like he was still trying to process the possibility five more vampires might have disappeared.

"Do you have a picture of Selene we might borrow, or copy?"

The girl looked around the room, then pointed to a small frame standing in a bookshelf. "There. She's the girl with the black hair. Hawke and Diana are to her left, Serpent, Scorpio

81

and Cougar to her right."

It wasn't much, but Miller took a photograph of it with his phone. At least we knew what they all looked like

"Thank you, Amber. Are you going to be OK?"

She swallowed hard and looked around the apartment. "I guess so. I just feel so empty, not seeing him for so long." She looked so lost I worried she was going to do something stupid. I reached forward and tossed one of my cards onto the table.

"He bled you, now you bleed him, and this place, for anything that will move. You call the number my friend just gave you and ask for help. Find somewhere else to be. This place is nice, but it's not good for you. You think of anything else, or you need any help, you call me on that number."

Amber looked back and forth between us, then nodded. I had done everything I could, other than taking her back to my house and locking her in the laundry. I stood up, and Miller joined me.

"Thank you, Miss Harding. I wish you well." Miller nodded to her and walked to the door. I leaned forward, tapping my card and the note he had given her. "Call."

I got a smile, and I thought I could see some life in her eyes. We let ourselves out.

...to Door

"Do we have an address for this Serpent?" I asked on the sidewalk. Miller looked in the leather notebook, then rattled it off to me as I tapped it into my phone, then I copied it into the map app.

"About a block south. Ride or walk?"

He looked up at the sky then rolled his shoulders. "My car is safer here. Your motorcycle, however, seems rather vulnerable."

"Try it," I dared him. "See what happens."

"Thank you, but no." He took a half step backwards. "The last time I underestimated a woman with a smile like that it cost me six months work in Yemen. Shall we?"

I compromised to the extent of leaving my leather jacket on the back seat of his car, then we set off.

It was longer than it looked on the mapping app, and the neighborhood seemed to deteriorate with each step. Not Dockside bad, but Miller wasn't wrong to suggest we leave the car and bike where they were.

Serpent's place was in another apartment block, but this had never been as up-class as Hawke's crib. Maybe I'd judged too soon, and there was something outside the vampire stereotype

I knew. Miller stared at the buttons on the entry phone, trying to find Serpent's, but I just ran my finger down all of them. Someone always pushed the button.

The door clicked and I pushed it open. "What floor?"

"Third. Apartment D."

He turned toward the stairs—no fancy elevator here—but I put my hand on his chest and stopped him. Stopped me, too. The skin beneath his shirt was firm and I could feel the muscles. I swallowed hard before I could speak.

"Can I ask a favor? Hold back. Let me run the conversation. Maybe even stay out of sight."

"If you wish, but why?"

I reached into my shirt and pulled out the Tongue. Really, we had to find a better name for it. "I need some confidence in this. I take your word on how it's supposed to work, but sometimes these things don't get the same respect out in the wilds as they do close to home."

He didn't say anything, but he did stand aside and invite me to climb the stairs first.

The door of Apt D looked like someone had busted it open more than once, and I pounded hard on it. If anybody was in there, I couldn't hear them moving so I pounded again.

"All right, all right," shouted a voice from within. "Gimme a second."

The door opened and a scruffy face looked out at me. "What?"

"Need to talk to you about Hawke. May I come in?"

"Don't know any Hawke. You a cop? Show me a badge."

He was wearing a vest, shorts, white sports socks, and looked like he hadn't shaved for a few days.

"Don't need a badge, I have this." My finger pointed at the

Tongue. He peered bleary towards my fingernail, then his eyes opened wide and he stumbled back a step.

"Shit. What?" His eyes narrowed. "Wait. No way they would give that to a stinking human, to *food*." He was building up into a rage and I loosened my fingers, ready to fire them up. "I should rip your damn throat out, drink your blood, then send your head back to the Citadel for the reward."

"Try it." I showed him my teeth and turned my clawed hands towards him.

"Enough," barked Miller, stepping into view. "Get inside, you dog. Or do you deny I exist too?"

So much for holding back.

"E... Emissary." Serpent bowed, sort of, and shuffled backwards into the room. "Forgive me."

"Silence." Miller closed the distance between them and backhanded Serpent across the face. He fell backward onto a coffee table, which collapsed under him. I had never taken on a vampire hand to hand, but I'd heard they were a lot harder to put down than that. Miller had skills. Or some power I hadn't felt. I wagged a mental finger at myself when I realized I hadn't paid that much attention.

Then Miller kicked him. In the ribs. That surprised me, as I hadn't pegged Miller as a shoot 'em in the back, kick a man while he's down sort of guy.

"Your sire will hear of this. And your house Lord. How dare you ignore the teachings. How dare you ignore one of the basic laws of your kind. Whatever you may think, whoever may hold it, the Duke's Tongue speaks in his voice. Would you prefer it if I took your name straight to *him*?"

I put my hand on his arm but had to tug at it before he paid me any attention. "Miller? We're here for a reason."

For a moment I thought he was going to kick Serpent again, but he snarled at him and turned away.

"Get up," I said. "And straighten yourself out."

Only then did a I get a chance to look around the place. It looked like the room of a slob in the worst frat on campus, the one on double secret probation and about to have their charter revoked. It was the room of someone who didn't care. I tipped a dining chair forward and dislodged the pile of empty pizza boxes it was holding up. I saw Miller sweep a half dozen or more beer cans from an armchair, then look at the cushion with a moue of distaste. He decided to perch on the arm.

Serpent shuffled backwards until he could haul himself up on to a couch that faced a fifty-inch flatscreen and a gaming console. I didn't know which one and I couldn't care less.

Odd thing was, the squalor was like a veneer, or a surface layer. Beneath it was a comfortable room with decent furniture and reasonable decor.

"What do you know about Hawke?"

"Rich kid and likes to make sure we all know it. Daddy is someone big, someone important, but he never says who. Been in that fancy apartment of his for six months, maybe eight."

"And you were friends?"

Serpent snorted. "He didn't have friends. He had groupies, hangers on. We hovered around him and snatched food from his table."

"Like his girl, Amber."

Serpent looked wary. "He never pledged her. She has no mark on her. No one possessed her."

I pushed my personal feelings down. Different culture. From his perspective, there had been no shame in using Amber. Now was not the time to make him see his error.

86

"Word is, members of your group left the area without mentioning it, without leaving onward details with anyone. Had you heard of that?"

His eyes shifted between me and Miller, then back again. "No."

"So you didn't know anybody called Selene?"

He flinched. His entire body twitched, and a terrible look crossed his face.

"Speak the truth, worm." Miller was still ice cold with rage, and I wouldn't have crossed him.

"She was one of us."

"One of your own kind, one close to you, goes missing and you raise no alarm? How many others were there?"

"What? I don't know."

"Liar. We have word you know of at least one more." His hand dipped into his jacket and came out holding an old Colt .45 automatic. Seemed a bit pointless to me, because you can't kill a vamp with a bullet. Can you? Serpent obviously thought you could, because he had gone grey and was cowering in the corner of the couch.

"Please, no. I didn't have anything to do with it. I don't know anything, except they disappeared. Four, including Selene. Five, with Hawke. I thought they were just stories, trying to spook each other out. Except it stopped being stories. There was a rumor, *is* a rumor. There's a new drug you can get if you go to the right bar and ask for Ruby."

"And Hawke went on a hunt for this drug?"

Serpent shook his head, in sharp and jagged movements. "No. He went looking for Selene. *She* went looking for the drug."

"Why? And the truth, now."

"Because I dared him. He'd been annoying us all night, bragging about this or that extravagance he bought for himself or his bitch ..."

He screamed as a ball of fire exploded in his crotch. "Call her that again and I'll burn them off."

His eyes darted between Miller and me, suddenly not sure which of us sacred him most.

"I told him Selene was probably in a drug house somewhere, either stoned out of her mind and too whacked to move, or locked down because she owed money she didn't have and was paying it off by ..." He glanced at me and red splotches stained his otherwise colorless face. "I could see it was winding Hawke up, so I kept making it worse." He sounded desperate, as though telling the story made him realize what he had done. "They never stopped me. None of the others said anything. They hated them as much as I did."

"Go on." Miller's voice was dangerously level. Controlled, but only just.

"He said we should tell someone, but I said he didn't have the balls to go in and fetch her himself. Pushed him that a single vampire should be more than enough to handle a half dozen humans, or more. Kept pushing it and pushing it until he took the dare. Until he said he would go in and get her out."

Miller reached into his jacket again, this time taking out a stubby tube he screwed into the front of the Colt. Serpent wept and begged for mercy. Part of me tried to argue it was murder, that I should intervene. A larger, wiser part of me told me to mind my own damned business and mentioned that it agreed with Miller.

Miller stood up, pointing the Colt at Serpent who finally fell silent, apart from a soft whimper.

"By the authority granted me as Emissary, and in accordance with the laws of the Citadel and of Night's Children, I find you guilty of conspiring to cause harm to another outside the Rules of Contest General, endangering or causing the termination of Charles Hawke, as sired by the duke himself, and failing to make the authorities aware of risk or harm to the one known as Selene, and to others as yet unknown."

"I didn't know. Oh Jesus and Mary. I didn't—"

The suppressor kept the discharge down to a discrete cough. A hole appeared in serpent's vest, but the only thing that trickled out was a liquid light I had never seen before. His face contorted in soundless agony as the light shone brighter, until his entire chest burned from within. He let out a brief, terrible scream as a soundless flash burst from his flaming heart, and his body dissolved into dust.

Miller used a handkerchief to hold the suppressor as he unscrewed it, then he looked about the floor until he found the discarded casing. That went into the handkerchief with the suppressor. He tucked the square of cloth into a pocket.

The rules seemed different in this world. I knew I should be shocked, that I would be if Miller had done that to a human, but the rules were different in this world. I glanced at the outline of dust that was all that remained of Serpent's body, and the only thought that passed through my mind was where I could get me some of those bullets.

Shoestring Forensics

E ddie burst through the door at the top of the stairs. "Please tell me you haven't opened it."

Tasha gave him a look that should have sent his privates cringing into his pelvis for safety.

"What are you talking about?"

"The bag. Those items have to go into evidence, and it's bad enough your prints and DNA are on the outside."

"Why?"

Eddie opened his mouth to argue but found nothing safe to say. Tasha pushed the bag toward him, across her desk.

"Take it, then."

Eddie reached towards it, hesitated, then drew his hand back like the bag had growled at him. "And what?"

"And get out."

"Ah, come on Nat. Not this again."

"Your call. I told you I didn't want in on this, but you kept pushing. You have succeeded in piquing my curiosity, but now you tell me you want to take our one and only lead and bury it in the evidence storeroom in the basement at Colingen Square."

"It's evidence. It has to be logged."

"Eddie, you told me yourself; they don't care. Connie tried to hand it in, they didn't want it."

"So does this mean you're in?"

"It means I want to have a look at what's in there. If it makes you feel any better, I have a forensic kit in the closet."

"Seriously?"

She rolled her eyes at him. "Don't you have one in the trunk? Wait, don't tell me. Leave me with some illusions you still know what you're doing."

Weston grimaced at her. "I guess you're right."

"Then wait here."

Tasha slipped through the door into the storeroom, found the forensic kit, and ripped the bag open. She skipped the bootees but wormed herself into the paper over suit and pulled the first pair of gloves over her hands and the mask over her face. Already feeling hot, she picked up a sealed clean-sheet and walked back to the office. Weston, living life on the edge as always, was stupid enough to laugh. Tasha glared at him over the mask until he shut up, then opened a drawer in her desk and took out a voice recorder. She switched it on and put it on the far side of the table. Ripping open the clean sheet bag, Tasha spread it out and pulled on the second pair of gloves.

"There's never a middle line for you, is there?"

"You mean I never cut corners? I suppose not. Bring me the bag, please?"

With fingertips gripping the tip of a corner, Weston brought the bag to the table and laid it in front of her. Tasha opened it and took out the items one by one, rather than just pouring them onto the table.

"Middle shelf of that cupboard." She pointed with her chin. "Fetch the camera. Take pictures of everything."

Tasha laid each item face up on the sheet, then waited while Weston figured out how to use the camera. It wasn't much to summarize the life of Ryan; the bag only held his work ID card, hanging from a dirty lanyard, his phone and his wallet. The wallet was empty, already skimmed by someone, but held his driver's license, a membership card for a strip joint out of town and a poker chip. Tasha plucked each out with tweezers and placed them on the table. She pointed at the poker chip.

"Have you seen anything like this before?"

Weston leaned over it, so close that she almost told him to mask up.

"Poker chips I've seen, but not this design, and not without a value or the name of the casino. What is that? A dog?"

Tasha shook her head. "Not sure, but it's no dog I can think of, nor a wolf. Notice the side, the pronounced molding seam? Could they be made to order, or 3-d printed?"

Weston shrugged and Tasha made a mental note to follow up later.

Last was the phone.

"Same cabinet. Phone cable, USB to Lightning."

"What?"

"iPhone."

"Why didn't you just say that?"

While Weston rooted around in the cabinet, Tasha angled the phone back and forth, making the light dance across the front and looking for grease marks from Ryan's fingers, but the screen was too dirty to see any frequent contact points. She pressed the home button until she got a keypad, then looked at Weston.

"We get ten chances, then the phone locks itself, permanently."

"I know."

"Where do we start?"

92

Weston thought for a moment. "You said she gave you birthdays?"

"Four of them."

Weston gestured she should try, and Tasha started tapping in numbers. Four birthdays later they were no better off.

"What now?"

Weston stared at the phone. "Just how stupid do we think this kid was?"

"You met Connie, draw your own conclusions."

"So, trailer trash?"

She scowled at him. "Judgmental much? No that's not what I meant. Connie doesn't have much in the way of an education, but she's smart in her own way. Tough. A little fighter."

"And her boyfriend was a doofus who let himself get set up as a patsy for a bunch of college kids, then stole from his partner and got himself killed."

Tasha scowled, but realized arguing was pointless. Besides, the portrait Eddie painted was not far from reality. She picked up the phone, poked it until the login screen came up, and tried the worst of the worst: 1234, 1111, 0000. The phone remained obdurately locked. She looked up at Weston. "Three left."

"And if we can't get the phone open, we have squat." He scratched at his head for a moment. "Did he have a driver's license, or his social security number."

Tasha snapped her fingers, which didn't work too well wearing gloves, and punched in the last four digits from the license number. The home screen opened.

"Good call, Eddie. Bring my laptop over from the desk, would you."

Tasha used the cable to connect the phone to the laptop and made to open an app. She hesitated. "You might want to look away at this point."

"Huh?"

"Plausible deniability. And I don't want to explain where I got this from."

"Oh." Weston wandered over to Jane's desk and sat on the chair. Tasha opened the app and clicked on the button to analyze the phone. "And don't mess with that chair. Jane will turn you into a frog or grow warts on your privates."

Weston raised his hands to show he was innocent, and they waited. The app chimed. Tasha disconnected the phone, then dropped it and everything else that had defined the life of Ryan Ellis into a fresh standard issue police department evidence bag.

"Here." She tossed the bag in front of Weston and stripped off her gloves.

"I thought you said—"

"I reconsidered. If anything does come of this, you need to be pure as snow. Check it in, then come back."

"You want me to go now?"

"The app will take an hour or two to analyze all the data we pulled off the phone. Besides, I'm starving. Bring food or suffer the consequences."

Who's Tailing Who?

We argued. Miller wanted to canvas the area, hoping for a lead not on Hawke, but on Selene. I wanted to retrace Hawke's steps, right down to looking for this 'Ruby'—whatever that was.

"The Selene thing still makes no sense to me," I said. "That trail is weeks old. If Hawke has been digging around where he shouldn't, people would be more likely to remember *his* face."

"I have my instructions." Miller was not going to budge, no matter what I said. I could see it in his face and hear it in every word. "If we start advertising Hawke has gone missing, people may start digging into who he is and why we are so interested. That in turn could reveal his familial connection to the duke, which in turn may lead to attempts at extortion or blackmail."

"You've been spending too much time with vampires." I frowned at him. Still, he was the boss, sort of, and he was paying the expenses.

We regrouped later that evening. I insisted he dress more casually and told him to park at least a half a block away from Cherry Tree Garden. I reverted to type with jeans, t-shirt, and my bike jacket. My girl got left three streets away with my helmet glued to the seat.

Right after we finished with Serpent, I had ridden around the area, just to get a feel for the place. It was nice, at least in the afternoon. Lots of bistro-cafe's, with outdoor seating and trendy young table staff. Several of the streets leading away from the gardens were trying to be darker or more edgy, and I texted a list to Miller. It was easier to leave him to arrange the schedule.

I walked into the first place on my list at a little after eight. Miller was already there. He sat at an out of the way table that still gave him clear look across the entire place. I walked up to the bar without looking at him.

"What can I get you?"

I gave her a smile but shook my head. "Sorry, business, not pleasure." I slid the picture of Selene onto the counter. "Trying to find this lady."

"Badge?" the server asked.

I shook my head. "Private. Mom and dad haven't heard from her in a while."

"My boss says we don't speak to nobody without a badge," said the girl, but I could see from her eyes that she didn't see anything familiar in the picture. I picked up the photo and put it back in my pocket.

"Hey, no problem. Thanks for your time."

I sauntered out and walked along the street to the next bar on the list.

"What can I get you?"

I tracked around the place like I was looking for someone. "I'll just get a coke until my friend shows up."

"No problem."

Soda in hand I took a table that gave me a view of the door. It also gave me an excellent view of the rest of the bar. Ten minutes later Miller walked in. We ignored each other and he strode up to the bar like a health inspector. I needed to have a word with him about that.

The server here engaged more than mine had and looked properly at the picture before shaking his head. Miller said something else. The server frowned, but I couldn't tell if he was angry or confused. Miller shook his hand and left.

Pretending to check my phone again and again, I kept my eyes moving all over the bar. I was looking for anybody acting out of sync with the mood of the place. Looking shifty, in other words. After ten minutes I gave up and sent a negative text to Miller before leaving my coke, grabbing my bag, and stomping out like I had been stood up.

That was what we did for the next half-dozen bars, and with no better result. I was getting disheartened and bored and was ashamed of myself for it. What sort of PI was I going to make if I couldn't do the grunt work?

My phone rang in my ear—I had made sure we both had wireless ear pods—just as I was setting up to watch the next performance by Miller. "Nothing," he said. "But that's the second time someone mentioned we are not the first to be looking for her."

"Understood. Ready." I hung up. People talking to themselves still drew attention, even today.

I walked into the next bar and had to turn covering my nose with my hand into an itch. I don't know who had picked the incense they burned, but they needed a second opinion. It was getting late now. Most of the bars were lively, despite it being midweek, but this place was half empty. I got my drink, picked a good table and waited for Miller to play his role yet again. And the sooner we could get out of this one the happier I was going to be.

Miller walked in and didn't so much as blink. Either he was uncomfortably good at controlling his reactions, or he hadn't smelt what I had. He did his schtick, and the bartender was helpful and informative. But when Miller turned his back to leave, everything changed. As he walked out of the bar, a customer three stools down turned to watch, then very obviously followed him. Meanwhile, the barkeep sees what the tail is doing, looks worried, and wanders to my end of the bar and picks up the phone. I couldn't hear what he said, but it was short and heated. Once he finished, the server turned and glared at the door.

I called Miller. "You have one on the hook." I hung up, tried to look like I wasn't hurrying as I got my stuff together, and took off after the rabbit we had just flushed.

Miller had already gone into the next bar by the time I was out and tailing his tail. I stayed in the fresh air, found myself a wall to sit on, and played with my phone while I watched. I sent him a text, too.

"Go to next bar. Check phone on entry. Turn back and go to cafe. Drink a coffee outside. Wait for text or call."

I didn't get an answer.

What I did get was a surprise. When Miller came out, his tail appeared at a window, looking casual but keeping an eye on him. Then a woman came out of the bar, looked either way, then stuck so close to Miller that she bumped into him when he changed his mind at the next bar. I tried not to chuckle. They had tried to switch and messed it up. She carried on into the bar, and the original tail stayed glued to the window, now looking worried.

I texted Miller and explained what I was seeing. He replied straight away.

"Coffee delicious. No hurry. Follow when I leave."

I wrote a snarky reply but deleted it. He might take it the wrong way. But he had coffee and I didn't, and I needed to pee. I looked along the street like I was waiting for someone. It wouldn't do for anyone to notice I was fixated on the bar window, though the original tail maybe hadn't heard of that rule. He still had his nose pressed to the glass, trying to peer sideways out of the window to keep Miller in view.

The street was busy. People wandered from bistro to bar, or vice versa. A few yards to my left I even saw a guy sharing his beer with an enormous dog that looked to have a lot of malamute or husky in its heritage.

I almost missed Miller finishing his coffee and leaving his table. I had no idea where he was going, but I waited to see who would come after him. It looked like window-boy drew the short straw, which made sense. Miller had been too close to the girl. Too much chance he would remember bumping into her.

But the window sitter was taking no chances. He waited until Miller had gone at least twenty yards up the street before he scampered out of the bar. After that, he slowed down, keeping Miller in sight but not crowding him. He didn't zigzag across the street like a crazy man, but he tried to keep at least a couple, if not a group of three or four, between them.

And he was concentrating so hard on not losing Miller he forgot to watch his surroundings. I sauntered along about twenty yards behind him, making no attempt to hide myself other than to keep looking at my phone like I was following the map.

Miller took a few turns, not too close together, but into smaller and smaller streets. The tail closed up on Miller and I closed up on him, until Miller took us into an alley, then stopped halfway along. As soon as window-boy realized what had happened, he tried to double back, which was when I stepped out and sprung our trap. I didn't have a carry permit yet, so I took out my telescoping baton and flicked it open. I thought the *snick-snick-snick* as the spring pushed it out to its full thirty inches was an ominous sound, like a rifle bolt being pushed home. The baton didn't look as threatening as a gun, but anybody who had been hit with one knew the damned things hurt. They could break bones easier than a baseball bat.

"Chill," I said. "We just want to talk."

But he didn't seem to be listening. Miller and I closed on him from either direction while he looked frantically for an escape. I held up my hand. We both stopped, still fifteen feet away from him. He was already spooked enough, and I didn't want to find he had a knife or a gun when it was too late to do anything about either.

That was when I heard somebody still moving. There were footsteps behind me, slow and cautious, and something else as well.

"Miller," I called. "Incoming."

His hand darted inside his jacket, but two dark shapes leapt at him from shadows. As they all rolled into the light, I saw they were dogs, and big ones, too.

No, not dogs. *Wolves.*

A figure walked out of the darkness behind Miller. He was tall, and the shadow from the peak on his baseball cap hid his face. It didn't hide the revolver he was carrying, though.

"I'll be asking the questions."

Still holding the baton in my right hand, I flexed the fingers of my left and drew strength from the ring on my thumb. I had stored a bucket load of wind energy in there for emergencies, and this counted. I would blow the guy across the alley and smash him into the wall.

Rookie mistake. I had seen the threat in front of me, seen a friend hurt, and forgotten my six. Just like the guy we had been following. Two pinpricks stabbed into my shoulder and, as I pulled the wind energy into my hand, fifty thousand volts slammed through me. I remember a bright flash, stumbling forward and hitting my head, then everything went white.

Echo from the Past

Halfway through chow mein and diet soda from Peking Palace, Tasha's laptop announced it had completed the analysis of the data from Ryan's phone. Weston picked up his box and sticks and walked over to her desk.

"Drop any of that on my Mac and you lose two months' salary."

Weston glared at her, then at the laptop, then put the food down at the edge of the desk and out of harm's way. "Anything?"

"Six hundred photos. App didn't find anything unusual, but we will have to eyeball each of them later to be sure it didn't miss anything."

"Great. Bet half of them are home porn."

"Animal. GPS tracking has come up with something interesting." Weston moved closer and Tasha tapped the icon that brought up a map of the city. Thin lines traced across the map like the finest spider web, but with several distinct loci. Tasha pointed at the screen as she named known locations.

"That's home, and there's where he worked."

"Let's go check out the others, then."

"Patience." She clicked on one of the clusters, and a street view appeared in a pop-up window. Centered in the image was a strip joint. "Care to bet that was where he met the college kids?"

"No bet. Also, no bet Connie didn't know that was where he was going. Want me to take that one?"

Tasha nodded and tapped the next locus. The fix was less precise, and the window showed a generic scene, the corner of a neglected block in the seedier end of the central district. That part of town was full of low rent, badly maintained apartment buildings, and populated mostly by minority families. The street image showed lots of parked cars.

"Looks busy," said Eddie.

"Maybe." Tasha had already tapped on the other locus. "No way of telling if that's the normal view or just a busy day."

Where there had been apartments, now the street picture was of warehouses from the streets paralleling the abandoned end of the dockyards. On one building was the logo of the delivery company Ryan had worked for.

"We'll need to eyeball those too," said Eddie. "What else?"

Tasha went back to the GPS map and stared at it long enough that Weston got edgy. "Not sure there's anything else to see here, Nat. We've checked out all three clusters."

She tapped on a single visit destination, right across town from everything else in Ryan Ellis' life. "Anomalies are always worth considering."

Weston shook his head. "I don't buy it. He could have given an Uber the wrong address or had to special delivery a parcel. We should be focusing on his haunts, his hotspots."

Tasha clicked on the map and got an image of a nondescript industrial unit. It showed no business name she could see, and in truth the place didn't look like it was being used. She made a note of the address and pulled up a different screen.

"Call records. Nothing stands out apart from these." The app had underlined a group of numbers in red. "Here's the first call to that number. And another a week later, both almost ten minutes long. Next call was barely sixty seconds, and the rest of these are unanswered."

"Man alive, there's at least one a day. Any text messages?"

"None. And I mean *none*. Either he wiped them from the phone's history, or Ryan hated sending them. I have no wish to disparage the man, but I wonder if he might have had literacy issues."

Weston nodded. "Could be. Do we have a name for this person?"

"Just the letter 'M' in the phone, but..."

Tasha copied the number and pasted it into another app. "There. Marcie Winger. Guess we'll have to pay her a visit too?"

"We? I thought you didn't want anything to do with this case?"

She looked up at him. "I thought I didn't either, but something about it worries me."

"You sure you're not getting the old buzz back?"

Tasha felt her heart sink. Part of her had been waiting for a comment just like that. Eddie was ginning, making like a joke, but his eyes were all puppy-dog and pleading. He probably wasn't aware he was doing it, nor how much he had really meant the question.

"Don't do that, Eddie."

"Hey, I'm just joking—"

"We have a lot of history, Eddie, and not enough time has passed to rub that out. I'm assisting you on this one case. It's not the old team back together again. I think that would be dangerous for both of us, particularly you. Stick your neck out far enough and someone in the department might think your head needs chopping off. If that happens, there will be no third name going up on our door."

"Kinda harsh, Nat."

She knew that. It felt like she was tough loving a wayward brother, making ultimatums and putting up walls. She still had the memories, and the feeling, of when they had been in a better place, but they were so overshadowed by the way things had ended.

"I just want to avoid any misunderstandings later on, Eddie."

He wouldn't look at her and his lips we pressed into a thin line, like he always did when he was mad at her but didn't want to start an argument.

"I'll understand if you want to reconsider working together on this," said Tasha.

Eddie snapped out of whatever was distracting him and raised open hands. "Hell, no. Can't do this on my own. I appreciate your input. And I guess I understand. Don't sweat it; one job, strictly pro. Got it."

Tasha let out a silent sigh. She wanted in on this and might even have worked on it behind Eddie's back, if he had decided to go solo.

Eddie gave an embarrassed cough and turned away. "Still think you should go see the Winger woman though."

Tasha held a photo of Ryan up so Marcie Winger could see it.

"Yes," she said. "I knew him."

"Then might I come in? I'd like to ask you a few questions,

if I may?" Tasha held out a business card.

Marcie took the card as she stepped aside to allow Tasha into the apartment. She closed the door behind them and led Tasha inside. She was not what Tasha expected. Winger was as tall as she was, and willowy. Every movement was elegant, and she seemed to glide rather than walk as she crossed to a table and put the card inside her purse. There was a naivety to her beauty that suggested she had never been anywhere near the modelling meat-factory, and that her movements were natural, not posed.

For the moment, all Tasha had were contradictions. It made no sense that Ryan would know anybody who lived in this part of town, and certainly not someone who lived in such an apartment. The floor plan was wide open, with long sightlines every direction you looked. Picture windows looked over a city that was almost beautiful in the mid-morning sun. The decor and furniture were very on-trend, and none of it seemed to bear the slightest trace of personality. *Lifestyle rental*, thought Tasha.

Marcie waved her towards the couch and took a seat on the opposite side of a black and chrome coffee table.

"Can I start with where you met Ryan?"

Marcie put a forefinger to her lips and frowned as she thought. For a moment, Tasha thought the action contrived, then she realized it, too, was entirely natural.

"It was the night I went to the blood people. They scared me. I don't like needles. He was kind. He held my hand while they took my blood."

Tasha shifted gears, changing how she was going to ask her questions. "What blood people were these? Do you remember the address?"

She shook her head, slow swings, slightly too wide.

"I don't know. Danny took me. Danny takes me everywhere. I like his car."

"Can you remember the name of the donation center?"

Another slow, wide shake, but this time with a bright smile. "Danny said we should go. He said my blood might be very rare and I might be able to help lots of sick children."

"Did you give Ryan your cell number."

An exaggerated nod. "He said we could be blood buddies, and that I could call him if I was afraid again." Her face collapsed into a deep frown. "He stopped calling. Danny gave me a new phone, and I lost Ryan's number. I wish I hadn't. I have to give blood lots of times. I get scared before, and it makes me so tired after."

She held out her arms, wrists up, and the split sleeves of her jumpsuit fell open. Even from the other side of the table, Tasha could see the needle marks were wide, like Ryan's.

"How often do they ask you to give blood, Miss Winger?"

"I go every week, and they take one bag of blood. Sometimes they take two. And they give me back one of lemonade."

Two? Every week? And what was 'lemonade'? Unless she meant plasma? The hairs on the back of Tasha's neck rose. They were killing this girl. "And where is Danny at the moment?"

"Oh, he should be back any time now. He said he had some business to attend to." She enunciated the last few words with great care, as though they were something he had taught her. Tasha hunched that now would be a good time to leave, but she couldn't decide if Marcie Winger needed to come with her. As if on cue, the door in the hall rattled and opened.

"Hi Danny," Marcie bounced in her seat and twisted to get

a view of the door. "We have company."

Tasha rose from the couch and stepped out into open space. The guy coming through the door was a big man, muscles bulging in the arms of a suit cut to show them off. The cut, by design or accident, also lumped out in a telling way under his left arm.

"Who da hell are you?"

From the corner of her eye Tasha saw the girl cringe down in her seat, face full of fear. Damn. She so wished she had acted just a few minutes sooner, because now she understood even more how much danger the girl was in. "Danny Morello. Been a long time, but I didn't think I'd changed that much."

He looked closer, then his eyes narrowed. "You bust—" His eyes flicked towards Marcie. "We had business five or six years ago. You got a warrant?"

"Eight years," she said and, as she did so, realized he was carrying a little more paunch under the suit than before. His close-cropped hair was too dark and too even not to have come out of a bottle. "No, no warrant. No badge, either. Not interested in you or the lady."

"Then what?"

"Someone I *do* have an interest in listed Miss Winger as a contact on his phone. He's..." It was her turn to look at the girl and wonder how she might take Ryan's death. "He's been missing a while. I'm trying to track him down for his fiancée."

"You want to talk to Marcie, you talk to my lawyer." He turned to the girl cringing in the chair. "What did you tell her? What?"

"Lighten up, Morello." Tasha struggled to keep her voice calm, unthreatening. "She told me how they met, then told me she couldn't remember where, and she told me how you replaced her phone to change the number." She turned to Marcie. "Thank you for trying, Marcie. I don't think you have anything we don't already know, but it was very nice to meet you."

"You, too, lady." But the girl wasn't concentrating on her. Her focus was on Danny Morello.

"Then I'll take myself out of your way." She raised her eyebrows at Morello, who stood between her and the door. His move.

He stepped back. Tasha walked to the door, opened it, and turned back to face him, making sure Marcie couldn't see her and maybe lip read what she was saying.

"You stay away from her and away from me," Morello growled. "If you know what's good for you."

"Danny, you sound like a bad gangster movie. I've no interest in her and less in you. But two things. Donating this much blood will kill her, and if I hear you've hurt that poor girl, I'll crush you like the roach you are. Think on it. No cop rules now."

She smiled, backed away until her back pressed against the opposite wall of the corridor, and stared him out until he flipped her the finger and closed the door.

Interrogated by Wolves

My left shoulder felt like someone had broken it, as opposed to the rest of my back and neck which just ached. Last time I hurt like this, my kick-boxing sensei had worked me over to make a point.

They had left me leaning against some kind of pillar. Someone had tied my hands behind it, and my ankles, also tied, were stretched out in front. A floppy bag, maybe a pillow slip, covered my head and the ground felt rough under my butt.

"About time." I didn't know the voice. "Who the hell are you people?"

"My name is Jane Doe and *ow*."

Somebody kicked me in the thigh and my entire leg lit up like fireworks.

"Don't lie to me."

"Back off, Babe."

Now *that* voice I knew. He was the bartender where we had picked up Miller's tail.

"Back off be damned. Harry's in the hospital because of her."

Say what? I didn't do anything to anybody.

"Sit down." He didn't raise his voice, but it cracked like a whip. "Now, you on the floor. Why were the two of you

110

following that man?"

How could two people get so many things in a row wrong?

"I wasn't following the guy in the front; I was following the guy following him. The one that ran out of your bar just before you made that phone call."

The silence was longer than it should have been, and I knew I'd scored a point. Then I realized something was missing. "Where's Miller. And where's the guy at the front?"

"Taser her," said the female. She had vengeance in her voice, but underneath was an eager desire to cause pain. "We're asking the questions, and I want some payback."

"Can we clear that up?" I asked. "What am I supposed to have done?"

"Harry's taser exploded in his hand when he shot you." The woman was shouting now, almost screaming.

Bar-boy spoke up again, but he sounded like his patience was about to expire. "How many times. The taser was junk. You bought the damned things on the cheap."

Now I had to make a choice. Play dumb and preserve my cover or scare the pants off these idiots and move things along.

"Yeah, that tends to happen when you taser a witch and she's holding a live spell in her hand."

"I will mess her *up*."

I heard movement, and knew she would get in at least one kick in before Bar-boy could rein her in. My turn. I put out my bottom lip and puffed air upward, like I was blowing hair out of my eye. I grabbed the air, toughened it up a little, and used it to whip the pillow slip off my head. She was sliding to a stop halfway between me and a pair of folding chairs. I waited until she stopped, then made the air around her feet solid, locking them in place.

111

Puffing out another stream of air, I grabbed it, toughened it up too, then wrapped it around her neck. Her hands went up to claw at it, but there was nothing there, and her eyes opened wide.

While Bar-boy was jumping to his feet to rescue her, I focused some heat between my wrists and burnt through the cord wrapped around them. Then cussed as I burned myself too. Air I was good with, fire still tended to get away from me.

"Hey," I shouted, just to make sure I had everybody's attention, then I made like Vader. I held up my fingers, pinched them, and thickened the air around Little Miss Angry's neck. Not enough to do her any damage, but she gurgled obligingly.

That was the moment I realized we weren't alone. I had been so busy looking after babe and Bar-boy, I hadn't looked around. I *really* needed to work on that. At least five more people lurked somewhere in the room. Sounds of movement came from behind me and on either side. In front, two men and a girl fanned out on either side of Bar-boy. A scream of magic hurt my ears, and two of them fuzzed in the air, like they were caught in transporter beams that reassembled them as wolves. What in all the hells had I stumbled into? Even Bar-boy upped the stakes by pointing his battered .38 at me.

"Anybody moves so much as an inch closer, and I snap her neck." I didn't shout, I went for low and growly. When in Rome, burn like a firework, right? Everybody hesitated. I could see intent firming up in Bar-boy's eyes, even though the barrel of the gun was waving about so badly I wasn't sure he could hit me.

"And don't get any ideas with that. I can still kill her before I die, and my death curse will torch this place before any of you can get out." And to underline the point, I lit up a small ball of fire in my free hand. I made a mental note to look up if there was any such thing as a death curse, assuming I got out of this. It sounded like a cool idea.

Now I had their full attention. The problem was, I hadn't had time to prepare where I was drawing energy from, and I was burning through my internal stores uncomfortably fast.

"Everybody, except you two, get behind those chairs where I can see you."

I ended up with two humans and three wolves, all of which were snarling at me like scrap yard killers. I recognized one of them as the malamute-cross I had seen the night before. It stared at me for a moment then it blurred. In its place stood a woman, a little shorter than me and just as tough. In a fight, I'd be a lot more worried about facing her than the crazy bitch out front.

"Now you, bartender, slide that gun over to me."

He thought about it, and thought about not doing it too. I squeezed the air a little tighter around Little Miss Angry's throat, and she hit him. "Throw her the damn gun. You know it doesn't work anyway."

Now who was bluffing who? The .38 skittered across the sawdust covered earth and bounced just as it landed to the left of my feet. I tried not to flinch, praying it wouldn't go off and randomly shoot someone. The crazy bitch was sure to blame me for that, too.

Undoing the heavy air around the girl's feet, I pointed they should both go behind the chairs and join their friends. I kept the air-noose around her neck, though.

Tossing the fireball into the air, I snapped my fingers and put it out, then reached down to the rope around my feet and carefully burned through it. No way was I going to scorch my boots. They were new and gorgeous. My thigh complained when I rolled onto my knees, burning where she had kicked me. That was going to leave a bruise, and it was going to slow me down.

Stretching forward, I picked up the .38. If it didn't work, why could I see the backs of shells in the drum? The hammer was already pulled back – which was why I flinched, remember? – and I aimed and fired so fast nobody had time to blink. For something that didn't work, it made a very loud noise and left a remarkably real hole in the wooden post right behind Little Miss Angry.

"Never, *ever*, lie that a weapon doesn't work if you are handing it over. That's beyond dumb." Shaking my head at them, I tucked the .38 into the back of my pants.

Her face flamed bright red, but the look she glared back at me left me in no doubt how much she would like to bite my throat out.

"The rest of you – oh, for heaven's sake stop snarling at me like that. If I wanted to hurt you, I could have killed you all while I was still tied up."

Not entirely true, but it seemed to work. The background rumble stopped, and the last two wolves shifted back into human form. Fully clothed. I only noticed that right now, and my idiot mind started trying to figure out how that worked before I brought it back to the task at hand.

"If my friend is safe to move, bring him here. Otherwise, everybody out except this pair." I stabbed my finger at the two who had been sitting in front of me.

"Fetch him," snapped Bar-boy, looking as nervously at my finger as he had the barrel of the .38. When the others left, I took a few seconds to look around the place. It was a barn, but then I pretty much figured that already. Wood beams and rafters, wood walls, a couple of stalls behind me, and hay bales stacked up to my left. Windows to my right, with a workbench and some toolboxes underneath. So we were on a farm, and a real one.

Reaching down with a hand, I brushed the sawdust aside and placed my palm on the packed earth. Questing downward through the ground, I felt the strength of the mother of all things and drew it into me. Combat magic works better in short bursts, or when you have time to arrange backup power. Everything I had thrown so far, I had drawn from within. I was in no danger of running dry, but one thing I learned already was working magic was like having an electric car; you never missed a chance to charge.

Throwing a little magical hook across the barn, I snagged one of the camp chairs and pulled it over to me. When I sat, I landed harder than I meant to. The chair creaked. My leg was really aching now, and it annoyed me I'd given Little Miss Angry the satisfaction of seeing that. I glared at them.

"Sit."

Stake Out

It cost her a hundred dollars for a room in the hotel opposite, but it was the ideal spot to watch the apartment block Ryan's phone led them to. Though the GPS hit hadn't been accurate to a door, it was obvious within minutes which house they needed to spy on. Weston, complete with camera and tripod took one window and kept the net curtains closed around the long lens. Tasha took the other and shifted the curtain just enough to give her an unobstructed view while she stood in the shadow.

"And you wanted to park outside and watch from the car?"

Weston muttered something under his breath. Tasha grinned and let it go. She had made her point.

The place was a classic stash house in some ways, not so much in others. A constant stream of cars parked and moved on, and a store would have been delighted by the foot traffic that passed through the front door. Enough to annoy the neighbors, but not so much to make them brave enough or angry enough to call the cops. Everybody on the street would know what was going on. What they wouldn't get from this stakeout was which apartment in the building the dealers worked from, and she would have bet her phone that nobody in there would say a thing if they were asked.

"Hey, I know him."

Tasha looked through the curtain.

"There. Short guy with the red jacket. Used to be a snitch for me. Quit about three years ago. Got his legs broken when he gave me a tip and word got back to the guy he'd snitched on."

"Car or on foot?"

"I guess on foot."

"Then what are you waiting for?"

Though she was faster, the man knew Eddie, so she let her ex-partner go first. The apartment they had borrowed was only on the third floor, and they threw themselves down the stairs before bursting out of the rear entrance. It opened onto an alley of dumpsters and wrecked autos.

The snitch headed along the street that passed the north end of the alley, and Tasha let Eddie play his hunch. They got to the mouth of the alley just as the snitch stepped into view.

"Floyd." Eddie stepped out into the sidewalk, arms wide in welcome. The snitch flinched, as anyone would when confronted by someone jumping out the end of an alley, but then his eyes rolled up and he shook his head.

"You gotta be kidding me."

"Long time no see, pal." Eddie deftly turned him into the alley and put one arm over Floyd's shoulders, steering him a half dozen steps away from the street before he realized what was happening. Tasha looked both ways along the sidewalk, then strode down the alley to catch up.

"Nobody saw anything, but if we don't get him out of sight the next person walking by will."

She grabbed Floyd's arm and between them they hustled him up the alley to a recess between two buildings.

"Aw, man. You said you'd leave me alone after last time."

"And you said you were going straight. I never believed you for a minute, so why would you believe me? We just need some intel."

"On what?" Then Floyd's eyes went wide and he pointed over his shoulder. "On those guys? They'll kill me."

"Just bring us up to speed on a few things and you can hobble on with your business."

"And if you don't, we'll drop the word that you did anyway," Tasha added.

Floyd looked at her. "Funny thing is, you don't look that heartless."

"We're following up on a guy who went missing," said Weston. "He turned up again a few days later, then died. We don't want chapter and verse. Give us something."

The snitch gave Weston a long look then chuckled. "You got bupkiss. You don't got the first clue what you've walked into here."

"We have a good idea they're pushing Ruby out of that flea pit," snarled Weston. "And I'll give dollars to dimes you have at least one about your person."

"You don't got no probable cause," Floyd blustered.

"Does this look like we are on the clock?" asked Tasha, and Floyd looked worried again.

"OK, OK. They're in apartment 2B. There have guns on the table, but I got no idea what they are. Could be fake for all I know."

"And how does a weasel like you get a taste for a hundred-dollar fix."

Floyd smiled and a tremor ran up Tasha's spine. He looked like he'd seen something holy. "You don't know 'till you've tried it, man. This shit turns you into a god. If I was on Ruby, I could have outrun either of you, even on these ruined sticks. Or beat you both to pulp. And it's the same every time. With coke, meth, you're always chasing after that first perfect high. With this, it's as good *every damned time*."

Tasha watched Eddie reach into a pocket and pull out the poker chip they had seen in Ryan's belongings. The liar hadn't taken them to the station after all.

"Know what this is?"

Floyd whistled. "People walking out of that rathole would kill you for one of those. They're like in that film. With the Golden Ticket. That, my friend, gets you a lifetime of free Ruby."

"And just how does that work?"

"Seriously messed up idea. You can give blood, if it's the right blood. They test you. If they like you, you get a chip. You take that to another crib; they test you again and bleed you. If it all checks out, they give you a different chip. Bring that back here, and you get one free ride."

"The other GPS hit?" Tasha asked. Weston shrugged, but Floyd shook his head.

"Heard two guys got shot for taking their phones, and that was by accident. Word got around after that. Look, any chance you might see your way to letting that poker chip drop on the floor right about here? I told you what I know. Give you more stuff. For a whole year."

"No, Floyd."

"Two years."

"I wouldn't put a dollar on you still being alive in a year, let alone two." Weston dug into another pocket and pulled out a clip of bills. He peeled off a hundred dollars in twenties and stuffed them into Floyd's shirt pocket. The snitch smiled.

"Still feeling guilty about the legs, Eddie?"

Weston slapped him gently on the face. "Get lost, Floyd. And keep your mouth shut, or I'll break them both again myself."

"You know he's just going to buy another fix with that," Tasha grumbled as Floyd hobbled swiftly away.

Weston looked down the alley after his snitch. "Don't they all, Nat? Don't they all."

A Mutual Sniff

"Who do you *think* we are?" I asked.

Seemed like a non-confrontational place to start. Get them to show their cards first. All stuff they teach in Confrontation Management 101.

"We know who you are, bitch-"

Bar-boy had put his hand on Little Miss Angry's shoulder and I saw him squeeze. I also saw her wince. Interesting relationship, but it shut her up.

"We didn't know," he admitted. "This was less about you and more about whoever it was you helped get away. It was him we really wanted to talk to." His face hardened up, and I could see that underneath he was just as angry, just as violent, as the woman sitting next to him. He just had better control.

"Things went crazy last night," he continued. "Nobody was supposed to get hurt. The plan was to hold you and the other guy doing the tailing, because you looked like a team. The other guy we wanted to scare off, with a warning about meddling in stuff that was out of his league."

He shrugged "Then you blew up the taser, and the guy at the front pulled a gun and pointed it at Chris, so Bree jumped him. They went over in a big tumble and he knocked himself out on a crate."

That did not please me. "So you rush your friend to the ER with a singed pinky, but the guy who knocks himself out on a hard edge you bring to a *farm*?"

"Didn't see any blood," the surly woman snapped.

"Cracked skull? Subdural hematoma? Concussion?"

The woman looked up at Bar-boy, and he looked worried. "We didn't think—"

"Obviously. This conversation will end real quick if I'm not happy when he gets here." I took a breath and tried to get the conversation back on track. "So why did you want this guy we were trailing."

"His pack are hunting on our range."

"You hunt?"

"We're wolves, what do you think we do?"

For a minute I thought she said 'werewolves', which would have put a whole different face on the game.

"You actually kill things?"

Bar-boy looked uncomfortable. "It's in our nature, but we do it out here, from the farm. It's been in my family for generations. We hunt up in the hills."

"And that's where this other pack is?"

"No, they hunt in the city."

"What? Somebody would have seen."

"There's more than one way to hunt, though there have been reports of dog fights on the southern edge of town."

He broke off when the barn door crashed open. The girl who had been the malamute, and the guy she hung with, helped Miller into the room. If they had untied his hands, it would have been a whole lot easier. He didn't look good; his skin was grey, and he didn't seem focused. I got up and pointed at my chair, then called out for a knife. At least they had uncovered his head.

Bar-boy slipped a knife for a sheath on his belt, flipped it over and held the handle out to me. I stepped towards him and reached out for it, but met his eyes as I did. "Honor? Until I've checked him over?"

He nodded and I turned back to Miller. I cut the ties around his wrists first, then turned his face towards what little light glimmered into the barn. We took basic paramedic training as part of the PI exams, but that was about as far as my knowledge went. His pupils were wide, but the place was dim. At least they were equal and didn't look blown. I made him do a finger track and checked his peripherals. He tried to bat my hands away. Good sign.

"Stop fussing."

"Stop fighting me and I'm done in a couple of minutes. Keep acting out and we go to an ER now. Irrational aggression is a sign of a brain injury."

He settled, but there wasn't much more I could do. His pulse was strong, he was coherent, and if anything his skin felt too cool rather than fevered. And he was grumpy, which was a good sign. My best guess, for now, was minor concussion but nothing too serious. I decided we could finish up here before we got him checked out at a hospital. I turned back to the wolves.

"We're not interested in your pack disputes," I announced, then I corrected myself. "Well, curious, but not officially interested. My name is Jane Doe. I'm an investigator. This is Miller. We have been trying to track down a missing person. Can't say who, but he is a friend of the woman Miller showed you at the bar. We were just canvassing the area when I saw Miller pick up the tail in your place, then saw you make a call.

We were also trying to encourage our mutual friend to stop for a chat and explain why he was so interested in us."

"But that's the thing," said Bar-boy. "I remembered another guy coming through with a picture of the same girl you were showing."

"Can you remember what he looked like?" Miller shifted in his chair and took more of an interest.

"Little shorter than you, slimmer, too. Overdressed, like a rich kid trying to show it. Pretty stupid stuff to wear trawling around the darker corners of the quarter. Likely to get him mugged. Typical vampire."

Sounded like a fair thumbnail of Hawke to me, but then the penny hit the sidewalk. "You thought he was a vampire?"

The tense woman in the chair snorted. "They stink of stale blood. We've given up warning the generics; they never believe you. Vamps smell so bad you can't believe the normals can't smell them too."

"We get a lot of vampires in the quarter," bar boy agreed.

"Was there anything else you remember about the encounter?" Miller asked.

"Not really. Pretty much the same as our talk. She started hanging around the quarter on her own. Made her stand out until she made a few friends. She kept asking for Ruby, but everybody knows you can't get that on the street. Then one day she left. Never heard anything more of her. The other guy was only around for one night. I assumed he checked everywhere and moved on, or found what he wanted."

"What's the story with the Ruby?"

Bar-boy gave me a look.

"Humor me. Just trying to get a fresh perspective on it from what I already know." Which was a lie, of course.

"It's new, only been around a couple of months," the smaller woman at the back piped up. "Supposed to be the new cocaine. You know, new fix for the rich and famous. Crazy expensive and you have to know the right people. Street dealers can't get it."

"Thing is," said Bar-boy, "she wasn't the first."

That got my attention, and I sensed Miller push himself straighter in the chair. "Oh?" I tried to sound like it was only mildly interesting.

"She was the third, or maybe the fourth. People come and go from the community, but mostly they don't ghost. Somebody always knows where they went, or who pissed them off. But these people stood out because they were so noticeable, then they just vanished. Maybe they were a bit larger than life." He bit the corner of his lip. "That's what we think this other pack is hunting. Vampires."

Narcos

"Eddie!"

A black Dodge van with a tinted windshield turned hard into the alley south of them, side door already sliding back. Tasha slid over the hood of Weston's, car and jerked the door open to crouch behind. No real protection, but better than nothing.

"Two" called Weston, slamming the lid of the trunk and crouching next to her. She turned to look as another van roared into the other end of the alley. Both stopped fifty feet away. Tasha had already drawn her Glock and pulled the slide. Weston drew, of all things, a revolver. She rolled her eyes and hoped he had loaders for it in his pocket.

Four men jumped from each van, and her heart sank. They were in black fatigues, with body armor and helmets. They covered their faces with goggles and scarves, and they were carrying PDWs, nasty little hybrids between a machine gun and an assault rifle. Then the drivers got out and backed them up with shotguns.

"We're outgunned," Tasha muttered.

"Ya think?" Weston did not sound pleased.

Whoever the uninvited guests were, they had tactical training, fanning out and finding cover where she would have sworn none existed. She might—might—be able to take out one team, but the odds of taking out the second without getting riddled were slim, and they would take Eddie down on a 'just in case' defense.

"Make your weapons safe and throw them out."

"We're cops," Eddie yelled.

"Don't care if you're the freaking president, toss your sidearms. And your spares. We search you and find anything, we use it on you."

Tasha didn't see any point in holding out. She slipped the magazine from her Glock, ejected the round out of the chamber and onto the floor, then slid it out the front of the car. A moment later, round pressed back inside, the magazine followed, as did a slim four-inch blade.

She heard the sound of Eddie's revolver, then the rattle-clatter of two speed-loaders. She waited. Surely, he wasn't that stupid, either to not have a hold-out, or not to admit it, but a few seconds later she let out a sigh as more metal scraped across the alley. And the flat slap of his badge. Well, it was worth a try, but Tasha didn't think it would make much difference.

"Phones."

They were good. Tasha took out her very nice and still new iPhone and sent it out to join her Glock.

"Hands and knees. Eyes on the floor. Crawl out until I say stop, then lay flat, hands wide. Anything else, we take out a leg and you do it again."

Tasha did as she was told. Stones and grit stabbed her as she shuffled forward. Something bothered her about these people. They were controlled, trained, but she heard a tension in their voices, and an excitement, like the one giving the orders was hoping she or Eddie would do something wrong. Like he was just waiting for an excuse to kill them.

Unless this was an ex-military unit gone rogue, or freelancing, it didn't make any sense.

"Stop!"

Tasha lay flat on the floor, arms outstretched. Boots crunched on the loose surface of the alley, then knees pinned her to the ground; one along her neck and over her shoulder, the other across her calves. Both hurt enough she wondered what would have broken if they had done the same to Jane. Then she grinned and wondered what Jane would have done to them if they'd tried.

Zip straps tightened around her wrists and ankles. Someone slapped a length of tape over her mouth and pulled a bag over her head. She breathed deeply in and out and got another surprise. Semi-permeable. This was the stuff of Black Ops and Special Forces. Suffocation hoods to leave the snatch disorientated and terrified, but not dead. Who the hell were these people?

They patted her down, one on either side, then picked her up, carried her to the van and threw her in. The van rocked, and she felt a thump as they threw Eddie in next to her. She waited for someone to roll them over, but either they were playing the positional asphyxiation game, or they had shown the first crack in their professionalism.

"Four and six, back to base. Ears on TAC6. You three with me."

The van rocked from side to side as people boarded and left, then they reversed out of the alley and set off at a sedate pace, driving normally, attracting no attention.

Tasha listened very hard, trying to filter out the road noise.

Next to her, Eddie's breathing was shallow and rapid. If he didn't control it, he could end up hyperventilating, but she had no way to warn him with her mouth sealed over with duct tape. She filtered that out too. She was listening for feet, for boots shuffling on metal or carpet. If the boots were close, two of the men were facing her. If they were far, the seats faced away.

It would be the work of a moment to break the plastic straps, to leap forward and crack the two heads closest to her together. They would have sidearms, and she would be able to draw one and have it to the driver's head before the passenger realized something was going wrong.

But only if they had their backs to her.

Her ears told her nothing conclusive. She stretched. Not testing the straps, just easing her muscles. The side of a boot tapped against her head as soon as she moved, and she let her body relax.

Now was not the time.

A warehouse door scraped open. The van moved forward a few more yards, then the engine died and the scraping noise came again, this time echoing and from behind them. Uncompromising hands dragged her from the back and dropped her. The floor was cold and hard under her knees.

She heard the sound of a pile of laundry being thrown on the floor. Somebody cursed, then she heard a punch and a groan. They were working on Eddie again.

"Stay up. I have to pick you up again I'll kick you in the face first."

Tasha's eyebrows raised. Less professional. More like a boy, but frightened by what he was doing and covering it with aggression.

"Quiet." The voice was mature, maybe mid-thirties.

"So what do we do now?"

"We wait for the boss," said the older voice. "And he said no damage unless they resist. They already have strap marks, so watch it."

Perhaps he was the one in charge in the alley, but she couldn't be sure. With so many voices so close together, and no visual clues, it was impossible to tell them apart.

By the time the door screeched open again her legs were cold and her feet numb. A fat, burbling engine rumbled to a stop and a door slammed.

"Trouble?" Crisp. Urbane. In charge.

"None."

"Who's that with him."

"Surprise." Someone chuckled, low and mean. Did one of these hunters know her?

Her hood came off first, so she saw the fury on Eddie's face when he found out who had snatched them. She didn't recognize the man standing in front of them, smiling down. Dark hair, tight beard and moustache, with oil-tint shades and a suit that cost way more than a cop should have been able to afford.

"It pains me to see a member of the City's Finest on his knees." He looked over his shoulder at one of his stormtroopers. "String him up."

The trooper doubled off towards the van, and Tasha took a look at where they were. There wasn't much to see. It was an empty factory unit, perhaps never yet used. No markings on the floors, other than tire tracks. No abandoned equipment. The place was unreasonably clean. The trooper hurried back with a hank of rope and tossed it over a beam. They tied one end in a loose loop around Eddie's chest, while the other end was used to pull him up.

"Get him on his feet."

Two of them hauled on the rope. Eddie grunted into the tape over his mouth, and Tasha saw his eyes clench as the rope bit into the flesh under his arms. The troopers tied the rope off around an upright, leaving Eddie shuffling on tiptoe. The suit reached up and tore the tape from Eddie's mouth.

"What the hell, Palmer? You've gone too far this time."

So this is Greg Palmer, mused Tasha. Nasty, narcissistic, and utterly untrustworthy.

Palmer slapped Eddie across the face, hard.

"Language, Detective." He straightened Eddie's tie then tugged at his lapels, though the rope under the arms pulled his jacket out of shape. "Look at you. Sad, old excuse for a police officer. You look like a sack of shit and you amble around like a zombie. *And* you think you know better than your superiors. Did the captain not send a memo to all detectives very clearly stating that all incidents relating to misuse of controlled substances must be referred directly and promptly to the narcotics team?"

He glared into Eddie's eyes, and Eddie glared right back. Palmer turned away. "Remind the detective for me."

A faceless trooper stepped up behind Eddie and punched him hard enough in the back to make his feet leave the floor. He waited until Eddie stopped swinging, then did it again. Palmer waved his dog away while Eddie struggled to find his feet.

"How's your memory now, Weston?"

Tasha ground her teeth, but her options were limited. Her legs were so numb that she couldn't move quickly. She might grab Palmer and use him as a human shield, but before she could draw breath there would be two barrels pressed against Eddie's head. Besides, if she tried to act, she would show them what she truly was, what she could do. She wasn't playing the secret superhero, but very few humans knew what she was, and nobody in any official capacity. And that was the way it had to stay. She shifted her weight to try to get some blood into her legs without catching a bullet in the back of her head. Palmer turned to face her.

"Something you wish to say, Miss Campbell?"

She hoped she kept the surprise out of her eyes. Damn. He knew her. Why in hell would he know her?

"While I think it's sweet that such old flames wish to work together again, the department has strict rules on this."

Tasha rolled her eyes.

"You disagree? You have something to say?"

Tasha shrugged. Palmer was behaving like the bad guy with the detonator in a Die-Hard rip-off. She wasn't sure if that made him dangerous or vulnerable. He caught the eye of a trooper, then he gestured to his mouth. A gloved hand held her head while another ripped the tape from her mouth. She worked her jaw and moistened her lips.

"He's no partner of mine." She kept her eyes away from Eddie and hoped Palmer would focus on her. Hopefully Eddie wouldn't be stupid enough to look hurt, or let any emotions onto his face, but he had a dangerous habit of living on the outside of his skin.

"Then what were you doing, staking out an active narco location?"

"I didn't know that's what it was. He didn't know that's what it was. He was working a misper, some forlorn waif trailer trash he felt sorry for."

"I still haven't heard what you, personally, were doing there."

Tasha sighed. "I owed him a favor. He asked me to crack the phone for him, which I did. Nothing useful in there except repeated GPS hits to that location, which is why we were watching. We were just leaving when your people rolled up."

"And the phone."

"Bricked after I downloaded it."

Palmer looked at her a moment longer, then turned back to Eddie.

"There is nothing more pathetic than having a friend prepared to lie to try to save your worthless ass. Except for putting your partner at risk for a personal crusade. Do us all a favor. Transfer to traffic. Better yet, quit, and get a job as mall security. It's more your speed."

Without warning, he short-armed Eddie in the gut, with a force that raised Tasha's eyebrows.

"Everything you have on this case, on my desk by Monday. You keep your fingers out of my pocket, or I will have every one of them broken. And I will be having a quiet word with the captain about this."

Palmer took a step back. "Next time, we'll shoot you at the scene and make it look like an accident. One?"

A trooper snapped to attention.

"Twelve reminders, nothing that shows, and make sure he can walk to my desk by Monday. Then leave them somewhere inconvenient."

Palmer got back into his car and, while one of the troopers opened the door to let him out, two more snapped out retractable batons and closed on Eddie.

Tasha could only grit her teeth and let it happen.

They were as professional at that as they were at everything else. Two strikes to each upper arm, two strikes to the front and rear of each thigh. They stowed the batons and switched to fists. Four hard blows to the back, one over each kidney, and one lower down on each side. Then they untied the rope and let him fall to the floor, groaning as he rolled from side to side.

The troopers loaded them back into the van, still bound but without the tape or hood, and they drove off. One rode in the back with them. He didn't take his eyes off her, and not in a good way. She could see him tracking along her legs and lingering over her breasts. If Palmer hadn't given instructions to release them, she would have tried to play him, get him closer and overpower him. But there was no need. She could ignore him and focus on trying to blot out the sound of Eddie's groaning.

The van stopped. The two troopers in back of the van cut the plastic strips, slid open the side door, and threw them out. Tasha's purse and their ruined phones followed, then the van pulled away with the door still open.

Tasha climbed to her feet, then helped Weston to his. The Narcos had dumped them in a truck stop. Exactly where, Tasha had no idea. She put her arm under Eddie's and helped him stumble across to the shabby diner, then settled him in a booth while she called for coffee.

"Do you have a payphone?" Tasha asked, when the coffee arrived. The waitress shook her head, and Tasha put a twenty on the table. "I really need to make a couple of calls."

The woman stared at the note for a few seconds, then over her shoulder towards the kitchen. "I'll bring it. Make 'em quick."

"You're calling an Uber?" Weston asked, as he ran his fingers over his ribs.

"No, I'm calling the police."

"What?"

The phone arrived, by which time Tasha had pulled a small notebook from her purse. She dialed.

"Yes, hi. I need to report a stolen firearm. No, I'm a PI." She rattled off her registration and name, then gave them to serial number of her Glock. "No, no further action. Someone rousted me when I was on a job. Didn't see who did it and there's no prospect of associating it with the john I was watching. I got sloppy. Just wanted to log the theft. Thanks."

She hung up and handed the phone to Eddie.

"What's this for?"

"They have your weapons, doofus."

It took him a moment, but she saw the penny land. He dialed, spoke to a desk officer, and reported his weapons missing too. Tasha held out her hand for the phone.

"*Now* we get the hell out of here."

Circle back

Someone knocked at her apartment door, but nobody had spoken to Tasha over the entry phone. That another resident would want to speak to her was unusual, likewise the building manager. She peered through the spy hole, scowled, and opened the door.

"What the hell are you doing here?"

"Untwist your panties, Nat," said Eddie Weston.

"Why, have Narco stopped watching my building?"

"Oh, you spotted that?"

"I'm a PI, Eddie. Of course I spotted it."

"Well nobody is watching the service door out back."

"You sure?" Tasha cocked her head. This was something useful.

Eddie nodded. "Pretty much. Maybe because it looks like it comes out of the block next door."

He had a point. The door was a foot exit from the underground garages, rarely used. More of an emergency measure shared by the two facilities. And very much worth knowing.

"I'll give you that one, but still: what are you doing here?"

Eddie's pulled a sheet of paper from inside his jacket. "Autopsy report."

"You made them do an autopsy? Are you trying to give

Palmer the excuse to have you fired?"

Eddie winced and Tasha knew he was keeping things from her.

"Have you crossed paths with him again?"

"Not exactly."

"Then what, *exactly*?" Tasha put weight on the last word, annoyed with him for trying to play things down.

"Captain's put me on administrative duties pending a misconduct hearing."

"Oh, Eddie. What did you do?"

"I guess Palmer had that talk with him. He hauled me in the next morning and ripped me a new one. Two, maybe. Told me to stick to my own patch."

"Which, of course, you did?"

He gave her a lopsided grin and Tasha groaned. "Kinda. I wasn't doing anything official, wasn't working any case. I was just gassing with some of the guys and asked if any of them had heard anything new about Ruby. Guess someone snitched, or the captain overheard." Eddie frowned. "I've seen the captain mad at me before, but this was different."

"How so?"

"I can't be sure, not one hundred percent, but he sounded scared. I mean, he yelled at me good, but there was something more. Like something scared him, but for both of us."

Eddie stared into the distance a moment longer, then shook his head and held the paper out to Tasha. "It's off the books. Not a full autopsy, but as much as my contact could get done under the radar."

Tasha scanned down the sheet. "But we know all this. Wait … Toxicology test showed metabolites of methamphetamine and an unknown substance that may or may not have played a part in the subject's death. Again? Even the hospital doesn't know what it is?"

"My girl said they have a standing instruction not to analyze it, and to refer to it as an unknown substance. Said they were told analysis was being handled by an out of state government agency."

"I don't suppose your contact knows where that came from?"

Eddie shook his head. "Down through admin channels. We could try pushing the point up through the hospital but ..."

"Neither of us wants another visit from Palmer's charming associates." Tasha tried to hand back the paper, but Eddie shook his head.

"Shred it. No use now both of us have seen it and I don't want anything getting back to my girl in the mortuary."

Tasha wandered across her apartment to her desk and fed the paper into the machine. By the time she turned back, Eddie had found two tumblers and poured himself a whiskey. The bottle hovered over the second glass, but Tasha shook her head. It was too early in her day. She sat on the couch, one leg folded beneath her. "So now what?"

"Do you want out?"

"If you keep asking me that I might say *yes*. I want to know if there's any point continuing to risk ourselves, our careers."

Eddie gave her a long, direct look. "Nat, I don't want to put you in any more danger. When we were partners, it was different. But in that warehouse ..." He drew out taking a hit from the glass. "I thought they were going to kill you."

"I can look after myself."

He grinned. "I know. Seen it and been on the end of it. But still, this is just a favor. I don't like getting people hurt, especially old friends and people who are doing me favors."

Was that Eddie-speak for an apology? If so, for what? Or when? Being on the stakeout together had made old memories bubble up from the past. It had been fun, a reminder of the days when they would spend hours watching nothing happen, ribbing each other or communicating with barely a grunt or a change of expression.

She pushed the memories away. He had let her down, let them rob her of something she loved. Besides, there were parts of her world now that Eddie would never be able to accept, never be able to stay silent over. She would help him this one time, then let the canyon between them widen out again.

"I don't suppose you're going to let this go now?" she asked.

For a moment, Eddie looked like he was giving the idea serious thought. He was still limping from the beating his legs took, and he moved carefully when he sat, rose, or turned. Palmer's dogs had done a professional job on him, and she doubted he would have mentioned it to the captain. Or maybe he did, and that's what got the captain frightened.

"If we stick with it, we only got two options. First, we lean on the Winger girl."

Tasha shook her head. "Danny Morello has her wrapped up tight, and probably more so after my visit." Which was true, but only part of why she didn't want to bring more trouble to Marcie's door. Tasha saw something vulnerable about the girl, that made Tasha want to go gently around her.

"Didn't we—?"

"Bust him for possession with intent to sell about ten years ago?" Tasha grinned, and Eddie chuckled.

"He was a scrawny little kid with a grand idea of himself back then."

"He's bulked out, but he's no smarter. Nastier, though, and I wouldn't be surprised if he sent word to whoever he's working with that I've been sniffing. I might be able to get a tail on the girl, but it would be long range and unreliable."

"So let's put that under *maybe*. Option two is we go take a look at that second GPS hit from Ryan's phone."

"What did you do with that?"

"Kept putting the wrong password in until it locked and erased." Eddies grin was fierce. "Right before I handed the bag in to evidence. Let Palmer try to get anything out of that."

"Staking out another location would be very risky, Eddie. If Palmer catches us, he'll just kill us and make it look like a blue-on-blue accident."

"So we're screwed?"

"Maybe." Tasha frowned. "Think back to that bag of belongings Connie gave us. Wasn't that much in it, was there."

"Not putting the clothes and stuff in made sense. Did us a favor in away."

"It was something she said. Not sure if you were there when she did." She screwed down her eyes as she tried to remember. "Something about not wanting Ryan's mom to find out he was a user."

"So she was hiding something from her?"

Tasha nodded.

"And you think she might be hiding something from us?"

"Enough to pay her another visit."

Switch tracks

Miller tried to pump bar boy for more information, but I could sense we had everything we were going to get from them. Besides I wanted to get him to an ER.

"Are we going to play nice on this?" I asked the wolves.

"Are you kidding? I still want payback for Harry." Little Miss Angry leapt to her feet but Bar-boy's hand, still on her shoulder, pushed her down so hard I heard her grunt.

"Enough. It wasn't deliberate, and it's as likely to be the trashy, cheap taser."

"*I* bought those."

"Exactly. You buy on the cheap and pocket the difference."

Her face burned red, but she didn't deny it, and I understood the dynamic between these two. They were the alphas, the pack leaders. And if I remembered my wolf lore, they didn't get to pick each other, they just got to their relative positions through seniority. My mind wandered off, wondering how that worked for the more personal side of things. I tapped my mind on the nose and told it to focus.

"You have a man down, I have a man down. We have complementary interests here, not competing. We don't care what you do with this other pack—are they wolves too?"

The girl curled her lip. "No. Don't know what they are. Once we find them, they won't be anything."

Bar-boy rolled his eyes.

"We are only interested in finding out what happened to the missing vampires," I said. "We'd like to recover them if we can. Maybe we can work each other's angles here? Share information if we get any?"

Bar-boy checked over his shoulder. The two who brought Miller in shrugged. He didn't ask his queen bitch.

"One question?" he said.

"Just one?"

That got me a grin. "Why are you working for the vamps? I mean, everybody hates them, right?"

Miller either hadn't caught the comment or was ignoring it, so he was no help. Winging it a little, I said, "No vampire has ever tried to do me harm, but I'm aware of their reputation. I've heard good and bad of wolves, too, but I don't work on gossip. Most folk get the benefit of the doubt, but I seldom trust anybody. And I have bills to pay."

That last wasn't true, but it made the point I wanted. He looked at me then stuck out his hand. Little Miss Angry snorted, but I ignored her, stepping close enough to them to take his hand and shake it.

"Jeff Baker," he said. "I own the farm and the bar."

I dug a rumpled business card out of my jeans and handed it over. "Text me with your number. We hear anything relevant, I'll be in touch."

I looked over my shoulder at Miller.

"Can someone give us a ride to the nearest ER?"

Miller made a big song and dance about being fine, but I dug my heels in. Jeff drove us to the Ellen J and dropped us right outside the ER doors. It's amazing how fast you can get a porter if they think you're paying. They rushed him inside. I made up a story that fit most of the events and timelines, and they dragged him away for tests. I made for the in-house bistro-cafe and took care of the critical issue of having not eaten or caffeinated for over fifteen hours.

Three hours of tests later the medics threw Miller back on the street with a hairline skull fracture and a minor concussion, together with a bucket full of attitude at me for being high handed and overly familiar. But he gave me a ride to pick up my girl.

"What do you want to do next?" I asked.

"We need to go back to these wolves. We have more to find there."

I shook my head. "We're better off with them on our side, not standing between us and anything they find. If we keep bothering them, we could turn them against us."

"You are assuming that this mysterious pack that has their hackles up is associated with the missing vampires."

"No, I'm thinking in all the bars we checked last night there were only two where we got any kind of positive reply."

"Then we should go back and canvas the general public. Someone might know something."

"We aren't the police, Miller." It was my turn to dig my heels in. "We could spend a month handing out flyers and talking to people, and still miss half those who visited at that time. And that's assuming nobody calls the cops on us for harassing the public."

"Then what do you suggest?"

"I suggest you take the rest of today off, and maybe tomorrow too." I had a good idea what his reply would be.

"Out of the question."

Told you.

"Tomorrow, then. We leave this with the wolves to see if they can sniff anything out. Meanwhile we go take a look into this other issue. We do have two jobs here."

"Priorities, Miss Doe."

"Exactly. We just threw a rock into the pond. If that guy who was following you is one of the kidnappers, he knows we are looking for him, and he knows the wolves are looking for him. He may suspect we are working together."

"So you think his people may lie low for a time?"

"Either that, or if they're stupid enough, they might decide to start a turf war with a pack of angry wolves."

He sat in silence for rest of the trip. The car pulled up in front of my bike. Where the BMW had gone, I had no idea, but he didn't seem to care. The driver held the door open for me, but I waited.

"Very well, Miss Doe. I'll send the car for ten thirty."

"No. Meet me at the Citadel at eleven, in the first courtyard. The last time I tried this Tongue thing it backfired. I still need to see it work. You'll send me the GPS?"

He nodded, and I slipped out of the car. Something made me turn back once I was standing on the sidewalk. He was leaning across the car towards me, and for a moment I thought he was unwell. He was looking at me, very directly and with an expression I didn't know how to read.

"Jane?"

Well that was a first. I raised my eyebrows as a *go on*.

"Thank you for taking care of me."

Then he nodded to the driver who closed up and got in. The

car pulled away while I was still staring at the door. Maybe he got hit on the head harder than I thought.

Things Un-Hidden

The Uber dropped them a block away from Connie's last known address. Eddie crossed to the other side of the street, so each covered the other for tails in cars or on foot. They went past Connie's apartment block and doubled back when they were sure nobody was watching outside. It wasn't perfect—Palmer could have had someone in the building across the street, like they had done at the stash house—but it was the best they could do.

Tasha tapped on the door.

"Who is it?"

"Tasha."

Voices muttered inside, and she head a window open and close.

"Just a minute."

They heard more scuffling inside, and the door opened wide enough to show the girl's face. Behind her stood a young man about her own age, still doing up the zip of his jeans.

"What do you want?" Connie's voice was squeaky and sounded like she was forcing herself to articulate every word.

"I wanted to check on those things we said I would look into for you. And I have a couple more questions you might be able to help me with. Ten minutes? Maybe fifteen?"

Connie looked behind her at the young man, then pulled the door open.

"You give me a half hour, hon?" she wheedled. "I'll make it up to you." Her face fell as Eddie's bulk filled the doorframe beside Tasha, who could see her mind working as she tried to find a way to back out on the invitation to enter. But she had nothing, and they filed into the room.

"Pardon us," Eddie said to the young man. "And you might want to grab that doobie off the window ledge before it blows away. Kinda gusty out there."

The kid actually thought about it for all of three seconds, then gave Eddie a look of pure hate as he strode past and out of the room. Tasha looked after him. She knew his type. Hispanic roots, from an even poorer part of town than this neighborhood. Probably affiliated with a gang if not a full member. She wondered what Connie was doing with someone like that and feared the worst.

"He your boyfriend or your trick, Connie?"

The girl scowled at her for a moment, but then her eyes fell away. "I got to eat and pay rent."

"Did the City help with the funeral?"

Connie barked a nasty little laugh. "Sure. Look, thank you for the hospital, and for the mortician guy. He was more help than the city, and cheaper, but I still owe him money. That lowlife's mom and pop aren't handing over a cent because I won't send their precious boy home to them."

"Is that a problem?"

"They won't send me the money up front. Say I'll take it and not send him."

"Where is he."

"In the kitchen, under the sink."

147

Eddie was wandering around the room, poking his nose into things, and Tasha wished he wouldn't. It was hard enough getting any rapport back with this girl. Especially when he opened the window and brought in the ashtray with the still smoldering joint. He caught her eye as he pinched out the coal, and she gave him a look that should have dropped him through the floor.

"What? I said it was windy, and the room stinks of it already." He put the ashtray on a coffee table already covered with beer bottles and soda cans, then looked at Connie. "What did you hold out on us?"

"Nothing," her voice was shrill, angry, but Tasha saw Connie fold in on herself, her arms wrapping across her chest.

"I just did you a favor. Rescued a good five dollars' worth of herbal in that smoke. My friend helped you out too. And we're very grateful for that. We're helpful people. But we like people we help to be grateful back."

"Why should I help you? Cops are all the same."

Tasha picked it up before Eddie. "Has someone else been here? Police officers?"

"They said they were. They showed me badges, cuffed me and took me down to a police station."

"Do you know which one?" Eddie asked.

"I wasn't looking," Connie snapped. "They kept me there for three days, trying to make me tell them stuff I didn't know about what Ryan was doing. When I finally got back, they had trashed my place. Took me a day just to straighten out."

Tasha said nothing, but by appearance the straightening out had taken about twenty minutes.

The anger was genuine, but Connie couldn't look either of them in the face. Whenever they got too close, she would look down at the ground, or up to the ceiling.

"How many did you find, Connie?"

"I told you and I told them, nothing. None."

"What are you holding out for?"

Her arms folded even tighter, and her mouth twisted into a sullen pout.

"He wouldn't have held more than one," suggested Eddie. "Did you think you would be able to sell it?"

"For how much," Tasha pushed the point. "It's only a hundred new. This one would be weeks old now. Let me guess; you tried to sell one on the street and everybody said it was just soda and food dye? Was that it? You thought it would be a meal ticket, and now you're afraid to take it out on the street in case the Narco squad hear of it?"

Connie's mask of defiance slipped, cracked, and she nodded. "At first I hid it because I didn't want anybody to know he was using when they found him. His parents would have disowned him. They didn't think much of him anyway."

"And you think they don't know now?" Eddie's tone was surprisingly gentle. Connie looked at him like she didn't know anything anymore and shrugged. Tasha didn't buy it. She had already misjudged Connie once.

"Hell, if that's all it takes, I'll buy the damned thing off you for a hundred and that's and end of it." Eddie reached into a pocket for his money clip.

"No," said Tasha, and both of them looked at her in varying flavors of surprise.

"Why not? Fixes the problem." Eddie looked defiant, but Tasha stood her ground.

"Fixes *a* problem, not all of them. Go get Ryan, then fetch the pill."

Connie glared at her but made off into the kitchen and returned with a simple metal urn.

"Now the pill."

Connie didn't move, but the trace of a smug grin hovered over her lips. Tasha shook her head. "In there?"

"They would have looked," said Eddie. "Those narco bastards would have tipped it onto the floor and spread it with their boots."

"So either that's Ryan plus the previous contents of the dust buster, or it wasn't here when they searched."

Connie unscrewed the top, then twisted the liner inside the lid. It unscrewed, and taped inside was a dope baggie and a capsule half full of red crystals. "It was loose when they delivered it. I put the Ruby inside and tightened it up good. They didn't notice. I saw them pull at it, but it doesn't move that way."

"This is how it's going to work," said Tasha, making clear the offer wasn't negotiable. "I'll square things with the parents. I make sure they get Ryan, and on condition they either pay you or me what they owe. Write down their address, and how much they owe. And I will check with the mortician."

Connie didn't move and looked like she was trying to find an argument. Eddie stepped forward and took the lid from her hands, then put it back together. He picked up the urn, sealed the lid back in place, then stepped back.

"This comes with us either way,' he said. "You tell anybody we have it, and it goes straight to Narco. I'd love to see the look on their face when they realize they missed it. Then they'll come back to see you."

Tasha raised a hand. "No need for threats, is there, Connie?"

Connie scrawled on a slip of paper and all but threw it at

Tasha.

"I'll bring the money when everything's straight," Tasha promised, but Connie was already at the door, holding it open.

"Mail me a damned check," she snapped. "But don't ever come here again."

And the Magic Ingredient Is...

They found a diner on the corner of the block. Tasha looked through the window, then pushed Eddie towards the door. Inside, the diner was old and worn, but not neglected. Rather than overused grease, the place smelt of baking and fresh bread. Four cake displays sat on the counter, and more on a shelf behind. Cake suddenly seemed like the best idea in the world, and Tasha eyed each of them while the waitress looked on patiently.

"*That* one," she said, pointing to a towering structure of chocolate sponge and cream, feeling seven years old again. Eddie asked for apple pie and they found a table. The food, with cream and coffee, arrived in minutes, but the waitress hesitated before serving. Tasha looked at her, realized she was staring, and followed her eyes to the urn containing the mortal remains of Ryan—which Eddie had put on the table, next to the window.

"Would you mind putting that down on a chair, dear," asked the waitress. "People might get the wrong idea about the place."

Eddie's cheeks took on a hint of red and he hurried to put the urn onto the chair next to him. The waitress delivered the food and backed away, still looking at the top of the urn where it peeked over the edge of the table.

Eddie tried to start a conversation several times, but Tasha silenced him with an upraised fork. Her metabolism was unconventional. She still needed food, and drink, and could process everything normally—but she needed less of both. Her other hunger she had to satisfy elsewhere. Consequently, she tried to make those occasions when she *did* need to eat special, and this cake certainly counted as that. Eddie would just have to wait.

Tasha even went to the extreme measure of scraping up the last few crumbs on her finger, then indulged in an eyes-closed sensual moment of cocoa and butter lingering on her palate. She opened her eyes and looked at Eddie.

"Yes?"

He shook his head. "Get a room next time. People shouldn't have to watch that."

Tasha sneered and turned to her coffee. "What's the next step in your grand plan?"

"*My* plan? I thought it was you who wanted to push the girl for more."

"Maybe, but now it's your turn."

Eddie stirred cream for his apple pie into his coffee, then added sugar. Tasha winced.

"I suppose we can get someone to analyze it."

"Who?"

"I don't know," snapped Eddie. "Someone. Maybe out of state."

"Assuming there isn't a warning out to every lab and university capable of analyzing it to leave it be and call it in. Palmer comes knocking while we sit in the waiting room."

"You have a better idea?"

"No."

The waitress came by, refilled their coffee, and walked away. Tasha held her hand out over the table.

"Give me the lid off that thing."

Eddie's eyes opened wide. "Are you crazy?"

"No more than usual. I'm playing a hunch. Come up with something better or go with it."

Eddie unscrewed the lid from the urn and handed it over. He kept his hand over the mouth of the urn as if he feared Ryan's ghost might spin the dust around the diner in a whirlwind. Tasha unscrewed the liner, took out the baggy, then put the liner back into place. Eddie screwed the lid back on like he was closing Pandora's new box and let out a sigh of relief. Until he saw Tasha open the bag.

"You've got to be kidding!"

Tasha raised her eyes but not her head, then lifted the bag to her face and drew a deep breath through her nose. She gagged.

"Don't waste the cake," said Eddie, but Tasha ignored him. Why had she heaved? She had smelled cremation ashes before. The odor was unique, but not that revolting, and though the plastic of the lid cast its own note into the mix, it wasn't pungent enough to cause that response. She took another, more cautious sniff. Same reaction, though not as violent, and still nothing she could identify. But it was familiar, and it was triggering a dark fear deep inside her.

Before Eddie could say, "What are you doing? Stop," Tasha took the capsule out of the bag and, holding it over the dregs of her coffee, pulled the two halves apart. A few crystals sprinkled into the cup, but the majority stayed in one half of the capsule. The burnt plastic taint of meth overwhelmed everything, but still something caused that undercurrent of nausea. Her body knew it. If she could just give it more of a clue. Knowing it was a reckless thing to do, Tasha touched her tongue to the lip of the capsule.

She threw up into her mouth. Dark horrors swirled around in her head, not from the Ruby, but from her memories, from her past. She had just enough time to drop the cap into the baggy before she dashed across the diner and into the rest room. She sank to her knees in front of the stinking toilet and heaved everything into the bowl. As she gasped in a breath of fetid air, she remembered to shove her foot against the door, then she heaved again.

Tasha had nothing left to come up, but the room still spun. She turned around, pressing her back up against the door and holding her head in her hands as she tried not to drown in the sudden flood of memories.

Being force fed, her mouth filled with vile effluent. A hand crushing over her lips as a finger stroked her throat to make her swallow. Except she didn't, she couldn't. She mustn't.

She forced herself to straighten her back, then crossed her legs and rested the back of her hands on her knees. They had taught her the meditation after they rescued her, shown her how to manage the fear, if not erase it. Breath by breath she rebuilt the wall around the nightmare and forced it back into its box.

Legs trembling, she turned the faucet on and swilled her mouth. The water tasted disgusting, but it was better than the lingering hint of corruption she had tasted. She dried her mouth on a paper towel and walked back out to the diner.

"You OK, dearie?" The waitress looked at her with more suspicion than concern.

"I'm fine, just ..." Tasha placed her hand low on her stomach and gave a little shrug. Let the waitress think what she would.

"You have everything you need?"

Tasha nodded and went back to her table.

"What was—?"

"Shut up. Take that baggy into the toilet and flush it. Twice. Take the cup with you and rinse it twice too"

"Are you kidding, that's our only lead."

She locked her eyes onto his. "Don't mess with me, Eddie. Do it, and do it now."

While Eddie was in the john, Tasha called up an Uber, then put her hands flat on the table so nobody would see them shaking.

Suspect in the Citadel

F inding the portal was easy enough, thanks to Miller sending me coordinates. The doors even opened for me as I rode towards them.

Finding the Citadel was more of a challenge. GPS doesn't work in the Dark—at least mine doesn't—and I didn't remember either of the forks in the road until I came up to them. I worried about the first one, then decided to do it on autopilot. Turning around, I backed up a mile or so then turned back. As I came up to each fork I all but shut my eyes. The first I went left, second one right, and rumbled on along the road in the hopes of seeing something.

And not much caring if I didn't. Something in the heavy air of the Dark made my bike sound wonderful. I normally ride quietly around town, but if you twist her tail, my girl makes a very satisfying rumble. Out here she *roared*, and I could have ridden around all day just for the pleasure of it.

But my choices seemed to have paid off, and after only a half hour or so, the Citadel loomed on the horizon. I stopped a distance away from the great door. Two guards on the ground. I was sure I saw two more in the battlements above, all paying me a great deal of attention. I slowly opened my jacket, so as not to trigger any gun reflexes, and hung the Duke's Tongue out where it could be seen. My foot hooked up to put the motorcycle back into first gear, and we rumbled slowly up the road.

I was still a good fifty feet away when the guards snapped to attention. The gate had opened for me by the time I got to it, but I pulled up between the guards. They saluted. Nobody ever saluted me before. I pushed up my visor.

"The Emissary is meeting me here in a few minutes. Where can I park and wait?"

"Anywhere you like, my lady, but might I suggest just inside and to the left of the gatehouse. We can keep an eye on your vehicle if you would prefer to leave it."

What a polite vampire. So this ridiculously named trinket did, literally, open doors. I swung my girl into the space suggested and glued the helmet to the handlebars, then perched on the seat until Miller arrived in his car. A tinted window purred down, and Miller peered out at me.

"Well this should raise some eyebrows."

I sauntered over to the car, smiled at the guard who had run to open the door for me, and slid in beside Miller. "What?"

"Hardly dress code for the Citadel."

"There's a dress code?" I gaped my eyes and mouth in mock horror, then sat back in the seat. "Relax. I'll leave the jacket in the car and look edgy chic."

We went up just two levels this time and stopped in a service area rather than the main courtyard. We got out and I left the jacket, as I promised. Underneath it I was wearing a plain white shirt, which went nicely with my black jeans.

"Simple yet elegant. I've no doubt there will be enormous gossip trying to discover who your designer is."

As I tried to decide how much Miller was mocking me, I

looked around the service entrance. "I'd say I fit right in. Isn't this a little low rent for you?"

"The individual's apartment is not far from this entrance, and I thought it might be best if we did not create too much spectacle passing through the rest of the district."

"Subtle," I said. "Not like you at all. Are you sure they didn't miss something when they scanned your head?"

"The contents of my cranium are unchanged, thank you for asking. Superficial bruising. Shall we?" He gave me an urbane smile that spoke volumes and gestured I should lead the way inside.

We passed through a storage and loading area, then alongside a kitchen, judging from the clattering. If that's not what it was, I didn't want a clearer explanation. A turn or two later Miller stopped me outside a plain door that wouldn't look out of place in an average condo. Whoever this guy was, he had either pissed off someone important, and real bad, or his family despised him. Miller rapped on the door.

It opened, and I could see into an apartment that was more like the one I shared with Bernie than either Serpent's or Hawke's. I knew right away this guy wasn't the end user; he was a mule, and he wasn't making much out of his trade. He looked like he was going to wet himself when he saw the Emissary standing at his door. Then he spotted the bauble hanging around my neck and his knees wobbled.

"Stand aside," I said. Not loud, not nasty, just ongoing testing to see how far this amulet would get me. Unreasonably far, it seemed. The guy faded to the left like a dancer and closed the door behind us once we were inside.

"Can I help you?"

I looked at Miller and jerked my head towards our host. I

hadn't seen him work before. He could have this one.

"State your name, for the record."

Good tactic. I didn't know what record Miller was talking about, but it made things sound very formal and official.

"Frederick, scion of House Hammerstein."

"Take a seat, Frederick."

He backed around us until he bumped into the dining table, then his hand fumbled until it grabbed a chair. He sat sideways on it, and as his hand went from the back of the chair to his lap, I saw it tremble.

"A Reliable Witness has made an accusation against you, Fredrick of House Hammerstein. Do you understand the implications of this?"

"Th—that I'm guilty, unless I can convince you I'm innocent?"

Harsh, but I kept my face straight. Their club, their rules.

"You are aware that the sentence may be reduced if you fully and freely admit your crime."

"Yes, but—" He bit off whatever he had been going to say and covered his mouth with his hand. I couldn't make up my mind if this guy was spineless, or if something deeper hid behind his obvious fear. And now it looked like he thought he was going to get something cut off for daring to interrupt the Emissary.

Miller glared at him for ages, but then his face softened. He took a chair from the table for himself and put it in front of Fredrick. I perched on the arm of a chair and kept to the background.

"Let's take this a different way, Fredrick. Freddie. May I call you Freddie?" Reasonable Miller sounded weird to me, and from the uncertain way he nodded, Freddie felt the same.

"Now, I don't know how bad you are, Freddie, but you don't look like an outlaw to me. I'm going to give you a chance to tell me all about it without asking you anything. Then I can say you volunteered the information, which will show you cooperated."

"Is it about ..." Freddie paused, and I wondered just how much naughtiness he had to sort through to decide which was worst. "Is it about the food?"

"What food?" Miller pushed gently.

"The food they make me bring in from outside?"

"*They* make you bring? Who are *they*?"

Freddie was already pale, like all vampires, but his face turned a horrible grey color.

"My lord, please. I can't."

Somebody had a serious hold over him. This was not turning out as I'd expected, unless Freddie was an Oscar-worthy liar. Miller leaned in harder.

"Let us begin by stating the crime, Freddie."

"I've been ..." His eyes closed and his face took on a 'how the hells did I get into this mess' look. "I have imported unlicensed food into the Citadel."

"Are you aware of the penalty for that?"

Freddie shook his head.

"The crime breaks several treaties that I cannot discuss. We also consider it to be an encouragement for kin to feed unlawfully, without the understanding or consent of the source. It is most serious. The penalty for this will be Exposure."

"But I haven't hurt anyone, not even a human."

Thanks for that, I thought.

"Are you sure? Do you know where your source obtains the

merchandise? Does he follow the same rules, or is he perhaps taking the food by force? Do they even survive?"

"I'm just the go-between, the delivery boy. They tell me where to go, when, what to bring back. I don't carry any money. They don't even *pay* me."

"Then why?" I asked and earned myself a look from Miller. "You knew there would be consequences. If there was nothing in it for you, why would you do it?"

He was squirming. It looked debased, but I pushed harder.

"Or are we talking about something other than money?"

A desperate hope flashed in his eyes but was crushed in a second. Hope about what I couldn't tell, but it was unmistakable. I turned to Miller, letting the focus come off Freddie for a moment, and giving him a moment to see the glimmer at the end of the tunnel.

"What is Exposure?" I asked. I could guess, but I wanted to see Freddie's reaction to hearing his death defined so clearly.

"In the old days, there would be ritual locations in the upper world, where spectators could arrive and depart without risk. In the center would be a post, or some other place where they could secure the condemned. An opening in the roof would be positioned such that a pool of light crawled across the floor until, often at noon, the full power of the sun fell on the condemned. Dramatic, but it is intended to make a point"

"Sounds Roman, something Caligula would do."

"The cultures are not dissimilar."

"But is that still done today?"

Miller nodded and surprised the heck out of me. "In some places, and for the most heinous of crimes."

"Could that happen to Freddie here?"

Miller hadn't taken his eyes off Freddie. "Possibly. His

actions have placed the nobility into a difficult position with the human authorities. They might make a spectacle of him to show good faith. But it would be far simpler to use the chamber."

I waited until he realized I didn't know what that was either.

"The chamber is in one of the basements of the Citadel. There is a post, to which Freddie is chained. High intensity sources of ultra-violet light illuminate the post when required."

He finally turned to look at me. "It can be much slower and more painful than natural exposure. For a vampire as young as Freddie, who still has some tolerance for UV, this form of execution is protracted and excruciating."

For an instant, Miller had described Freddie being tanned to death, but the extra detail made me feel shallow and a little sick. When I turned back to Freddie there were tears running down his cheeks.

"I didn't know vampires could cry," I said, but it came out quiet as a whisper. I cleared a lump out of my throat with a cough. Something wasn't right here. Freddie was terrified, but it didn't feel personal. If we had Tasha here, she could help him see beyond his terror, to find more rational answers. But if Tasha was here, we would have a war on our hands, so maybe it wouldn't be too helpful.

Could I do something? My stomach churned at the thought of messing with someone's head. It was training that Peterson kept telling me I needed to work on, that it would be much easier to protect myself if I knew what Corvax did and how. It made sense, but something inside me always rebelled against the idea. The thought of knowing how badly Corvax had screwed me was too much to bear, but now I wish I'd listened to my Grumpy Old Man.

"Miller, can I get a moment? Over here? Freddie won't try anything, will you?"

Freddie jerked his head from side to side. Miller gave me a look but followed me to the far side of the room.

"What is it?"

"Something's not right."

"He has admitted his guilt, and is understandably terrified by the consequences—"

"He's the wrong kind of terrified," I interrupted. "Can't you feel it?" And it clicked inside my mind. "He's not terrified about what will happen to him, but of what will happen *because* of what happens to him."

Miller frowned. He didn't get it, but the subtle distinction shone out as clear as day to me.

"There's something I want to try. Magic. I've never done it before, and it might go horribly wrong, but right now Freddie isn't going to tell us a thing."

"You may be right. And technically, you are in charge."

Was I? I hadn't noticed. "It may take me out of the conversation, so I need you to be gentle, ask sensitive questions, push to find out what he's protecting." I got another flashbulb moment. "Or who."

I took Miller's chair and moved it until I was knee to knee with Freddie.

"Let me help."

His eyes flicked between mine and Miller's, who was looming behind me. I looked over my shoulder. "Go sit where I was. Give us some room."

"What are you going to do?" Freddie stuttered.

"Honestly? I'm not sure. This may do nothing, but it won't

164

make things worse. You have so much fear in your thoughts right now that you can't focus. The Emissary is here to get to the bottom of what's going on. If you do wrong, then there have to be consequences, but we think there is something more, and we have to understand it."

"Are you going to hypnotize me?"

"Wouldn't know where to start. But I want to try to take some of your fear, if I can. Give me your hands."

My hands reached toward him and, as I waited for him to take them, I tried to figure out what the hell I was going to do. Peterson had tried to explain some of the theory of neurothaumaturgy to me, but it made me too uncomfortable. The idea of doing to someone else what Corvax had done to me made me feel sick.

But what I wanted to do here was different. As Freddie reached for me, his hands trembling, I realized how reckless I was being. If this was all an act, I was about to open my mind to him, fully and without protection. If this was a ruse, and he had some magical accomplice nearby, I could be a cabbage in the next ten seconds.

As I reached my thoughts toward him, his terror engulfed me like an inferno. My heart hammered and my chest felt like Miller was sitting on it. His raw emotions washed over me, and I didn't have a clue what I should do with them. I closed my eyes and saw a different vision of him; a charred but moving corpse, crouched on the floor with his arms wrapped around his knees and rocking from side to side.

Wind didn't blow out the flames of fear, but fanned them higher. Water turned to scalding steam, as did ice. Nothing I could manifest seemed to have any effect unless it was a bad one. I was out of ideas and making things worse. Time to get out of there and think of something else, but I couldn't go without an apology, without a farewell. My failure might be condemning him to death. My mind reached out with its 'hands' and cupped his face as if I was about to kiss him.

The fear-fire around him changed. It was tiny, but it was there. And the same time, my virtual hands burned. Was that it? To help him I had to hurt myself, to take his fear into me? And do what with it? I couldn't eat it, like Tasha, and I couldn't radiate it away or store it. Or could I? Could I use the Magni ring?

My hands took a firmer 'grip' on Freddie and I felt his fear flow into me. It burned. In my own body, my back cramped and I hissed with pain as my adrenals kicked my kidneys. Every muscle I had tensed up and bile burned in my throat.

My magic had a limit, one that the Grumpy Old Man had been trying to break me of for months. I only had two actual hands, so I only had two magical 'hands'. I could only do two things at the same time.

With one hand still 'holding' Freddie, I used the other to shape his fear and channel it into the ring on my thumb. The ring fought back, trying to reject the fear and throwing it back at me. I pushed harder, and the ring submitted, but I could tell it wasn't happy by how it clamped around my thumb and squeezed.

"Do you feel better?" Miller asked, though his voice sounded at least a room away. "Calmer?"

"A little, yes."

"My partner has a theory. Are you being compelled to act as a cut-out? Is someone in the Citadel using you as a Judas goat?"

"Yes. I am the go-between that protects them."

"Why? They are going to put you to death for another's crime. Name them and save yourself."

Things were under control until he said that. The fear poisoning Freddie erupted, engulfing him again. I pulled it away as fast as I could, but it felt like I was losing him.

"Tell us," Miller insisted. "We can help, whatever it is."

The fear burned higher, breaking away from me, and I forced my real hand to wave, hoping Miller would get the message and ease off.

As soon as we got close to the core of the situation, Freddie lost it. Whatever it was, it was more important to him than anything rational. I looked at his avatar again, at the image his mind held of himself, and realized I had got something wrong. He wasn't cowering to protect himself. He was curled *around* something, cradling it. *That* was what he was protecting.

If he realized what I was doing, he might resist me, force me out, and all this would have been for nothing. Something glowed deep in his avatar, a sparkling light where his heart should be. I eased a little closer and saw it was a memory, the image of a woman, perhaps in her twenties or early thirties. She was ordinary, mid brown, mid length hair, glasses, fun smile.

What in the name of anything was an image like that doing in the heart of a vampire?

The distance grew between us as I backed away. The fear-storm had died down since Miller shut up, and I had things stable for now. I searched around until I could reconnect my brain to my mouth and braced myself for it all to kick off again.

"Who is she, Freddie? Who is that woman, and why is she so important you'll die for her?"

Time to Believe in Fairies

Eddie tried to get her to talk in the Uber, but all she gave him was a snapped "Later". Once they were back inside her apartment, he slammed the door and snapped. "Want to tell me what the hell that was all about? Maybe explain why you made me throw away our only grain of evidence?"

Tasha heard him, but his words drifted over her head. She was fighting to stay on her feet, to bottle the screams in her throat. She tried to make it to the chair, but her knees gave out before she got there. Her hands clutched for the back of the chair, missed, and she slumped to the floor.

"Oh, crap." Eddie leapt towards her, catching her head just before it cracked onto the corner of the chair. He knelt beside her, then she felt him pull her arm over his shoulders. He grunted as he rose to his feet.

"Come on, Nat. Two steps to the couch."

He lied. She counted four before he eased her down into the cushions. Her head weighed as much as the moon, but she raised her eyes in time to see him pulling out his phone.

"No," Tasha croaked. "No paramedics. Just need a minute."

Eddie looked uncertain but killed the call before it could connect. He crossed the room to the kitchen and filled a glass of water from the dispenser in the refrigerator door.

Tasha pulled her knees up to her chest and wrapped her arms around them, rocking from side to side as the nightmares replayed across her mind. The worst was not the being strapped down, or the dreadful contraption that clamped over her face, its metal jaws scraping across her teeth as they forced her mouth open. Nor was it the foul taste of the ichor they poured into her mouth. She could still taste the tang of it in the back of her throat.

When Eddie knelt next to her, glass in hand, she snatched it from him and took a mouthful, but swished it around before she spat it on the rug. She put the glass to her lips and did the same again, but the water wasn't taking the taste away. She waved the glass around until Eddie took it, then wrapped her arms around her knees again.

It was bad enough to be what she was, a half-thing, neither human nor vampire. What they tried to do to her was evil, shredding the remnant of her soul and turning her into a monster worse than she thought possible. They taunted her with what she would become, and laughed at her as she drew on the deepest dregs of her courage and determination to deny them.

"Whiskey," she croaked. "Rum. Brandy. Anything."

Eddie, mopping the floor with a towel, stumbled across the room to the cupboard where she kept the spirits, then hurried back with the first bottle his hand closed around. She spun the top off, throwing it over her shoulder, then swigged from the bottle.

When her head, and the bottle, pitched down from the ceiling, Eddie had a wastebasket ready. She swilled the bourbon around her mouth until it burned, then spat it into

169

the basket. The booze helped, but nothing on this earth could take the memory of that ichor from her. She spat again, not wanting to swallow even the slightest trace, then filled her mouth from the bottle a second time.

Tasha continued to spit, but her stomach picked that moment to rebel. She heaved, dropping the bottle to grab the wastebasket with both hands. The bottle fell straight, and Eddie caught it as it bounced. He climbed to his feet and rushed to the kitchen.

Abandonment overwhelmed Tasha. She wanted to wail like a child but held it back. Her body started to shiver, and then Eddie was back, a damp cloth in one hand and the comforter from the back of the couch in the other. He gave her the damp cloth and took the wastebasket. As she wiped her mouth, he placed the basket on the floor and draped the comforter over her. Then she felt the couch sag, and Eddie's arm was over her shoulders. She settled back into it, trying to let her mind focus on the feeling of closeness, of belonging, while the trembling drained from her muscles.

It took a half hour until Tasha came back to herself. She took Eddie's hand, still draped over her shoulder, in hers, and kissed the back.

"My hero," she said, but it came out as a croak.

He placed the back of his hand against her cheek for a moment, then she felt the couch shift again as he stood. The absence of his body heat sent gooseflesh tickling across her back.

"The lengths some people will go to get out of answering a question." He shook his head as he sat in the chair facing her. She chuckled, a weak and fractured sound, but real. "You better?"

She nodded. "Some."

"But not OK."

There was no point denying it. She shook her head. "I'll live." Her breath caught in her throat as soon as she had spoken. *For now*, she thought.

"I still want to know what this is all about."

Cop, through and through, thought Tasha. Which was going to make this all the harder, because he would smell a lie while she was still making it up. How could she help him believe the truth?

"Why don't we start with what you think you tasted in that cap of Ruby."

"I don't think, I know."

"So why the reaction? I've never seen you behave like that."

"Eddie, do you remember the day I got stabbed?"

He shifted in his chair and looked away. His face lost all its color, and Tasha felt terrible for putting the memory back in his mind. Eddie had not taken the event well and blamed himself for what happened. Unfairly. They had both made the decision to go into a bust where they were outmatched, and he had been out cold when the man—beast?—they had been chasing stabbed her through the heart.

"The doctors couldn't figure out why I wasn't dead?"

"Why are you dragging this up, Nat? Sure, I remember."

"Weapon at least sixteen inches long, moderately sharp, rounded. Entry and exit wounds in front of and behind the right ventricle, yet no damage to the heart itself. Estimated five pints lost at scene, but my heart kept beating. What did the ER doctor say to you?"

"Medically impossible. Do you have a point?"

"The other woman. The one our perp was stalking, trying

171

to kill?"

Eddie's face screwed up for a moment. "Yeah. Tall, thin. Pale, with white hair and goofy colored eyes. Looked like she was on her way home from a horror convention."

"I lied."

"About what?"

"About what happened that night."

Eddie said nothing, but his eyes bored into hers and he slowly straightened until he was sitting ramrod straight.

"Everything I said was true," said Tasha, "but I left something out. Yes, the beast stabbed me, and he stabbed me through the heart. Yes, I raised my sidearm as he stood there and put a bullet through his brain. Yes, he was gone by the time you got there."

"Then what did you miss out?"

"The woman he had been chasing?"

"The freak?"

Tasha nodded. "She came back. I was on my ass, leaning against a wall. It was cold and my sight was fading. She knelt next to me and asked me if I wanted to live. I nodded. She told me I had to actually say the words, and that there were consequences. I didn't think. I knew I was dying, so what could be worse?"

She looked at Eddie, hoping for understanding, but his face was flat, expressionless.

"She slit open her wrist. Using one of her own fingernails, she cut right into it. Except there's no fountain, just a steady flow. In the streetlight it looked almost black. She put her wrist to my mouth and told me to drink. It tasted sweet, like maple syrup. The more I had, the more I wanted, and each time I swallowed I felt a little stronger. She took her wrist away and told me again there would be consequences. And she told me if I wanted to stay myself, to never take a life."

Eddie still didn't speak. Tasha searched for better words than the ones she had queued up and ready, but she could find no other way to say what she had to, and no way not to make it sound like she was insane.

"She made me a vampire, Eddie."

"Ah, hell." The words were soft, regretful. He sat next to her on the couch again, taking her hand and putting his fingers to her wrist, turning her face gently to the light and looking into her eyes, then resting the back of his hand against her brow. Tasha let him. She knew what he was looking for.

"Want me to do a roadside sobriety test too, Eddie? I'm not high from the Ruby."

He went back to the chair. "You must be high on something if you expect me to believe that. What's next, going to show me your fangs?"

Her lips twisted into a lopsided grin. "Don't have any."

"Not much of a vampire then."

"There are three different kinds. They all feed on humans, if they get the chance, but they don't all feed on blood. The woman who turned me, her kind feed on emotions."

"And the third kind?" Eddie threw his hands in air. "I can't believe I asked that."

"You don't want to know." A shiver crept along Tasha's spine. "You really don't."

"You get how crazy you sound, right?"

Tasha nodded. "You need proof."

"Damn straight."

Tasha looked around the apartment. "Think you can get to the door before me? You're closer. I'll even let you start

173

standing up."

"Nat—"

"Humor me."

"On three?"

"Go when you're ready, no cou—"

But Eddie was already on the way. Tasha pushed off from the couch so hard it slid two feet across the floor. She unleashed everything she had. It felt like she flew across the room and every muscle in her body tingled at the release. Her life these days was all about holding back, concealing her abilities. It was exhilarating to let them loose. She thumped into the door, ass first, and Eddie slid to a halt three steps in front of her, eyes and mouth gaping.

"Gotcha," she hissed, and grinned. "Hold tight. Going up."

She stepped up to him between blinks, put her hands under his arms, and lifted him two feet into the air. It would have been easy to bump his head into the ceiling, but she didn't want to leave a dent by accident, either in the plaster or Eddie's skull. Tasha lowered him to the floor then, before he could turn around, ran back to the couch. By the time he turned she was already pushing it back into place—using one hand. Then she sat and waited for him to do the same.

Perversely, the exhibition made her feel better. Letting herself go released some kind of endorphin rush that was better than anything a narcotic could have given her. And it was why she so rarely took her strength off its leash. It would be too easy to fall in love with that high, to use her strengths simply for how good they made her feel. Which in turn would need her to feed more. Which in turn put her in increased danger of inadvertently, or even deliberately, taking a life.

Eddie, stunned, had taken his seat.

"Believe me now?"

He shook his head. "How can I? Vampires, for Christ's sake? Easier to believe the pope assassinated Kennedy."

It was Tasha's turn to feel stunned. The man couldn't ignore the evidence of his senses, could he?

"Tough audience. How about this? You *pretend* you believe me. Put the cynical cop to sleep for an hour. There's no other evidence I can show you right now, not without feeding from you, and you may not even believe that."

"*Feed* from me?"

"Leave it, Eddie. This is the rest of the story. Remember I had a medical leave of absence after the stabbing?"

"Of course. Hit you hard. Why wouldn't it. Wondered if you would ever come back. So did the captain."

"I had some adjustments to make, some things to come to terms with. There were some people who were trying to get me to be one thing, others trying to convince me to do something opposite."

She took a deep breath. This was more difficult than she had expected. "But then the blood suckers joined in. They kidnapped me. They wanted to turn me as well. I don't know everything, but I know they spent days trying to get me to drink *their* blood."

"Couldn't they just tube it into your stomach?"

Tasha shook her head. "It has to be a deliberate act. You have to choose to swallow it for it to work. I don't understand all the ins and outs. I had only been a vampire for two weeks and even then, I wasn't fully converted."

Echoes of the horror threatened to overwhelm her again, but she focused on her report, like a good cop should. "They strapped me down, and hour after hour they filled my mouth with their disgusting blood. It was foul and putrid; made worse because I knew by then that if I took it, I had no chance to resist making the full change. It was three days before someone rescued me."

She took a deep breath. "I can never forget that taste, and what they did to me still haunts me."

Eddie was frowning, his lips turned down at the sides.

"Are you trying to tell me what I think you are?"

She nodded. "The unknown ingredient in Ruby Meth is vampire blood."

Tasha's heart gave three slow beats before Eddie roared with laughter. "You had me. You actually had me for a moment." He wiped his eyes with his thumbs, and Tasha waited. He shifted in the chair and settled his jacket on his shoulders. And Tasha waited. He looked around the room, at anything other than her. And still Tasha waited. Eventually he would remember the last hour, the coffee shop, her reaction.

He finally looked at her. "You really believe that?"

"I do. The taste I will never forget, but knowing what it is, the effects of Ruby drop into place."

"They do?"

"The behavior changes Connie told us about match vampire behaviors: arrogance, huge self-belief. Not the crazy egomania coke- and crack-heads display. This would be true confidence, and that would enhance the user's ability at planning." Tasha slouched back on the couch and chewed at the corner of her thumb nail. "Add that to the addictive nature of meth and the energy boost it gives. Pretty irresistible."

Eddie's fingers were drumming on the arm of the chair. "Say I believed you; how the hell can I take that back to the Captain? I'd be out on a section eight before I finished speaking."

"This can't go back to him, or Palmer." She raised her eyes and rocked her head from side to side. "Though I have a feeling he may already know."

"Then what?"

"Then it looks like I've got a partner again. At least while we get to the bottom of this."

"You're in? All the way in?"

She nodded and Eddie's face creased into an enormous grin. Tasha scowled at him. "Calm down, detective. I said just until we fix this mess."

"So what do we do we do next?" Eddie shifted in his chair, not meeting her eyes.

"We have the other GPS hit, we have the Winger girl, and we have the poker chip."

"You said Morello has her wrapped up. Putting an eye on her would be dangerous, maybe lethal."

"And we don't know how to use the poker chip." Tasha added. "Plus the GPS hit we are putting so much faith in is a single hit."

"But Floyd said they banned phones for anybody going there, so the location, if that's it, would be important."

"And well protected."

They lapsed into silence for more than a minute.

"I can't see a clear best path," Eddie finally admitted, but Tasha felt the corner of her mouth lifting.

"I can."

"What?"

"We need help. And I know just the witch for the job."

Break (through?)

"How did you find her?" Freddie gasped.

The whole 'holding her in your heart' thing might make the two grown men yak. "I saw her in your thoughts, and that she's very important to you."

The fear-fire died away, as though us knowing was a catharsis, or he had given up.

"How is this person important to you, and why does she need protecting?" Miller came on a little hard, but I couldn't give him a signal to back off. There was no way I could make eye contact. Freddie needed a moment and so did I. His fear was still swirling around my system, and my back was still in painful spasm. As I took my hands from Freddie's, needing to arch my spine and stretch it out, he clung to me for an awkward moment. But he let go, and as I raised my hands over my head, I caught sight of the ring on my left thumb. The gem was so clear that, for a moment, I thought it had evaporated in protest. Grumpy Old Man would kill me if I broke the ring.

"Fredrick." Miller's tone was authoritative, and I raised my hand to stop him. That wasn't what we need now.

"Freddie," I said. "We can only help you if we know the full story. If you won't help us, we can't help you, and they will execute you. We can't stop that. Unless you level with us."

He raised his face and looked into my eyes. I let him. He held the look for ten or fifteen seconds, then sighed and turned his face to the floor. I smothered a curse. We'd lost him.

"She is my daughter."

Well that was a surprise, and on more levels than I could count.

"Impossible." Miller exploded. I held my hand up again and wondered how many more times I could get away with that.

"And why are you so afraid for her?"

"They know about her, and they know I still love her. They came to me one night, told me what they wanted me to do. At first, I refused. Then they said that if I didn't, they would drag her in here and make me watch while they turned her, and that her first meal would be her own child. My granddaughter is only eight."

"But this is not possible," rumbled Miller.

I wasn't listening. Maybe some of Freddie's fear was still rattling around in my head, but incandescent fury had set fire to my soul, and I wasn't really running things anymore. Something inside me reached down into the earth, deep, deep down and far below the usual energy plane.

"Miss Doe?" Somebody—Miller—shook my shoulder, but I was busy elsewhere. The energy was drawing up towards me, and I could feel questing probes reaching up, trying to find a way through to the source above. The Bloodfire was coming, and I couldn't do a damned thing about it.

My body jerked as the chair twisted around, then pain exploded across my face. I saw Miller raise his hand to strike me again, but I snatched his wrist in midair and squeezed. He cried out and sank to the floor, his other hand scrabbling in his jacket for his Colt. I squeezed tighter. He cried out again.

"Jane, *stop*."

That wasn't going to happen, though I had no idea where this was going. Until I felt hands on me again, but this time gentle.

"Stop this." Freddie stood in front of me and stared into my eyes. "I don't know what it is, but I don't want it on me, or my daughter. Please."

And the Bloodfire faded away, gone in an instant. Compassion trumps fury. I let go of Miller's hand and he swore as he cradled it in the other.

"Oh, I'm *so* sorry." I reached out to him, but he flinched away, and somehow that hurt me more.

"We are finished here," he gritted out through clenched teeth. "The matter is closed."

"Wait." Freddie was subdued. Maybe I scared him sane. "I can't tell you who in the Citadel is making me do this. I can't risk my daughter's life." He reached over the table to a pad of sticky notes and picked up a pencil. He wrote for a few seconds, then held the note out to me. "This is where I have to pick the blood up: the address, the number, and the name. Please, try to make it look like I'm not involved."

"And what's to stop you warning them as soon as we leave? Tell them everything you told us?" Miller's voice sounded angry, but I think it was more his pain, or his anger towards me.

Freddie shrugged. "Then they will turn my daughter anyway. Are you going to call the custodians now?"

Miller looked at me, but this was internal. That made it his call.

"You are the strangest vampire I have ever encountered," Miller said, and his anger seemed to soften. "Normally, I would never take the word of anybody in the Citadel, but I'll take yours, if you swear to keep this meeting to yourself."

"Who would I tell? But I so swear, if that helps you."

Miller said nothing but got to his feet with the help of his good arm. He crossed to the door and waited for me. As I passed, I squeezed Freddie's hand, then caught up with Miller and opened the door for him.

"I know someone who can fix that?" I said, as he walked past me.

"So do I; the ER at Ellen J Fenway." He was cold, not looking at me. I closed the door behind us, and we retraced out steps.

"I mean fix it in twenty minutes. As far as I know Ellen J doesn't have a department of magical medicine."

He ignored me a moment longer, then stopped at the next door and turned back to face me. His eyes were still cold with anger. "What happened in there?"

"I have no idea."

"Don't play with me." Miller snapped and I flinched back from him.

"I'm not. I do not know what happened. And don't speak to me like I'm one of your servants."

"If you cannot control yourself, there is no place for you on this case."

Well, that was like another slap on the face. Storming off in front of him, I hurried outside, but the cool air didn't stop my cheeks burning. Both doors of the car were open, and I walked around to the far side before I slumped into the seat. It only took a few minutes for the car to get to the courtyard where I had left my girl, and during the ride I said nothing. The driver opened the door for me, as usual. Once I got out and he closed it, I turned back to him and gave him Doc's address.

"Take him here if he'll let you. I'll try to get there before you, but the response to the entry phone is "Bite me, Louis." Tell them to charge it to the Campbell and Doe account."

"I'll try, miss, but he's not one for doing as others suggest."

Rolling my eyes, I nodded. The driver got in and the car purred away while I took my helmet and pushed it over my head. I caught up with the car in minutes. I could have roared past it, but he knew where he was going, and I had already nearly gotten myself lost. Besides, they were making a good ninety miles an hour, and I was comfortable with that.

Also, it gave me time to think, to try to figure out just what the hell had happened.

Grumpy Old Man had pushed me to dig into the Bloodfire, but I refused. He didn't know about the note I had left myself, hidden in the base of a model motorcycle. The last line of the note read "He must not know. He must never know."

Dramatic.

Thing was, I had written everything else in a code I had no clue how to read. In a sense, that suited me. If I didn't know it myself, how could I tell anyone else? And I was fine with that. Until today.

Though it hadn't happened since that night when he tried to kill me, the Bloodfire had called to me today. Yeah, I said that the right way around. *It* called to *me*; I didn't summon it. And I felt like it had been in control, not me. Though that could be an excuse.

Which left me thinking. Where the Bloodfire was concerned, I had believed ignorance was bliss, was the greatest safety. But if the damned magic could fire itself up like that, was I a liability? A danger to those around me? Did I have a duty to find out more about it? I guess I felt like someone who is really sick but doesn't go to the doctor. Until someone tells them how bad things are, they can ignore it, pretend its not as bad as they think. Except each day they put things off, the problem gets bigger. How big dare I let the problem get before I admitted I had to do something about it?

Miller's limo slowed to go into the cave, and I pulled back even farther. I didn't want to slam into the back of it if they stopped for any reason. Once we left the barn, I swung in front of them. I wanted things to be as smooth as possible when they reached Doc's—assuming the driver could talk Miller into going.

I twisted the throttle hard, and my girl roared away down the road.

Poking Sleeping Bears

Tasha looked out the window and onto the street below, at the front of the apartment building. The same Dodge was sitting there. At least he had the craft to park between the light pools cast by two streetlamps, but the shape of the driver was still visible. To her eyes, anyway.

Eddie had just left, making for the Uber they arranged to meet him out back of the building. It seemed Palmer's crew were only looking for cars in and out of the garage. A crack in their previously remarkable professionalism.

Tasha dug around in a cupboard until she found a travel mug, rinsed it, then filled it with the dregs from the coffee machine. She added milk and sugar, screwed on the lid, and ambled down to the sidewalk.

She felt his eyes on her as soon as she opened the doors to the foyer, tracking her as she made her way along the sidewalk until she was level with the car. It was a quiet street, and late at night, so she crossed the road and stood next to the driver's door. The man inside looked directly ahead, expression slightly panicked, refusing to acknowledge her existence until she tapped on the glass. Only then did he buzz the window down and look at her.

"Wow, who did you piss off to get stuck with this duty."

Tasha kept her voice light, even sympathetic. "I just thought I'd tell you I'm staying home for the rest of the night. I've got Chinese being delivered in about thirty minutes, and I'll be going to bed around eleven." Which was a lie. She held out the travel mug. He took it automatically.

"So, I brought you this to help you stay awake. I promise I won't tell Palmer how easily we made you, but can you ask him to send a different vehicle and driver next time. It's not that I don't like you, but the building has excellent security cameras. We have this vehicle's license plate, and a nice clear picture of you, both of which are already with my attorney. A new face would help keep him interested." She smiled sweetly.

The driver unscrewed the top of the mug and tipped the contents onto the road—an inch away from splashing her slippers. He screwed the lid back on and handed the mug back to her, all without uttering a word. The window rolled up, the engine started, and he pulled away into the night.

Tasha grinned as she rode the elevator back to her apartment, wishing she *had* ordered Chinese food and wondering if it was too late. Taunting the guy was a risk, but sometimes, you just had to poke the bear to see what would happen.

Back in the apartment, Tasha went to her purse and took out a tiny silver whistle. Opening a window, she leaned out and blew. Several dogs began to bark, but otherwise the whistle didn't make a sound. She left the window open and went back to the kitchen, taking a spoon and measuring out a portion of local, organic honey into an egg cup. She went back to the window, placed the eggcup on the sill, and waited.

Minutes later, announced by a metallic buzz, a glittering red dragonfly hovered outside the window for a moment, then resolved into a fairy form before settling on the ledge. Tasha gestured at the spoon.

"And offering, in return for a small favor."

The fairy, petite and female, eyed her and then the spoon with great suspicion. "What favor?"

"I seek parlay with the one who calls himself Maximus."

The fairy rolled her eyes upwards at the mention of the name. "What can the Great Bombast do for you that I cannot?"

"Very little, I would imagine." Tasha weighed her options. Having another helper would be useful, but Maximus might take offence. "Hear me, then, little sister. Can you make the pictures of great detail?"

"Better than he can."

"Then here is the task. Go to a place I shall describe. Watch for a female of my species, whom again I shall describe. Follow her when she leaves her stone box. Make note of any other stone boxes she enters. Tell me of these each night. I shall leave an egg cup full of nectar on my window. You are welcome to it if it pleases you. How do you say, little sister?"

The fairy frowned at Tasha for many seconds, appraising her, then produced her silver spoon and sampled the honey Tasha had set out.

"I shall do this. For how many nights?"

"At least two."

"Very well. Describe to me these things."

It took a while. Maximus was used to her shorthand, but the new fairy was young, even if she was ambitious, and Tasha had to go over things more than once to make sure they understood each other.

"Until the morrow, then," said the fairy, turning to leave.

"Wait, what shall I call you?"

The fairy looked over her shoulder. "Names hold power,

and I do not share power with those I do not yet know. Ask me again at the end of our business. If you need me, make that horrible noise three times and I shall come to it."

She jumped from the ledge and her red wings flickered into the dark.

Hook the Next Fish

"Hello ... We have a mutual friend ... Yes, Fredrick is unavailable, and I have been asked to step in ... Yes, most inconvenient, and I would rather not be involved, but ... Don't be ridiculous. I don't have any more names than Freddie did, and we both know he knew nobody ... What he did with them once he got them inside the Citadel is none of your business or mine. No, I can't give you the order over the phone ... Because they didn't tell me. I've no idea what I'm collecting, and I don't want to know. I'm just supposed to smuggle it back in ... and I don't care if you don't like the word."

Miller looked at me and rolled his eyes. He was on the phone to Freddie's contact, and he was letting his voice rise and become more panicked with each new exchange.

"This is absurd. I'm going back to the Citadel and tell them you just tried to extort a fee from me. I'm doing this because I have to, not because I get anything out of it, but it's not worth you trying to ... Eight tonight?"

Miller took the phone from his ear. "How impolite, he hung up."

I grinned. "But you have a meeting?"

"As you heard."

Now the bait was taken I picked up my phone and booked a rental car. Everything in Miller's collection was too flash, and my bike wouldn't work for the idea we had. But Miller was looking at me across the table, rubbing at the wrist I had broken. It was fine now—Doc had fixed him up good in half an hour—but Miller kept rubbing it when he looked at me, like he had some deep, residual ache. I didn't like it, but it was of my own doing, so I put up with it.

"What's the matter?" I asked.

"Are you up to this?"

"Again?" I tried to keep the irritation out of my voice and failed. I understood. He had seen me lose control, and almost do something with incalculable consequences. For all I know, I could have torn down the Citadel. "It's never happened before. So long as I stay clear of draining buckets of fear out of impossible vampires for a while, it's not likely to happen again."

"And you won't tell me what it was?"

"You must have this on file somewhere, but for please the last time, no I won't tell. I don't understand what it is, and I hope nobody else knows. All I could do is make guesses."

"The ground shook."

"You said."

"The actual walls of the Citadel shook."

"Things were a little busy. I didn't notice."

I knew he was weighing me, judging what value I brought to the investigation against the risks, the consequences. It was an uncomfortable feeling, and worse that I knew Tasha would do the same—if I ever told her what happened.

"So am I fired?"

"I should." And I knew he meant it. Probably wasn't wrong,

either. "But I would rather leave that up to you. You need to consider if you are an asset, or if you are likely to lose control to that extent again. And if you might, you should resign. I'll make sure they pay your expenses."

Big of him. The pig-headed side of me wanted to quit there and then. Let them figure out the rest of this mess without me and crawl off to lick my wounds. And that would give Tasha an option on the biggest 'told you so' ever.

But I wanted to stay on. I wanted to finish my first solo job, and maybe I wanted to do something to help Freddie.

"I don't quit."

Miller's face stayed poker straight. "Very well. Then we should move to the next stage of the plan."

Though I nodded, I felt achy inside. I hadn't quite realized it, but I liked Miller, and it was tragic to find that out only because I'd hurt him.

"On my way."

We knew the address of the apartment Freddie picked up the deliveries from, and we had figured out which windows belonged to it. We needed to be sure the contact was in place. And this all fell on me. Miller waited in one of his cars, down in the office garage.

I hauled up in the rental car, parked out of the way, then found somewhere I could watch without being too conspicuous. Miller had set the meeting for eight. I got there thirty minutes early.

Our dealer was an early bird too. Twenty minutes before the scheduled meet, the lights came on and I saw a shape moving around inside. I picked up my phone and dialed.

"What?" The voice was flat and suspicious.

"You've been set up."

"Who's this?"

"Meet with a guy, rich voice, Freddie out of action?"

"I said who is this."

"He's Citadel security. They're going to bust you."

"Shit. How'd you know?"

"Big yellow bird told me. You want out, or you gonna talk?"

"I got my car."

"Already bugged. They're covering the garage in case you run."

"This is bogus. Who sent you?"

This was always the weak spot, and we hadn't figured a way around it other than bluff. "Stop wasting time. I'll be outside in four minutes. White rental Ford. I wait fifteen seconds at the door. If I don't see you running by then, I drive away. I get paid either way. He said not to leave the goods."

I hung up. I had been walking towards the car since I saw the light come on, and now I picked up the pace while I sent a text to Miller. Three and a half minutes later I pulled the Ford up to the sidewalk outside the apartment block door, smooth and calm like I was somebody's sister come to pick them up.

A shape scuttled across the foyer, then the door burst open and he ran out like a bank robber after a heist. He hauled the back door open, threw in a sports bag, then dived in himself, screaming "Drive, drive".

I eased the car out into traffic.

"Floor it," he yelled from the back.

"Want me to put a sign on top and run a siren screaming 'bust me' too? Amateur. You could have blown it back there. Nobody ever tell you the best way to hide in a crowd is to be part of it?"

One eye was on the road, and the other watched him in the mirror. Sure enough, he dug into his jacket and pulled out a gun. I was waiting for him to do exactly that, and as he leaned forward to put the gun to my head, I stamped hard on the brake. That got me a braying of horns from the traffic behind me, but it made him lean too far forward. As the gun passed over my shoulder, I grabbed it and twisted until the trigger guard bit so hard into his finger it was lose the gun or the digit. He let go and I floored the gas, throwing him back into the seat.

"Amateur," I snapped again. "One more stupid move and I'll drive you to the Citadel myself." I looked at the weapon I had torn from his hand. 9mm, but ancient and a piece of garbage. The only way I would have used it was to hit somebody over the head. I threw it into the passenger footwell.

"Here's what happens. I drive you to a garage about five blocks from here, and I leave you and the car there. Where you go and what you do is up to you. So long as I get a picture of you in the car in the garage, I get paid. So sit back and enjoy the ride. And clean your damned weapon before it kills you."

Focusing on the business of driving, I prayed that there hadn't been a patrol car behind me, while I occasionally glared at my ride in the mirror.

He was a perfect middleman. He didn't look like anything. Mr. Average in every way. Except for his eyes. Right now they looked feral, like a wild dog cornered in your yard. They had a nasty edge to them, too. I wouldn't turn my back on this guy in an elevator.

We turned into the garage under the office. I slowed as I drove down the ramp, then pulled up near the door to the stairs. I didn't park, and I didn't switch the engine off. "Out."

"No. Why?"

"Because, moron, this is where we switch, and you can't drive from the back seat."

He grumbled under his breath, but he opened the door and climbed out. Only then did I switch off the engine, grab the keys, and haul ass out of my own door, baton already clicking open.

"Bitch," he growled, and turned to run. That was when Miller stepped out ahead of him, taser in hand. He pulled the trigger, and the courier fell twitching to the floor.

Dead weight bodies are conspicuous and a pain in the ass to carry, even when they aren't dead yet. Miller was all for dragging him into the elevator, but I remembered seeing a utility room down here. It only took a moment to pick the lock with a quick spell, and inside was a flatbed cart. Result. We bundled the pusher onto the cart, then I took his bag while Miller wheeled him into the elevator. Once we got him into the office, we hauled him into the couch, then bound his hands and feet with plastic strips.

He woke up after a few minutes, fighting the strips and swearing.

"Enough with the potty mouth, or my friend will spark you again."

Miller held up the taser, now just a stun gun, and pulled the trigger. A pretty blue arc crackled and spat between the pins.

The courier hadn't locked the bag, so I opened it and started taking out blood pouches. I held each one up and read the label before I put it on my desk.

"Virgin, virgin, virgin male, virgin female teen." I stopped. The next one I had to read twice, then I had to do a ten-count before I put it down. It was that, or I would have hurt him. I still might. I glared right into his eyes. "Virgin female pre-teen?"

"I don't collect it, and I don't use it. Hey, wait ..."

Miller threw himself at the pusher, stabbing the sparking taser into the courier's neck. Crap. The guy screamed and jerked, but Miller didn't stop. I hurried around from my desk and hauled on his arm.

"Miller. *Miller.* Ease up."

Brute force was getting me nowhere, so I called up a little electricity of my own and shocked his bicep. His arm jerked away from the pusher's neck, and he turned to scowl at me. "You ever mention me not being able to control myself again," I murmured in his ear, "and I'll slap you into next month."

I put a finger to the pusher's neck. His pulse was strong and his breathing regular. He could wake up in his own time. I went back to my desk and got the rest of the blood out of the bag. It was more of the same, forty or so pouches, but no more kiddy stuff. There were a few rare blood groups, but most of it was pretty generic. The bag was thermal, and there were ice bricks in the sides to keep the blood refrigerated.

"We need him alive to answer questions, remember?" I said. "Go sit over there," I said, pointing at Tasha's desk. "I don't trust you so close to him." I glanced at the desk again and realized I didn't trust him not to get nosey. "And don't touch a single thing. She'll know and she'll blame me again."

Miller glowered at me, but I ignored him and he moved, eventually.

The pusher woke a few minutes later and rubbed at his neck with his bound hands. "What is *wrong* with you people?" Then he looked at my desk. "Hey, you need to get that stuff back in the bag. It'll go off, be worthless."

"Oh, it's already worthless," I said. "As is your life, unless you tell us what we want to know."

His face took on that stubborn look they always get when they think they're harder than you and I sighed.

"Your choice. Miller, call for the car."

"I thought we were going to question him."

"Thinks he's a hard man, and I can't be bothered. Call the car, stuff him in the trunk, and we'll let the Citadel break him. Once we show them the food in the bag, they'll fry him alive."

"What?" The courier lost a little of his bravado.

"Mess with fire, you'll get burned. That's what's going to happen to Freddie. You know vamps can't stand daylight, right? It's the ultraviolet. Very bad for them. Freddie's being executed, burned alive by high intensity UV lights. Slow and painful."

I pointed to Miller. "See him? He's the Emissary, the duke's right hand."

Then I pulled out the amulet and dangled it where he could see it. "This? This is the Duke's Tongue. Disgusting name, but it means while I wear it, I speak with his voice." It could have been a St. Christopher for all he knew, but we had him scared enough to believe me.

Doing my best to look bored, I sat back in my chair. "They know about Freddie, and they know about you. They know your customers in the Citadel, though there are some they can't act against. Yet. We take you back there, we tell them to take the flesh off you one bite at a time, all they'll ask is how long to keep you alive."

"But—"

"They don't want you. They don't really want poor Freddie, except to make an example of him. Did I tell you his execution was going to public? Big crowd; doesn't happen often. Where was I?"

"Who they want?" Miller offered. I gave him a smile for following my lead.

"Quite." I turned back to the courier. "You could walk out of here in ten minutes—if you tell us who is supplying you and how the system works."

The pusher had turned a little green. "I can't. They'll kill me."

"You're dead anyway," rumbled Miller. "Once you get to the Citadel. Once they get bored with you."

"Your call," I added.

"Tell us, and the Citadel will get you out of the city, relocate you to anywhere in the country. Even some settling in money." Miller dangled the carrot while he idly sparked the taser in short bursts.

"I ain't no snitch."

"They always trip over that same mistake, don't they?" I shook my head. Miller nodded, but the courier looked confused.

"You know that's all bullshit, right?" I gave him a moment, but he just glared at me. "All that crap about snitching? Everybody sticks together, nobody gets hurt? You really think that anybody higher up the food chain than you, which I guess is pretty much everybody, wouldn't sell you and your grandmother out in a heartbeat? The rule of snitch only ever protects the big guys, while the little guys all get burned."

Looking down at the desk, I kept talking as I started to repackage the blood. "You think about that while I put this stuff away, because when I'm done, he calls the car and there's no more deals."

He held his nerve until I was two pouches away from

finishing.

"Look, I don't know anything. I'm just a runner."

The second to last bag was in my hand. I paused with it in the air. "From whom to whom, little rabbit? From where to where?"

"I get a call. I go to a place. They give me the bag. I take the bag to the apartment and hand it over."

"Your apartment?"

"You think I live in a dive like that?"

The outside had seemed nice enough, but I guess we all have different standards. "So they pay you?"

"Damn straight. Good money, too."

Damn. All we had was another cut out, and I felt bad for Freddie, on account of this one getting paid. Wasn't a total loss though.

"What's the number?"

"Comes up as no caller ID. On a burner phone they gave me."

"And what's the address?"

He hesitated and I put the pouch I was holding into the bag.

"2806, an industrial unit on Mulberry Drive. There's a smart door in front, but I have to go around back. Always a few people lined up outside for something."

"For what?"

"Don't know. Don't care. My job is to stay out of shit that's not my business."

"Who do you see? Is it the same person every time?"

"Could be any of two or three."

"Names?"

"See answer above."

I picked up the last pouch and dropped it into the bag, zipping it shut.

"Hey, you said no car. I get to go now, right?"

Miller and I both laughed, for real. Either he was an idiot, or he thought the two of us were.

"You walk when we see if your information is any good. Miller, sit on him."

It wasn't graceful, but it worked. Miller darted over to our snitch, knelt on his legs to pin them down, then grabbed his wrists and forced them against the pusher's belly. I hurried around to the back of the couch and put my hands on either side of his head. Like I said, I don't like messing around in people's skulls, but the day I saw this used on someone, I decided I *had* to learn it: Fenwycke's Somnambulance. Or as I call it, the zombie spell.

It didn't take long, just wrapping his mind in a suggestion and adding a twist for control. He stopped struggling and Miller climbed off.

"A most undignified position. Are you sure this will work?"

"If I've done it right, and I think I have." I fetched scissors from my desk and cut the plastic strip around the courier's ankles.

"And he won't run away?"

"Not unless someone tells him to. Watch." I touched my zombie on the forehead and said, "Ambulus." His eyes opened and his head lifted.

"Do you need the toilet?" I asked.

A slow shake of the head.

"If you need the toilet, it's over there." I pointed and his eyes slowly followed. "Otherwise, sleep on the couch."

He closed his eyes and lay down on the couch. I turned to Miller and smiled. "See, safely contained with no nasty chains or ropes."

Miller took one more look, his face suggesting he wasn't convinced. "Do we check out his story now?"

My watch told me it was almost midnight. I hadn't eaten in hours, and I was getting tired.

"Can we stop at a drive-thru?"

"In my car? Absolutely not." He frowned, then looked thoughtful. "We can take your rental."

Intersection

The phone shrieked at me. Normally I would have ignored it, but this was Tasha's ringtone. Not sure how pleased she would be if she found out it was the violins from Psycho. I fumbled for it, knocked it off the nightstand, then had to actually open my eyes to see where it had fallen. I pressed green.

"Why is there a man sleeping in our toilet?"

"Ah. I can explain."

"I can't wait."

My eyes were bleary, so I blinked them awake. "Are you there now? For the next hour?"

"Yes, and I can be." She came back with curious caution, which was better than I expected.

"Wait for me. I'll be there in less than an hour."

"Bring chocolate. And a danish."

Even better. She wouldn't have asked for food if she was still pissed with me.

"And how do I wake this idiot in the back room up."

"Fenwycke's," I said, trying to fight my way out of the bedding. "Try tapping his forehead like you did for that girl who tried to kill me."

I hung up and headed for the shower.

Hot chocolate and pastries in hand, I made it through the office door in fifty minutes. Tasha was sitting on the couch, which wasn't a good sign. Where was my zombie drug courier?

"Didn't work?"

A slow shake of her head and a frosty glare was all I got back.

"I got hot chocolate. With marshmallows."

"Adding to a problem usually doesn't solve it."

"Right. You'll have to move though."

"Trust me, I will."

I carefully deposited the emergency supplies on Tasha's desk, then I went into the bathroom. He was asleep on the toilet, trousers around his ankles. I tapped his forehead, and muttered "Ambulus." He zombied awake and sat there, looking at me.

"Finish up and go back to sleep on the couch," I ordered, then stepped away. I heard him shuffle along behind me and turned, ready to tidy the bathroom if I needed to.

"And pull up your pants," I snapped. A flush and a spray later I was back in the office and Tasha was a passing breeze on her way to the john.

"Who is he?" she called through the door. At least she was still curious.

"Don't know his name," I called back, sharing the goodies between our desks. The door opened and closed after appropriate sound effects.

"So why is he here?"

Things were calmer now that we were at our desks, facing each other.

"He's a cross between a pusher and a delivery boy in the one of the cases we're looking at."

She raised her eyebrows. "One of? How are they working

201

out for you?"

I had been thinking about this moment since last night, and not looking forward to it. Miller and I had gone to check out the address the pusher had given us. It didn't help. There were lights on inside, but the lobby was dark. From where we stopped, we couldn't see any names or logos. We did see security cameras all over the place. If we had moved any closer, a camera could have made out our faces, so we munched the burgers and I admitted I was, for now, out of ideas.

Miller wasn't. He wanted to haul the pusher down to the Citadel and hand him over, but I didn't think that would do any good. Besides, I had kind of promised him we wouldn't do that.

And so, reluctantly, I brought up the idea that asking Tasha what she thought might be our next move. And I'd been dreading it ever since.

"Stuck. Both of them. Yours?"

Eyes on the uneaten half for my danish, I waited for the *finished*, or the *going* well, or *which one I've done three*.

"Same."

It was hard, real hard, to keep the relief and a small amount of smug off my face. I looked up and saw her trying to do the same thing. We both burst out laughing, and the awkwardness that had lingered in the room since I arrived blew away.

"Want to share?" Tasha asked.

It was tempting. Just the two of us, going over each other's cases sounded like fun. But Miller would get huffy about being left out, and I figured the same for whoever she was working with. I scrunched my nose.

"Think we might put some egos out of joint? Besides, I have a rental to get back before noon. How about a full war council, here, at one?"

Tasha looked like she would have preferred just the two of us as well, but she nodded. "Makes sense. I can nap here. But please, before you go, take him to the toilet again."

Miller was waiting for me outside. I told him I wanted to meet, with a place and time, but I hadn't told him why. He left the car and strolled towards me.

"You have news?"

"Not exactly."

"Then why the meeting?"

"You won't like it," I said, resting a palm on his chest. "But I've asked for a war council."

"A what? With whom?"

"I was going to see if Tasha had any ideas I could use. Turns out she's stuck on something she's working on too. It seemed fair that if we want her to help us, that we should help in turn."

He was not in the slightest bit convinced by my argument. "Three hardly constitutes a war council."

"She is also working with a third party," I admitted.

"Miss Doe, what we are engaged in is sensitive and very confidential. I cannot approve of sharing it with some nobody I have never met. Who is this person?"

Only then did I realize I hadn't a clue who Tasha was working with. I improvised. "We meet, we sniff each other's butts, and we talk if we like them." I took the hand that was still resting against his chest and patted him. "Besides, this is me being professionally courteous to you. I could have had this meeting without you. Might even have been easier. I just thought it fair you should be here."

He looked down at me and, to my surprise, nodded. "I

appreciate the thought. Shall we go meet the rest of the council?"

The main office was empty, but the light was on in the side room we used for consultations and meetings. I led Miller there, walking into the room first.

When I saw who was sitting with Tasha, I felt my jaw clench and knew my body language must be screaming how unimpressed I was. The idiot grinning at me across the table was the cop who had tried to bust me for setting fire to my own house a year ago. Tasha hadn't been too complimentary about him at the time, so I couldn't imagine what he was doing here. They were both standing. He gave me an uncomfortable half wave.

But when Miller walked through the door behind me, the temperature in the room dropped like it had turned into an ice box. Tasha stiffened and her face set in lines of disapproval, so I got a good idea of how I must have looked to them. Nobody moved. It was like gunslingers waiting for the church bell to strike noon. I decided to draw first.

"This is Emissary Miller. I believe you know my partner, Tasha Campbell."

Miller gave her a small bow. "Investigator. A pleasure to meet you. Your accomplishments are most impressive."

Tasha nodded back to him, and opened her hand towards the cop. "Senior Detective Eddie Weston, Metro police. You've already met my partner, Jane Doe."

He made the awkward wave again and shuffled his feet. From the corner of my eye I saw Tasha glaring at Miller, and realized I was doing the same to Weston. This wasn't going to get us anywhere.

"Ground rules," I clapped my hands and spoke loud, like

a kindergarten teacher. "Only one, actually. No history. No baggage from the past, who we are, who we were, what we did. For the purposes of this meeting, clean sheets. Do we agree? Because if we don't, we may as well all walk out right now."

Weston pushed out his bottom lip and nodded right away. I sensed Miller shift his weight beside me, and for an instant I thought he was turning for the door.

"I agree."

And that left Tasha, and she was having none of it. I wasn't sure if she even heard what I said. Her eyes burned the air as she glared at Miller. I felt him shift his weight again and got a feeling that if Tasha didn't back off soon, he would walk. I would have.

"Tasha? Whatever they did, *he* didn't. He just works for them."

"You don't know," she breathed.

I hunted for something to say, but Miller beat me to it.

"Actually, I do. I have been briefed on the pertinent details. It was barbaric, and unforgivable. It was also without sanction. Duke Ladislav has given me a statement for you, should I ever be in a position to deliver it. Those who perpetrated that assault upon you were subsequently hunted. Several were caught and dealt with. The instigator was never found or identified. The Citadel made a number of attempts to reach out to you, but it is understandable that you weren't in place to receive those approaches. I am pleased that I am able to bring this to you now. Of course, you may choose to dismiss this as a convenient fiction, and I can only assure you, as one human to another, it is not."

It was my turn to stare at Miller. In fairness, we all were, in varying degrees of surprise and disbelief. "Is that true?" I didn't know what the hell he was talking about, but I could sense how huge it was.

He turned away from Tasha and looked me in the eye. "Every word, I swear."

He sat at the table, took a pen from his pocket, and put it next to the legal pads we left in front of every chair.

"Shall we begin?"

But I was watching Tasha. She wasn't there. She had turned inwards, staring into space. Her face was blank.

"How about I get some coffee first," I suggested. "Won't take a minute, and we could be in for a long ride. Tasha, want to give me a hand? Tasha?"

The cop, Weston, had noticed that Tasha was acting weird. He was starting to look all confused and angry, like he was looking for someone to take it out on. I hurried to the other end of the table, grabbed Tasha's arm, and eased her out of the room with me.

The kitchenette was right beside the conference room, but out of sight of it. I kept my voice low. "What's wrong, are you OK?"

Her eyes still had that 'thousand yard stare' and she didn't reply, didn't even look at me. I grabbed her hands in mine and squeezed them. They were corpse cold, as usual, but I remember her mentioning that skin contact was like having her hands doused in hot water. She took a deep breath, looked around her in confusion, and tried to pull her hands away. I wouldn't let go until she looked at me.

"What? Let go."

Better, but I held on a moment longer. "You zoned out, after Miller said those things to you."

"He's lying." Her voice was flat, angry, and uncompromising. She twisted her wrists free of my hands and crossed her arms tightly over her chest.

"I've never caught him lying to me. At least, not yet." I tried to make it not sound like I was bragging, but I still got a hurt look.

"You don't know these people. He's telling you exactly what he needs to."

I thought about that for a moment. The criminal psych course I took did cover that, and how difficult it could be to detect. If I was honest, it wasn't something I had been watching for, at least not consciously, but flicking my mind back through the week or so we had worked together, I couldn't see anything.

"Maybe. You think he'd be able to make all that up on the spot, or believe it would make you OK with him?"

It was her turn to look a little less certain. "Perhaps not."

I was done. "You easy now?"

She nodded but didn't look sure. "Enough to get by."

"I'll take the tray. You get the door and bring the cookies."

Suspension of Disbelief

"**B**efore we start," said Miller. "I must ask a somewhat indelicate question. How well briefed is the Detective, and what is his role here? While nothing we are doing is illegal, I question the need for the involvement of the police department. No offence intended, Detective."

Weston gave him a frosty nod, but he folded his arms and leaned back in his chair. Thing was, Miller had a good point. It was going to be difficult to discuss things openly.

"Detective Weston's—" Tasha began, but the cop interrupted her.

"Eddie. We aren't in court and you ain't my captain."

Tasha looked surprised, and I thought he was bordering on aggressive. Miller didn't seem to react.

"Eddie has been told I am an emophage vampire. He has been made aware of haemophage vampires too. I believe we are still working on some credibility issues." She glanced at him, her eyes narrowed, and I realized she wasn't sure if he believed her.

"Who wishes to present first," asked Miller.

"Us," I said. "We're working two cases. We can break between them."

I looked around for approval. Nobody grumbled, so I went

on. "First case is a misper, or maybe a cluster of them. Only really came to light because the most recent has connections. Five in total so far, and what we have suggests they were all last seen in or around Petite Paris."

"Why isn't that a police matter?" Eddie asked.

"Maybe because the department doesn't have a stellar reputation on minor issues like missing persons," Tasha suggested. I was glad she said it before I did.

"Hey!" Eddie looked hurt, but I saw an underlying resignation that said he knew she was right. "If they were rich and knew who to grease, it would have been checked out." The last came out as a reluctant mumble, but I admired the honesty. Time to make things even more awkward, at least for Eddie the Cop.

"Couldn't involve the cops. These people are vampires. Haemophages."

"I will accept the use of 'bloodsuckers' around this table," offered Miller, with a half-smile. "Haemophage is, frankly, something of a mouthful."

"You people are as crazy as her." Eddie threw his hands in the air.

Tasha turned and gave him a look that should have killed him. "You bastard. You were humoring me? After what I showed you?"

"Ah, come on. You're faster than me and stronger than me. So you work out."

Tasha was already going through something, and this just hurt her more. It must have, because I could see it in her eyes, and she would normally never let her emotions show so much. I think Eddie the creep must have seen it too, because he wouldn't look at her. He was appealing to me and Miller, and his face dropped when he realized he had no support here.

"Come on, don't tell me you buy into this. Or are you vampires too?"

"Not at all," said Miller, his face neutral as always "I am as human as you are."

"See," said Eddie, thinking his point proven.

"But I am the human Emissary for Duke Ladislav, hereditary ruler of the largest enclave of haemophage vampires in the north, covering the northern states and most of the West Coast."

Eddie's face dropped. It seemed appropriate for me to rub it into something else unpleasant.

"I'm not a vampire, either." When I saw a flash of wary hope in his eyes I stomped on it. Hard. I don't like people who hurt my friends. "But I am a witch. Well, technically a Combat Mage."

Without touching it, I lifted my pencil in the air and fired it at his face. He flinched, but I had already stopped it four or five inches from him. I threw at little heat at it, and it burst into flames, the ashes dropping onto the notepad in front of him. Miller passed me his pencil.

"Excellent fine control, Miss Doe."

See, he appreciates me.

Eddie, however, was looking from one to the other of us with wide eyes. "You're all crazy."

"And you're stubborn," I shot back, but Tasha raised her hand.

"You have two choices, Detective Weston. You can start treating us all with respect, and not denying who and what we are." She took a breath. "Or you can get the hell out of here. I'll turn over what material we have, but you can work this case on your own."

"Ah, come on, Nat. You can't blame—"

"I can and I do. You have offended me, and these people who have come here to help you. Same old Eddie. I should have known."

Anger flashed across the cop's face, but I'll give him credit that he crushed it. "I apologize if I have offended anybody. These—issues are difficult to absorb. And I can't say I believe any of it without lying, and that I don't do.

Tasha snorted, but he ignored her.

"How about you just pretend you believe for now?" I offered him a way out if he wasn't too stupid to see it.

Eddie looked doubtful. "I can try."

"Better than nothing. Starting again, our first case involves missing vampires, young and wealthy, most last seen in Petite Paris. The second case involves contraband human blood being imported into the Citadel, some of it rare and specialized."

"Specialized how? Blood group?" Eddie asked.

"Some rare groups," I agreed. "But a lot from virgin sources." I was about to mention the children, but I glanced at Tasha. She was still wound tight, lips pressed together. "Some others too."

"And why's that contraband? I thought that was what vampires did."

At least Eddie was taking an interest.

"There are rules," said Miller. "Agreements with the government. Unlicensed blood contravenes this and puts the agreement at risk."

But now Eddie looked thoughtful. He reached into a pocket and threw a poker chip onto the table. I saw Tasha's eyes open wide.

"Nat, didn't Floyd say junkies were using these to buy Ruby?"

"By giving blood. And the unknown ingredient in this drug we've been trying to track down is vampire blood." Tasha slapped an open palm onto the table and looked disgusted with the entire universe. "Damn it, we've all been working the same case."

It took a lot longer than one jug of coffee for us to bring each other up to speed.

"So we agree we can ignore the stash house?" Miller suggested which got nods from everybody. "And what value do we put on the Winger girl?"

"Danny Morello isn't going to let us anywhere near her, so we can't ask her anything."

"I have a tail on her that hasn't reported in yet. She's due soon, though."

"She?" I was intrigued. "Not Max?"

Tasha gave me a wink and I burned to find out what she had been up to. "Shouldn't we follow that up? We need all our intel before we can move forward, don't we? Do you have any honey here?"

Eddie had looked like most of the conversation had gone over his head since we started, but now Miller looked at me like I was speaking in tongues too.

"It's not very good." Tasha frowned. "I don't want to make a bad first impression."

Now I had to find out what was going on. "Maybe use what we have as a bonus payment?"

Tasha shrugged. "Worth a try. Gentlemen, you'll have to

excuse us for a while. Please don't leave the room until we open the door again."

"Unless anybody needs a pee break," I added. "In which case go now."

Miller was burning with about as much curiosity as I was, but not quite for the same reason. I could see he really wanted to come with us. I gave him a look that told him I was enjoying that he had to stay put.

Once we were outside, I raided the cupboard in the kitch-enette for honey and something to put it in, while Tasha went to the window and blew three toots on her magic flute. I had a suspicion it was just a dog whistle, but she used it to summon fairies, so that made it magical to me.

I found the top from a bottle of cough medicine and the honey and hurried back to the table closest to the window. Tasha had bought paper, and we waited quietly.

"Are you OK?" I asked. "I mean really OK?"

I thought she was ignoring me, it took so long before she answered.

"No."

"Because of what Miller said?"

She nodded but didn't say anything more for minutes. When she did, I wished she hadn't.

"Do you trust him?"

My turn to take my time searching for an answer. "No." And that surprised me too. "I think he's very loyal. But I have to ask myself would he—could he—build such a complex lie so quickly? Which will make his employers look even worse when the lie gets out? I don't think he would want to put them in that position."

She nodded, and we left each other with our thoughts until a deep scarlet dragonfly rasped toward the window. A moment later a red-garbed fairy stood on the table, glaring at the honey I left out.

"This is not the same place, or the promised item."

"And for that I apologize, but events have moved on and I need to know if you have seen anything of note yet. You can trust this one. She is known to Maximus." Tasha gestured towards me.

"The blowhard trusts too many too easily."

"No. You are welcome to this poor substitute as an additional consideration for your inconvenience."

"What is it that you would know?"

"Did you find the woman?"

"Of course." The fairy crossed her arms and lifted her chin.

"Did she leave the stone box?"

"Only once, in a metal box. She went to a different stone box for a time, then went back. I do not see why she bothered."

"Did you make memory of the place where she went?"

The fairy touched her spoon to the end of the pencil and sketched on the paper. It took her no time at all to render the street names. 127th, and Mulberry Drive.

"Pardon me," I said quietly, "but did you see any numbers or writing on the front of the box she travelled to?"

A fresh sheet of paper, and another sketch; this one was the front of a regular, industrial unit. Beside me, Tasha was fizzing with some barely contained emotion, but she was holding it together so as not to spook the fairy.

"Most efficient," she said, and we both offered bows with our heads. Tasha reached for the pot with the honey in, ready to hand it over.

"If you choose to go there, beware the beasts," said the fairy, eyeing the honey with something close to lust.

"The what?" I blurted, and the fairy frowned at me for being too loud.

"Beasts guard the building, many inside, many at the rear."

"Can you show us?"

The fairy sighed. "My arm grows weary."

"We are in awe of your skills and will not need you to watch this woman further, but the agreement for compensation still stands."

The fairy gave Tasha a long look, then started on a fresh sheet of paper. Again, a pretty generic industrial unit loading bay. A truck door, closed, but an open side door. Next to the side door was a man, or a woman, holding a nasty looking gun I couldn't make out, but Tasha was looking over the other side, in the shadows.

"There, can you make that bigger, and lighter."

Two humped shapes grew to a quarter the size of the sheet, the somehow the fairy shifted the contrast and the lumps resolved.

"Very precise. We have finished here." Tasha slid the pot over, and the fairy made short work of emptying it. "Your work is of the highest quality. May we work together again?"

"I would consider it."

"Then may we know what we may call you?"

I'll swear I saw the fairy roll her eyes. "Scarlet, of course."

With a metallic buzz, the fairy took wing and was a sparkling red dragonfly before she cleared the window.

"So that leaves us with pretty much everything focused on 2806 Mulberry Drive?" Nobody disagreed with me when I looked around the table. I had taken charge of the drawings

215

and slid the first two on the table. There should have been some groans of injustice at the cosmic level of coincidence, but everybody was trying to out-cool everybody else.

"And what's our next step?" Tasha asked.

"SWAT? Call it in and get support?" Eddie suggested.

Tasha shook her head. "Palmer will kill the request, then come out with his own team. Besides, I have a hunch he's involved in this somewhere."

"We have dirty cops in this too?" That was not something I wanted to hear. Tasha raised her hand and twisted it from side to side.

"We cannot storm the building," said Miller. "Unacceptable. Any vampire inside must be recovered and removed as a priority. Nothing else must risk their safe and discrete extraction."

"That sounds like an ultimatum, mister." Eddie bristled. "These creeps are killing people, real people. Shouldn't that be our priority?"

"Strike two," said Tasha, her voice cold as ice, beating me by a split second. I was getting tired of the cop's reality issues. It took him too long to realize what he had said, too, but he at least had the grace to blush.

Miller either let it pass or didn't notice. "Unless I get a clear understanding that the missing vampires get priority, I will have no option but to have a Citadel-controlled ring of personnel around the unit. In an hour."

Tasha fanned her hand in front of her face. "The stench of testosterone is getting overpowering in here."

She was right and I was half-ready for one or other of the men to draw a weapon. Time for me to distract them with something else. "I think I may know someone who can help us."

I slid the third picture onto the table. Eddie grabbed it first and stared at it for a moment before sliding it back to the middle of the table.

"Can't make it out."

"That's the opposition," I said.

"I thought they were guard dogs," said Tasha, while Miller drew the picture towards himself and stared at it.

"Not dogs," I said, and I couldn't help another smug grin on my face. "Those are—"

Miller stole my thunder.

"Those are hyenas."

Here, boy

Tasha sneezed when she walked into the bar. The ambient aroma was ... well 'musky' was as kindly as she could put it. Still, she would be surprised if most humans would smell it; those that did would be dog owners and think it smelt 'homey'.

Jane strode up to the bar, looking for somebody and, from her body language, not seeing them. Tasha hung back a step. This was Jane's show.

"We close in fifteen minutes, ladies. Have to be a real quick one."

"We were looking for Jeff. Business."

"He's out back. I can call him for you, but he might be too busy."

"We'll risk it."

"Got a name for him."

"Jane."

The bartender picked up a phone, pressed a single button, and murmured into it before coming back up the bar to them. "Can you give him twenty minutes or so? I can get you a coffee. No alcohol though." He looked apologetic. "You'll be here past closing."

Jane said, "No problem," and led them to a table right

at the back of the bar. Tasha thought it a good move. No point advertising their presence to any enforcement agency looking for license violations. The bartender arrived with two enormous cappuccinos and a side plate of chocolate biscuits, then went back to tidying up and closing the bar

The war council had ended after some major debate, not least triggered by Eddie having his credibility stretched. When they tried to explain the difference between shifters and were-beasts, they hit his limit, especially when Jane tried to tell him they were going to engage the help of a pack of shifter wolves to deal with the hyenas.

Miller, on the other hand, fixated on getting his precious vampire prince out quietly and intact. Tasha argued against what she called 'typical bloodsucker mentality, of always looking after their own first'. The conference had not ended well, and she let her mind wander along all the potential arguments they were going to have tomorrow, and what her comebacks were going to be.

"So what's with the cop? I thought you didn't like him anymore?"

"Excuse me?"

Jane gave Tasha a lop-sided grin. "You were looking miles away, and I know you don't want to talk about what's really bugging you, so I thought I'd distract you with something else."

Tasha gave her an exasperated look, knowing that was what Jane expected. In truth, she would have preferred to brood alone. On top of everything else, the Miller statement needed analysis, interpretation. More evidence of its truth would help, and a second source would be ideal. Only she could not for the life of her think of anybody she would trust who would have the information she needed. So she accepted the diversion Jane offered.

"Eddie came to me, asked me for help."

"I'm surprised you would even talk to him after what you said about him last year."

"Said the woman working for vampires?" Tasha saw Jane's eyes flick up from the coffee froth she was sculpting with a spoon. Not long ago, Tasha would have expected a cheeky half-grin. Today Jane was guarded, looking for any nasty edge in Tasha's comment. Tasha knew she was doing the same. They had to fix this. Jane was the only friend she found in ten years. "Eddie was a good cop, once."

"Ever thought it might have been you that made him one?"

"Perhaps. What he came to me with sounded more like the old Eddie—an off-the-books crusade that would get him into trouble with his boss, but that might help out someone the system was letting down. I was only helping with this one small thing. Guess I got sucked in."

Jane gave her a half-smile. "And for free?"

Tasha waited for the snark, the criticism.

"Good for you. Being impulsive is healthy for the soul sometimes."

Tasha wanted to get mad. This girl threw knives around like paper planes, without knowing or understanding the consequences of things she said. Tasha didn't do impulsive, never had. And as for souls ... Did she even still have one? Hurting someone without intent was still hurting them.

Tasha took a gulp from her two-handed cup. Or was it her own fault? Was she looking for pain in everything anybody said to her, even where there wasn't any? It was a great way of putting up barriers, stopping people from getting too close.

"You could be right. Perhaps I'm going soft in my old age."

That got a laugh, which was nice. Jane had an infectious laugh, uninhibited, and Tasha didn't hear it often enough.

The door of the bar opened. Tasha turned to see who would be entering the place after it was closed. The woman was tall and well built, but not overweight. Mid-thirties at a guess. She looked like she had thrown her clothes on and dragged a brush through her hair once before she left. And she looked angry, especially when she saw the two of them sitting at the table.

When she turned back, Tasha caught Jane rolling her eyes. "You know her?"

"Kind of. She's the alpha bitch."

For a split second Tasha thought Jane was using a euphemism, then she remembered why they were there, and raised her eyebrows. "With whom is she so annoyed, or is she like that all the time?"

"Us, or both. Haven't seen her not angry yet."

"Does that help us?"

"Absolutely not."

The alpha went straight out back, and a moment later they could hear raised voices. The argument went on right to the moment a man burst through the door from the office, his face flushed, eyes wild. Tasha assumed this was the other alpha and felt sorry for him. He looked several years younger than the bitch. Life, she mused, did not always provide us with the partner we would choose.

The door swung closed behind him, almost catching the bitch in her face, and tightening her anger another notch. They made their way to the back of the bar, then sat at the table next to Tasha and Jane.

With us but not with us, Tasha mused, and wondered how reliable these people were going to be as allies.

"Jeff Baker," he said, without offering to shake hands. "This is Abbie."

"My business partner, Tasha Campbell," said Jane. "She's a PI too. How's Harry?"

"Like you care?" snapped the bitch, Abbie. Jane ignored her and looked at Jeff.

"He'll be OK. First and second degree burns over the whole hand, but he should get all the function back."

"Good." And Jane moved on to business as slick as a sales rep. Tasha felt a little proud. Jane had learned so much in the last year. "We have news, and a proposal. You won't like how I say what I'm going to, but you'll see why before we finish."

"And you couldn't do this at a reasonable time of day." The alpha bitch threw another snide comment.

"What can I say, we're night owls." Jane again looked at Jeff, and Tasha wondered if she realized how much that was making an enemy of Abbie. "Do you want to do this some other time? We thought you would want to know as soon as we knew, and figured end of business would be best. We can arrange something another day."

"Now is fine." Jeff's tone was short, but Tasha didn't think it was because of their timing. As arranged, Tasha took a folded sheet of paper and handed it to Jeff. She would be the one to present, to cement her as part of the group.

"What's this," snapped Abbie before Jeff had opened the page then, as soon as he had, "Can't see a thing. It's not very clear."

But Jeff scuffed his chair across the floor until he was directly under one of the lights recessed into the ceiling. He pointed first to the shadow of a man with a machine pistol, then peered even more closely. He pointed to the other side of the loading dock, to the other shape that they had seen in the shadows. "What the hell is that?"

"We think the other pack you are concerned about are the same people we are interested in, and we think they are Hyenas."

"Are you stupid, or just freaking crazy? Give me that." Abbie snatched the paper from Jeff's fingers, tearing it, then found her own light to view it under.

"Where are they?" Jeff asked.

"We'll tell you," said Jane, "just not yet."

"You're holding *out* on us?" Abbie snarled. "I *knew* it."

Things got nasty so fast Tasha had no time to react. Abbie dove toward Jane, lips curled back in a snarl, hands out and clawed like talons. Jeff was caught out as badly as Tasha, but Jane's expression didn't even flicker. It was like she had been expecting it. Her right hand came up to chest height, palm out, and Abbie bounced off a wall of something. More than bounced. Jane's hand pushed away, just a fraction, and Abbie flew across the room, sliding over the top of two tables before coming to a halt in a tangle of chairs.

Jane waited until Abbie was looking at her. "First, last, and only warning, Abbie." Then she turned to Jeff. "Sorry."

"Don't be." He looked over his shoulder. "Get back here and pay attention."

Jeff didn't raise his voice, but at that moment Tasha would have thought twice before taking him on. There was a subliminal growl in his words, and he looked like a man who just passed his tolerance for stupid. He turned back to Jane. "I assume there's a reason?"

"Two, actually, and I'll be honest with you; if we tell you where they are, you have no need for us, and this arrangement could end like that."

Tasha fought off a smile. Jane had lifted her hand and snapped her fingers, except she had added a little spark and a puff of smoke, and Jeff's eyebrows crawled toward the back of his head.

"So you need our help?"

Tasha decided to step in. "We *want* your help. It will make everybody's lives easier and safer. But if you don't want in, that's up to you. We have other resources we can call on."

Jane nodded. "Do shifters have an honor code? Like if you are going to fight another shifter, is it expected you both take the same form?"

"Pretty much. Doesn't happen often and I can't guarantee it."

"And ..." Jane frowned, then looked embarrassed. "Look, I only came into this world a year ago. There's still a ton of stuff I don't know, and I just as much I *think* I know and have wrong. So I'll apologize now, and you guys don't take offense if I accidentally say something rude."

Jeff grimaced and shrugged, while Abbie sniffed and curled a lip.

"When your folk shift, apart from taking on your other form, does anything else change?"

"We are bigger than our true natural animal," said Jeff. "Twenty, maybe twenty-five percent. We are still who we were before, but your instincts change depending on what form you're in. I don't know where you're going with this."

"She wants to know if we can only be killed by silver bullets, and if we howl at the moon," mocked Abbie. "She wants us to do their dirty work for them, be their little doggy army."

Jane went red. Tasha wasn't sure if she didn't have a comeback, or if she was trying not to turn the bitch into a Pekingese.

"My partner is trying to assess the risk to you if we tell you where this other pack is, and you try to attack them. Just like you are attacking her now." Tasha kept her voice level, reasonable, but noticed Abbie wouldn't meet her eyes.

"We can look after ourselves," Abbie snapped.

"Really? A hyena queen masses forty or fifty pounds more than a grey wolf male. And they have firearms, very many and very modern. If we tell you where they are, they could cut you down in an ambush."

"So what are you suggesting."

"A distraction. We don't want things to descend into a general melee," Tasha explained. "We want a presence at the rear of the building while we make a quiet entrance elsewhere. Nobody gets hurt. The hyenas lose their ability to make their drug and move on."

"And if they don't?"

"Chances are one night a vampire SWAT team will block all the doors and set fire to the building," said Jane. "They've made some powerful enemies."

"*We're* powerful enemies" Abbie snarled. "We should be the ones to kill them."

"Enough," Jeff snapped, slapping his hand down on the table. "You're reckless, dangerous. You would risk all of us for your stupid pride and stand there while we fought for your damned honor. That's not the way. That is not *pack*."

"You're weak. The way doesn't run in your blood. You are a coward."

"I'm careful, and I protect my pack. That's what an alpha does."

"You're no alpha," Abbie all but spat on him. The contempt in her face was vicious.

"You've made no secret of wanting Karl, not me. You think you can manipulate him, wind him around your finger. We contested. I won. *I* am alpha."

"You played *pool*."

"His choice. We're friends. We're pack. Nobody needed to get hurt."

And Abbie spat at him, for real. She missed, but Jeff rose to his feet, fists clenched. "You're the coward. You know I can't fight back, not in this form. And you hide behind your gender."

"Then fight *them*." Abbie pointed at Jane. "Make them tell us where those hyenas are, then we make war.

"Me. Take on the woman who just threw you across the room like you were a puppy?" He laughed. "You *are* insane. Maybe too much. Maybe it's time we had a contest to see who is truly alpha bitch for this pack."

He turned back to Jane. "Do you have a plan?"

"Working on it." She told the lie with a perfectly straight face. Tasha knew they had a plan, but Jane wasn't telling him what they wanted him to do. Given his mate's hostility, probably the wisest thing to do. "Needed to know if you were on board first."

"I'm happy to provide a distraction. All out confrontation is too dangerous for my people."

Jane nodded, and Tasha agreed.

"Then wait for our call. It won't be long."

Alternative Plan

Tasha drove me home after we had finished with Jeff and his crazy bitch. I invited her in, expecting her to make another excuse, but she said yes. I hoped I didn't look surprised. As I walked up the path to the door, I looked up to Amanda's apartment and saw that damned curtain twitch again.

"Something bothering you?"

We were in the kitchen and I was fixing hot chocolate—small and intense, as we just had a huge coffee. I might have been banging things around a bit, annoyed by Amanda.

"My tenant seems to have a morbid fascination with what I'm doing."

Tasha looked at her watch. "This late?"

My eyes flicked over her head to check the clock on the wall. It was past one in the morning. "Crazy is as crazy does," I said.

"Do you think she's just curious, or is there something more sinister there?"

That hadn't occurred to me, and it should have. Maybe I still wasn't as good as I hoped I was getting.

Tasha stirred her chocolate and added some marshmallows. "You should invite her down for coffee and put some truth potion in it."

"There's no such …" My voice trailed off as I started to wonder.

Tasha wagged her spoon at me and chuckled. "But I'll bet you go down and check before you go to bed."

She got me. I probably would. Still, something to think about. Could someone be using Amanda to keep tabs on me?

"Can we trust them?"

For a moment I hadn't a clue what she was talking about, then I realized she had switched tracks.

"You mean the wolves?"

She nodded. "That woman is too unstable. He may be on the level, but can he control her?"

"Find another option," I said as I shook my head. "One that doesn't involve the Citadel taking over or turning the whole thing over to the cops."

And that got me a reaction I hadn't expected.

"I'm not convinced Narcotics isn't already involved," Tasha growled. "And not on our side. They busted us when we were staking out the dealing house. Roughed us up and threatened us, particularly Eddie."

"Surprised you let them get away with that."

"There were too many witnesses. And they were good at what they were doing. I didn't think they were going to do us any actual harm." Tasha looked thoughtful. "But if they catch us meddling in their affairs again, I'm not sure it will end so well."

"Speaking of witnesses and reliable." I realized I was drawing little circles with my finger on the top of the counter and put my hand flat. I had to as an awkward question, but a necessary one. "How far can we trust Eddie Weston? He seems uncomfortable with some of the truths. Can we trust he's not going to turn everything over to his captain?"

Tasha shook her head. "Eddie's on a crusade. He used to do this in the old days, get caught up in some sob story only to find someone had fed him a line. The girl he was trying to help has already moved on and doesn't want anything else to do with him, or her dead ex, but he's committed. Eddie will see it through. Not saying he won't involve the department, but he won't until we finish our business."

She finished the chocolate, put the mug on the drainer, then kissed me on the cheek. "This was nice, but you need to sleep."

She was going too soon. I opened my mouth to protest, but it turned into a huge yawn right on cue. I gave her a sheepish grin. "Let's get everybody together again tomorrow, at the office."

She was already at the door, letting herself out. "Leave it with me."

I finished my chocolate, put the cups into the dishwasher, then locked the front door. I thought about checking out truth potions in the workshop, but my eyes were gritty. I headed for a bed I don't even remember lying down on.

"We need to get into the building, preserve the scene, and secure everybody inside. That has to be the priority." Eddie was getting loud. "If we don't, then the DA will throw the whole thing out and they'll be back on the street in hours."

"And what is to stop them killing the captives as soon as they see your assault force, or burning the place to the ground?" I didn't like the look in Millers eyes.

"You don't even know if they have any captives."

"And we never would, with your plan."

"Gentlemen," snapped Tasha. Her lips were set in a thin line and her eyes were narrow. "Enough. The plan is to cause a distraction on one side of the building while we make an entry somewhere else and evaluate what we find inside."

"And we can't even decide if the distraction is at the front or the back," snapped Eddie. "If they realize it's a distraction, they could just fade away into the night, and we lose everything."

"We're supposed to be working together on this." I thought I should throw my hat into the ring, but Eddie shot it as soon as it landed. Figuratively. I mean, he didn't pull his sidearm or anything.

"That's what I thought, but all I hear is doing what *he* wants, and nothing about catching these guys."

"We are talking about rescuing hostages," snapped Miller. "As a police officer I would have assumed that would be your priority, not making yourself look good with an impressive bust."

"What hostages? Even if they are there, they ain't even human."

Oops. Strike three.

The room fell so silent you could have heard a staple drop, let alone a pin. Miller sat back in his chair, arms crossed as if he had just proven a point about Weston being an ass, and Tasha—well I couldn't tell if she looked more hurt or mad. Either way I was glad it wasn't me who made her look like that.

Geez, the guy was an asshole. I had hoped I was wrong, but it looked like my first opinion of him was the right one after all. I clapped my hands to break everybody's concentration.

"And that concludes today's meeting, people. We'll think

about restarting tomorrow, but for the present, everybody out. Now." I knew it would cost us a day, but if things kept going this way, it would cost us everything and people would go off and do their own thing. And that would be a disaster.

"I thought we all knew this was important," grumbled Eddie as he took his jacket from the back of his chair.

"It is, and it's even more important we get it right. Which means nobody does anything stupid tonight? And I'll have everybody's word on that right now." I know I sounded like a scolding schoolteacher, but they were acting like kids. I decided the men might need things made a little clearer.

"Eddie, you do anything that gets those vamps hurt, the Citadel will strike back. I know you don't want to believe in all this, but just imagine, for a second, if it's all true, and how many people they could hurt. Miller, same for you. You get those vamps out but let the drug runners get away, Police will be all over the vampire population of the city."

"Unlikely."

"They will because I'll damn well make sure they are." I got in his face as I snapped, and he took a half step back. "We can do all of this, and do it right, if we leave our damned egos at the door when we come back. Now get out, and think of something new to bring back with you tomorrow."

I marched over to the meeting room door and held it open for them. The men filed out; Eddie looked sheepish, but Miller looked thoughtful and that worried me more than if he had looked mad.

Tasha was trying not to laugh, which almost set me off.

"You can't mean me too."

I kept a straight face and held the door open. She gave me arched eyebrows and a 'come try it' look, and I cracked up. For

231

a minute. Then we both stopped laughing and gave each other serious looks.

"Leave him to me," said Tasha, and I knew I had to do the same with Miller.

But it was Miller who reached out to me. Tasha had gone off in search of some information she thought would help, though she wouldn't say what, and I was still in the office, tidying up. My phone rang.

"Are you busy?"

"Not particularly. Cleaning up."

"Can I pick you up in the car? I need to show you something."

"Anything good?"

"Not over an open line."

Well that tickled my curiosity. "Sure. When?"

"I'm parked outside."

I shook my head even though he wasn't there to see it. The man was incorrigible. Maybe that was why I liked him so much. "Ten minutes."

It was more like fifteen, but I doubted he minded. I left my helmet and leather jacket in the office, and found the limo outside, not the BMW. His driver already had the door open for me, so I slid in.

"What's up?

Miller made to hand me some papers. I turned to look.

And something sharp stabbed me in the neck right before my head exploded in crackling agony and everything went white.

XX

I couldn't move. I could feel the rest of my body, I just couldn't communicate with it. Which at least got rid of the specter that someone had snapped my neck. Next problem was when I tried to ask what the hell was going on, I couldn't speak. Enough was enough, I'd just fire up some magic and ...

Except I couldn't. Just like the rest of my body, I couldn't talk to whatever it was that made me able to do magic. I was screwed, and given the fact I was still in Miller's limo, I had a good idea who had screwed me. Bastard. Tasha had been right all along, and I felt like a child; I'd been stupid, naive, and willful. If Tasha ever wanted this guy, I'd hold him while she hit him, or *vice versa*. Hell, we could take turns.

"I conveyed the proposals from our meeting to the Citadel. They told me they considered them inappropriate, and I should devise an alternative plan."

And that was all he said. His voice was no different to any other time he had spoken to me, and with twenty words he betrayed me. To whom and for what I would have to wait and see.

It didn't take long. I recognized the route the driver was taking, which reminded me I needed to get even with him too.

It was only a few minutes until we pulled up in the back-yard of 2806 Mulberry Drive. I hoped it wasn't coming to this, that the bastard had more respect for me than that, but I was wrong again. And now I was getting scared.

From the corner of my eye, I got a glimpse of two thickset men with stubby assault rifles walking toward us. The car turned a little, pointing towards an exit before it stopped. The driver did something on the dash and passed a microphone, like a cop radio, back to Miller.

"That's close enough." His voice reverberated outside the car. "This vehicle is armored, and I will leave if you come any closer. But before I do, tell somebody with authority that I have a donor for them. One they will not be able to resist. I will wait five minutes."

What could I do? I was scared enough to pee myself, and would have taken some pleasure in ruining his upholstery if I could have, but he denied me even that small satisfaction.

The outside mic worked both ways. I heard the squawk of a radio and a voice I couldn't quite make out, then the longest three or four minutes of my life, listening to Miller breathing. Eventually, footsteps crunched over gravel, tinny through the external pickup.

"You got some balls, man."

"Let's pass over the pleasantries and trash talk. You have something I want. I have something to trade in return."

"Such as?"

"You give me the vampires, alive, and I'll give you a bona fide Combat Mage to tap."

"Bull. Shit."

"I assume you can test her blood?"

"Why don't you come inside, and we can talk about it?"

234

I fervently hoped Miller wasn't that stupid.

"Don't be absurd. There is a disused truck stop on the edge of town, along the Middleton road. Be there in two hours. If I see more than one vehicle, I leave. Bring what vampires you have kidnapped. One of you can approach to test the mage. Assuming everything is satisfactory, we exchange."

"And what stops her from turning us all into cockroaches?"

"There is an inhibitor around her neck. She can neither move, nor perform magic, until someone is foolish enough to remove it."

"Never heard of one of those."

"I'm leaving now."

The mic flew forward onto the front passenger seat as the car eased out of the back lot and drove off down the street.

If I thought four or five minutes were an eternity, two hours was an introduction to hell. We drove to somewhere I didn't know. The driver got out and Miller took his place before driving us further out along the Middleton Road. *That* road I knew. I used it to get my bike out into the country, where we could have some fun, and I remembered the broken-down shell of a truck stop about fifteen miles out of town.

And that was where Miller took us. He left the engine running, presumably for the air con, but turned the mirror down so I couldn't glare at him. He never met my eyes during the drive, either. Coward.

Unless he had backup, there were holes all over Miller's plan. I couldn't believe he didn't see them, and he had left me in no position to warn him. But he should have seen things were going to hell when they turned up in a Hummer. Three gunmen got out with those nasty snub assault rifles, and it surprised me there weren't more.

Once they had fanned out, another guy left the Hummer and dragged an emaciated, hooded body out with him, pulling it quickly over to the shelter that used to cover the fuel pumps when the place had been working. Another, perhaps female, followed, and both hid in the deepest shade.

Miller took a Glock, rather than his usual Browning, out of a shoulder holster, popped the mag, and tossed it onto the passenger seat. From the glove compartment he took out a magazine that must have held thirty or more rounds. I heard it slip into the Glock, and Miller snapped the slide. He opened his door and got out.

"Send your tester," he shouted. "*One* person."

The last door on the Hummer opened and a girl stepped out onto the gravel, about my age and maybe a little shorter. She started to walk between the two cars, carrying an expanding box. Someone shouted at her, harsh words that made her pick up the pace like someone whipped her. Miller opened the door next to me and I heard a soft crunch as she set the box down.

"She can hear you, but she cannot answer or move. She will still feel pain if you are careless."

"Hi, my name's Tracy." Her voice was sing song, like a child's. I don't know if it was natural or if she put it on to make people feel at ease. It didn't work.

"I'm going to take three vials from your arm. You'll feel a pin prick."

A strap tightened around my bicep and I felt her tapping around the crook of my elbow for a vein. She was good, and I felt nothing as the needle slid in. She counted the vials as she drew them, then taped something into my elbow.

"I'm just going to test these. It will take five or ten minutes."

She could have been talking to me or Miller, but I heard him grunt. There were small sounds beside me as the girl worked her own kind of magic, then the tackle box rattled closed and I sensed her stand up.

"Is he on the level?" said a faint voice from a distance.

"Yes."

Well how the heck could she tell that?

"Damn. Da bitch is a witch?"

"Yes."

"We exchange. Now." But what Miller got back was laughter. It was blowing up in his face and he hadn't realized. Or had he. Someone squealed, like he had grabbed Tracy.

"You want to exchange? Sure thing." The one doing all the talking grabbed the guy he had been holding, tore the hood off his head, and pushed him out into the sunlight. But it wasn't Hawke, and from the way he looked up at the sun, he wasn't even a vampire.

What a surprise. Miller had been double crossed.

They caught the fool with his pants down, with no backup and on the wrong side of the car.

"Nobody move or I shoot her."

"I got a dozen more where she came from. Besides, you got to keep what you catch."

The air fizzed with magic and Miller let lose an uncharacteristic "Shit," just as something snarled near my ear. In front of me, two others were blurring, becoming indistinct, only to reform as hyenas. Dear lord, they looked big. Miller's Glock barked and there was a howl of pain, then I saw Tracy, or what she had become, entered my narrow line of sight, scuttling back towards her own people. She was running away. Miller wouldn't shoot her.

But he did open up on everybody else. Or he tried to. The obvious threats were the approaching hyenas, and they seemed able to dodge everything he fired at them. Meanwhile, another guy still held his assault rifle and was taking the occasional pop to keep Miller pinned down where he was.

"I want them alive. Both of them." Somebody thought they were in charge and screamed at everybody. Comforting. Sort of. Except the hyenas were drifting out of my sight-line, so Miller was letting them flank him. And once they did that ...

"Now!"

Now what? It wasn't Miller, and nobody else moved. From behind us came a soft pop, like a suppressor. Miller cursed again and fell against the car. Damn. He was hit and I was in huge trouble. The car rocked again, and he fell through the open door and across my lap.

A dart stuck out of his neck.

Commodity

T he shame almost killed me. That, or the anger overload. Miller had collapsed into the car with his face in my crotch. The bastards took time out so just about every one of them could take a picture of it on their phone, though I had no idea where they were going to post it. Until the idea of a dark-net Facebook popped into my head.

They hauled him off me. I heard the trunk click open, and assumed they threw him in there. Good. Served the treacherous bastard right.

The one doing all the talking got in back with me, but I couldn't see much of what he looked like. Not easy when you can't turn your head. Another got in to drive, and we pulled away while everybody else was still tidying up. Nobody spoke, except for one call on a cell phone.

"It's me. Yeah, everything went like you said it would. Bringing them in with their own wheels. A freakin' limo, heh heh. Worth a hundred K to the right shipper, maybe two. Right. Get someone to clear the back yard, would ya? Thanks, boss."

So he was making all the noise, but he wasn't in charge. Interesting.

When we got back to Mulberry Drive, the back yard was deserted and so was the road leading up to it. From the corners of my eyes I caught glimpses of men standing at strategic places with their assault rifles right out in the open. I guessed they were there to keep people away, but they were taking a terrible risk. One call to 911 would have the place crawling with cops.

Or would it. Something Tasha said came back to me, about Palmer and the Narco squad. Maybe these hyenas had a reason to act like they were untouchable.

We pulled into the yard and there were people at my door while the car was still rocking on its springs.

"Careful," snapped the one who had led the operation. "You knock that thing off her neck and she'll let lose a shit storm that will burn you up."

He wasn't wrong.

They hauled me onto a gurney then trundled me up the loading ramp and in through a small door. The loading bay was like the donating room at a blood bank, complete with four chairs with high backs and padded arms. They may have looked sharp and clinical once, but now they had duct tape patches and looked like a good fire was the only thing that would make them sterile again. Two tall cabinets looked like refrigerators, and a couple of racks were half full of boxes with crosses on them, probably medical supplies. That was when I realized I wasn't sure whether Ruby was their major market, or if it was selling the blood to the vamps.

They wheeled me past all this and through a door in the back wall of the warehouse. Things started to look a little cleaner, but the smell was intense, like when a dog owner has gone nose-blind. It got better when we took an elevator up a floor.

I got rolled into another donating room. This one looked clean and safe, and smelt of plug-in scent diffusers. Lots of them. So they had different facilities for different donors. Made sense. Who would want a stream of raggedy, stinking junkies fouling up a room like this?

Two guys lifted me out of the gurney and set me down on a cross between a sun lounger and a therapist's couch. Well, if I was going to die, at least I'd be comfortable. Still, it felt very spooky when everybody left the room. I tried to keep myself calm but being alone ramped my anxiety level up by the minute until my heart was doing about 140 and my lungs were trying to hyperventilate.

My lounger was on one side of the room, facing inward. On the other side of the room was a conventional couch and a matching chair, for people to wait their turn or wait for those they were with to finish. I could still see the door from the corner of my eye. When it slammed open, my brain tried to leap off the couch but my body, even though it flooded with biochemical fear, didn't even twitch. It felt horrible.

Then the room was full again, like it was somehow trying to make up for the earlier emptiness. First through the door was a wheelchair. Someone had used half a roll of duct tape to strap Miller to it, and used the other half roll to cover his mouth and eyes. I would have smirked if I could. The tape over his eyes was going to rip his eyebrows off when they pulled it. First, I wanted to hear him scream. Second, I wanted the satisfaction of laughing at how he looked with no eyebrows, even if I couldn't do it out loud.

Next came the medic-girl from the double cross, Tracy. She was wearing scrubs now, and wheeled in a surgical trolley full of bags and needles. She turned to the side and stood somewhere behind me, waiting.

The last to enter was a woman. Late thirties or early forties, stocky but fit. Not attractive, but the hard-hitting power outfit she wore suited her well. Everything about her said business came first, no matter what it was.

She was the boss.

She walked across the room to the couch, sat, and placed her cellphone on the table next to it.

"So this is a Combat Mage?" She sniffed. "Doesn't look like anything special to me."

Take this damned collar off me and see what happens, I thought. I have no time for people who talk big when they know they're safe, and when I found a way out of this, I was going to make sure she understood that.

"Hook her up. I want three bags."

"Three?" Tracy squeaked. "That could kill her."

"Then make sure it doesn't."

"Yes, Gina."

Tracy set to work, but being in front of her boss must have made her nervous because the second cannula hurt like hell as she put it in. An enormous bag of saline passed in front of me, then I felt cold creep up the inside of my left arm and into my chest. It was horrible. Tracy stood up and walked towards the door.

"Where are you going?" Gina snapped. "He'll be here in a few minutes."

"I have to get her a blanket. She's getting cold saline and we're taking too much blood. She could go into hypothermia."

So that was two ways they were going to kill me. Nice.

"Hurry. And make sure we have a glass. One of the crystal ones."

"Yes, Gina."

She stared at me across the room like she was weighing me,

judging me. I glared back, but wasn't sure how threatening I looked blinking angrily at her. A few minutes later, Tracy rushed back into the room.

"He's here, Gina."

Tracy set an elegant crystal wine glass on the surgical trolley, then draped a blanket over me. She had warmed it through, and I hadn't realized how cold I had got. If they were taking three bags of blood from me, I was going to get a lot colder.

A man walked into the room. Tall, lean, expensive suit, pale skin. Gina rose to her feet, so he was important.

"Welcome—"

Was as far as she got. The guy had been looking around, but it wasn't me he had seen. It was Miller. He moved crazy fast, like between two blinks: one second standing in the middle of the room, the next behind Gina with his hand over her mouth. Two goons appeared at the door, weapons ready, but Gina raised a hand and they stopped.

The tall guy, obviously a vampire, released Gina then pointed to Miller, and the door.

"Take him out," she said, her voice a little shaken. "Put him somewhere and watch him."

While they wheeled Miller out, the vampire tugged at his shirt cuffs and brushed imaginary human dirt from his suit. Only once they shut door did he speak.

"My profound apologies, madam, but you have unwittingly seized a tiger by the tail. Were you to mention my name, or had I spoken, an opportunity might have been missed."

"How?"

"Are you aware who you have captured?"

"Seems not."

"His name is Miller. He is Emissary for the Court of the

Citadel." The vamp waited for a reaction and got none. A hint of exasperation crept into his voice. "He is the right-hand man of Duke Ladislav and manages all of his affairs in the mundane world. He is highly thought of and beloved."

"So a ransom opportunity?"

"Perhaps. Mishandled, it will result in a vampire army overwhelming you and feeding on you for the rest of your life."

Cry For Help?

ina's eyes went wide, and she blinked until the bravado came back. "They can try."

The vamp laughed. "Such misplaced confidence. So endearing. Now, where is this rare delight you have promised me?" He pointed towards me, eyebrows raised.

"That's her," Gina looked like she was sucking a lemon. I don't think she liked me or being laughed at. "Word is she's a witch."

"Witch? The message I received was that she was a full Combat Mage."

Gina shrugged as if the terms had no difference for her. I itched to demonstrate. He walked closer then, scary as hell, *behind* me. I could smell him, expensive perfume masking a subtle stink of mummified flesh. It got stronger, and I could hear his breath in my ear. Damnit, he was *sniffing* me.

"Ah, if only I could take a sample from the source." Regret, with the hint of a request.

"You know the rules."

"Not from the neck. From the wrist, perhaps?"

"You're the one that told me vampires release something into the blood that taints it."

He sighed cool, fetid air into my ear and walked back to the other side of the room. "Sadly true, and we must protect our investment."

Gina snapped her fingers and Tracy appeared beside me. She took the glass from the trolley then did something to the cannula in my left arm. After a few seconds she put the glass back, only now it was half full of my blood. The trembling medic picked it up and carried it to Gina, then scuttled out of the way while Gina presented the glass to the vampire.

He raised it to his nose, the locked his eyes on mine. "This is a rare treat. One so rarely gets to see the expression on food's face when one savors its produce."

He swirled the glass, leaving a red sheen up the sides, and raised it to his nose to savor the bouquet. I tried to look away, but I couldn't even blink.

"Authoritative on the nose. A-negative, I believe, which is deliciously rare in itself." He took a sip, and what blood I had left in my body ran cold. His eyes rolled up in his head and he shuddered, then sipped again. "The magic sparkles on the tongue like champagne, and the sharp edge of fear and impotent anger only adds to the experience. Priceless." He took another sip and put the half-empty glass on a table. "Now, what to do with her?"

"We keep her locked up here and milk her." Gina looked a little green, but greed apparently made it easier for her to push through her mild distaste.

The vampire waved his hand in a camp gesture that could have been indecision or dismissal.

"You, servant."

"Me?" Tracy squeaked.

"Remind me, how long does your kind need to replenish blood?"

"About two weeks for every bag, sir."

His face collapsed into a moue of discontent. "Oh, that won't do at all."

"She can make it faster," snapped Gina, glowering at Tracy.

"A little, but it doesn't always work, and only speeds things up by twenty-five percent, sometimes less."

The vampire raised a finger. "We have two options. We make a limited but regular supply, for which we charge a significant premium, but the demand will fall off over time as the quality of the product deteriorates." He tapped his lips with his finger.

"Or?" Gina prompted, after the pause for dramatic effect had gone on too long.

"Or we make it a one-off vintage. Drain her dry. Eight bags only, perhaps ten, one each to the highest bidders. And mark the bag on which she actually dies. It should go for twice the price of the others." A sly grin crept over his face. "Or keep it a secret. Market it as one of the ten secretly contains her death blood. The drama would be exquisite."

He got to his feet, almost in a rush. "I must return to the Citadel and assess the market. I shall be in touch before the morning, regards her and Miller. Draw a quarter bag for me now. I can use it for samples before the auction. And take that bag of water out of her arm. No point diluting the product if we are going to drain her."

Well, that sucked.

Gina snapped her fingers and pointed somewhere behind me. A pink-cheeked Tracy hurried over to me. Something tugged on my left arm, then I saw the saline bag as she put it on the table. It looked about half empty to my uneducated eye. Hopefully I'd had enough to stop me going into shock. As the girl went around my other side to change the blood bag, one

247

of the goons stuck his head through the doorway.

"Priority donor just came in, boss."

"Do they have an appointment?"

"Says they do."

Gina scowled then rose from the couch. "Well, she can't say anything, so I suppose it's safe enough. Bring them in. Who is it?"

"Morello, and the Winger girl."

Gina's expression softened. "At least they're not wasting my time. Let them in."

She crossed the room to me, took my jaw in her hand and turned my head from side to side. "Nothing special."

In my mind I bit off her thumb.

"Tap the Winger girl for two bags. Play the sob story and ask nicely. Do not let that creep Morello interfere with the witch. Scream and security will shoot him."

"Yes, Miss Gina."

She swept out of the room. I heard a brief mutter outside the door, then the *tap tap* of her heels receding along the hall. A moment later a couple walked in. He was a stereotype; a nobody who thought he was a somebody. His suit was expensive but looked shitty, like something out of the 70s. His hair was cut long on the top with a skin fade on either side, and a kilo of tacky jewelry cluttered his hands and neck. I saw a shoulder holster, but it was empty.

The girl looked like a shell. She was tall, slim but big boobs. Blonde, perhaps even for real, and pretty—apart from the dark smudges under her eyes and the overly pale skin. She was eye candy, but maybe not for much longer.

He went over, dropped on the couch with an arrogant bounce, and sat with his legs spread like his balls were too big for his sack. I hate manspreaders. She waited passively until Tracy asked her to sit on the couch next to me. She said "Hi," as she passed and looked hurt when I didn't answer.

"Don't mind her," said Tracy, voice bright and breezy. "Poor thing has ALS, she can't move."

"At all?"

"Not a bit."

And suddenly I was an object in the room, not a person. Another log on the bonfire of emotions crackling in my head.

"I have a big ask of you today, Miss Winger."

"Oh?"

"Can we take two?"

"Must you? Two makes me so tired for days." The girl sounded close to tears.

"I understand, but the facility in Germany desperately need a unit too. We don't want to say no to one of them, do we?"

"Think about the poor kids, babe. They gonna die if you don't." The guy—I had already forgotten what Gina had called him—used a whining, wheedling voice that would have driven me out the door. But it did tell me the cheesy little gangster was the one getting paid, and I would bet the girl didn't know that. More fuel for the anger fire when the girl, voice full of fatigue and resignation, agreed.

What the hell was I going to do? I couldn't move, I couldn't act, but I couldn't just lie there while some bastard vampire decided if I was going to die today, tomorrow, or while they milked me like a cow for some indefinite nightmare. I was missing something, but even if I figured it out, what the hell could I do about it?

A memory belched up from my deep past, so strong it almost felt real. A book smacking me around the back of my head while I sat, cross-legged, in the middle of a silver circle. The voice I most hated in the universe barked at me from a forgotten corner of my brain.

"How do you expect to achieve if you cannot quiet your mind? Still your thoughts. Focus."

It came back so loud and so real that my heart stuttered—but it was just a memory. I had killed the bastard a year ago, incinerating him in a rage of Bloodfire.

Corvax was the foulest creature in the universe, but he had taught me to focus. He had forced me to learn how to still my thoughts and fall to the deep, quiet center of my mind, no matter how much I was distracted or distressed. Mainly because if I didn't, I wouldn't eat that night. That recollection, and the ability, were stolen when he blocked my memory. Since I killed him, the barrier holding the memories back was weakened, and occasionally something would break through when I really needed it. Seemed this was one of those occasions.

The damn thing around my neck wouldn't let me pace my breathing, which made things more difficult, but I remembered the mandala I used as a focus and made it sharp in my mind. I couldn't make the fear go away, or the anger. They were still there, on the surface of my mind, but I was sinking beneath them and their voices were fading.

Problem was, I couldn't think of the trouble I was in or about any way to get out of it. As soon as I did, I rose back to the chaos of my thoughts and had to start over. Eventually I decided to sink to the bottom and see what happened when I got there.

It was quiet and dark. Not the dark of a basement, or a sealed box. This was the dark of a forest at night or looking up at the moon from the bottom of a lake. Peaceful. And crazy easy to get down here. I had struggled for hours to do this as a kid and getting this deep was a rare treat. It was nice here. I could stay down here forever, and a part of me wondered if I should. If I could find a way to disconnect from my body, to ignore it no matter what, it could be a better solution to my problem.

But something was different. Something was here that hadn't been before. It was like a connection between this place and another place. I certainly didn't remember it, but that didn't mean much since Corvax salad-tossed my memories.

The calm slipped and I threw my anger away from me before it could pull me back to my body. As soon as I settled, I went back to contemplating the whatever it was that disappeared into the distance like an infinitely thin guitar string, glinting into the darkness.

"... you might find some interesting and unexpected benefits ..."

A different voice echoed through the vaults of my memories, newer this time and it took me a moment to place it. Grant Peterson, my Grumpy Old Man, had said the words when he found out that Tasha had saved my life by feeding me her blood. Was this one of the unexpected benefits? Vampires knew when those they had turned died. Might this work the same way?

I reached for the thread but passed through it with only the barest resistance. It was nothing I could get hold of, nothing I could send a message along. When I tried to focus on anything as organized as a message, my fear would bubble up again, and my focus would slip away.

But the guitar image came back to me. Yes, the resistance was slight, but it was there. And if it was all I could do, then do it I must. I settled down and began to pluck the string that I hoped connected to Tasha.

Moody Blues

S omeone thumped on the apartment door. She opened it and glared through. "Where have you been? And what do you want?"

Eddie held up a sports bag. "Peace offering."

"What is it."

He hauled the bag into her apartment, dropping it heavily to the floor and stretching his back before turning to her. He scowled at the glass in her hand. "Jack? At ten in the morning."

"Morning for you. I haven't slept yet." Tasha took a sip from the glass, then turned away and sat on the couch, one leg folded beneath her.

"Still nothing?"

"Both phones are off." Tasha frowned. "I can track hers, but she switched it off yesterday, right outside the office. His I can't track. I can't find any record of him pinging off any cell mast within fifty miles in the last seven days." She took a swig from the glass and screwed up her face, not sure if it was helping, but unwilling to put it down. "What's in there?"

"In a minute. I want to show you this first." Eddie opened a side pocket in the bag and took out a squashed roll of paper. He took it over to her dining table and started to unroll it, using mugs Tasha hadn't cleared away the day before to hold down the edges.

Tasha ambled over, standing near him but not too close. "I'm getting tired of asking what things are, Eddie."

"This," he said with some pride, "is the floor plan of 2806 Mulberry."

Suddenly more interested, Tasha put her glass down on a still unruly corner and peered closer. "Useful. Look, here is the main utilities access."

"Yeah, outside and down the least exposed side of the building."

"Any way in other than the loading dock or the front door?"

"I checked. No way up to the roof, and the only outside access we didn't already know about is the fire escape from the second floor."

Tasha didn't bother to point out she could probably jump high enough from the fire escape to get onto the roof. She saw no point triggering his prejudices so soon.

"It helps, but we have no idea what they're doing in each room." She pointed at the upper floor. "These designations won't mean anything now."

She glanced at Eddie. He looked hurt, just for a second, like a dog that had brought in a marvelous stick and was being scolded. She could be a bitch sometimes. "On the upside, we have the utilities access, and precise layout. That's worth a lot. We'll still need that diversion, though, and I don't want this to degenerate into a free for all."

Eddie nodded. "They'd be ground into dog meat."

Tasha froze for a moment, then scowled at him. The grin Eddie had been trying to hide faded.

"Aw, come on. That was funny."

"It was inappropriate."

Eddie shook his head. "Tough crowd."

Tasha ignored him but admitted to herself she was being hard on him this morning. She was going to be even harder on Jane for switching her phone off when she saw her. She had some nerve, warning everybody not to do anything stupid, then switching off her phone to do something she knew Tasha wouldn't approve of.

"So what else do we have?"

"You said you didn't like the idea of your SWAT team going in unarmed? How about this?" He reached into his bag again.

"Eddie, what the hell are you thinking? That's an AK47. And where's the stock?"

"Close. It's a movie prop. Here." He tossed it to her.

"This movie prop could land you in jail, Eddie. I can't tell it from the real thing."

"Fires blank rounds. Looks right, sounds right."

"How many of these do you have?"

"Two that go bang. The rest are just mock-ups that wouldn't fool anybody from ten feet."

"And if you get stopped with your trunk full of this?"

Eddie shrugged and Tasha raised a hand. "Sorry. It's a good idea. We want the hyenas to stop and think, and this might be enough to keep them from jumping straight into a firefight. We still need to get their attention." She handed the fake Kalashnikov back to him.

Eddie put the rifle back into the bag then rummaged inside again. He drew out a grey tube, about five inches long and two across. Tasha caught a flash of blue around the middle.

"A *stun* grenade. Where did you steal a—" She raised her hands. "Never mind, I don't want to know. Isn't that a little extreme?"

"You said you wanted their attention. This going off in the loading bay will certainly do that. And it's not real, it's a special effects pyro. Makes a bright flash and a big bang, but there's almost no shockwave."

"Which will bring in cops from all over the area?"

"Not if I call it in."

"Eddie. You promised."

"Nat, we can't let them get away with it."

"Eddie Weston, for the very last time there may be innocent victims in that building. I get this is a personal crusade for you, but dot you *dare* pull that greater good bullshit on me. Trading in an innocent to catch the bad guys never was and never will be an option. I need your word on that. Right now."

Tasha's phone rang. She came within a hair of tapping ignore, but half-recognized the number. One hand took the call on speaker, while the other raised to silence Eddie.

"Hello?"

"Hi. My name is Marcie Winger."

"Yes, Miss Winger. Of course I remember you. How are you today?"

"I'm tired. I gave lots of blood yesterday. That's why I'm calling you."

Tasha realized Winger was almost whispering. "Are you safe, Miss Winger. Please, do not take any risks on our account."

"You said to call if ... There was this girl yesterday, where they take my blood. They said she couldn't move because she was sick, but that didn't look right. She didn't have thin arms, or hollow cheeks or anything. She just looked angry. Real angry. And they seemed to take so much from her. I think it was more than two bags. I thought you should know."

"Thank you, Miss Winger." Her thumb hovered over the disconnect button, but Eddie was drawing his finger around his face in a circular motion. "Can you tell me what she looked like?"

"Not really. She was wrapped up on the couch. She was like me, but not so tall. Oh, and she had these tight braids around her head with things woven ..."

Eddie picked the phone up off the floor, tapped the button to end the call, then took Tasha's trembling hand in his own.

"I think it's time we kicked somebody's ass."

He held her hand a moment longer, then went to the dining table and brought her the glass that still held a finger of Jack. She downed it in a single swallow, then held out her other hand. "Give me the damned phone."

She made a call, arranged a time and place, then turned to Eddie.

"One more loose end. Go down to the garage. Wait for me there."

Eddie gave her a long look, his face a study in neutrality, then nodded and left her apartment. Tasha changed into black yoga pants and a tight black top. She opened the bottom drawer of her nightstand and took out four spare mags for her Glock. Last, from the same drawer, she lifted out a thin black ski mask. A pale face did not go well with covert night ops.

Her jacket more or less covered the Glock in its shoulder holster, and she stuffed the mask into a pocket already over-flowing with ammunition. Grabbing her keys, she went out the front.

On the other side of the street was the ever-present black SUV, with its bored Narco cop on intimidation watch. It wasn't that they were going to follow her. They might try, but she always lost them. This was all about letting her know they were watching her. And right now that pissed her off.

It had fallen into a routine. Every day or so, she would walk out the front, sometimes with a coffee, and taunt the driver. Some took the coffee, some didn't. One or two actually drank the coffee, which had shocked her to the core the first time it happened. So the window was already sliding down ready for a lazy exchange of insults before she crossed the dividing line.

She sauntered up to the car as normal, put out her hand to lean on the roof. While the bored cop was still turning his head to look at her, she reached snake-fast in through the opening window and seized the cop by the throat.

It was nothing subtle, nothing controlled. She devoured him, drinking the insecurities that made him hurt people, the lost loves, the regrets and the fear of dark secrets as yet undiscovered. Tasha consumed it whole, without filter or reservation.

The rush was intense, brighter, stronger than ever before. With wild abandon, she drew harder and harder, until she could feel his heartbeat stumble and his soul fluttering under her hand.

In the back of her mind a voice screamed louder and louder for her to stop, but this was too good, too rich. Why should she? What did anything matter if she could feel this good whenever she wanted?

Hands clamped on her shoulders and pulled her away. She screamed as she spun around, lashing out at the enemy who dared interrupt her while she fed. Eddie flew twenty feet through the air and bounced of a hedge before falling to his hands and knees on the sidewalk.

"What the hell are you doing," Eddie gasped, winded. "Are you killing that guy?"

The fever swept out of her mind like fog before a breeze. "No. Just making sure he can't report on us for six or eight hours."

Eddie had made it back to his feet and pushed past her. His hand reached out to the cop's neck, feeling for a pulse. "Fast and thin. What the hell did you do to him?"

"What I had to," Tasha snapped, elbowing him aside so she could open the door and close the window. She slammed the door and walked away. "Let's go. We have things to do."

Argues with Wolves

"You drive like an old woman," Tasha snapped.

"Feel free to get out and walk. I drive like a man with a trunk load of contraband munitions that does not want one of his fellow officers to pull him over and ask a bunch of career-ending questions."

Tasha tsk'd and stared out the window. She needed to do something. Energy buzzed through her, and the urge to put it to use was overwhelming. A smile twisted her lips. Why not? Wasn't this what she should be? Was this not how fate meant her to live her life, above the mediocre and mundane?

Settling back in the seat, she mused over what she was going to do to Miller once she got her hands on him. Jane was blind, naive. She was soft, and it was time she was shown what to do to vampires, or their toadies, when they dared approach her. Tasha knew him for what he was, and she'd take enormous, prolonged pleasure in extracting who gave him that lie for her. And then, she would find that individual, and take her time with them, too.

Eddie pulled into an empty lot a couple of blocks away from their target. A dozen cars and pickups had pulled up in a rough semi-circle, and Eddie stopped facing them. Perfect. The center of attention, where she needed to be and should be.

Everybody got out. There were greetings, but they were few and half-hearted.

"Where's Jane?" asked Jeff, looking past them to peer into Eddie's car, as if he hoped she was hiding on the back seat.

"They have her," said Tasha. "The man she was working with double crossed her, and us."

The pack muttered. The alpha bitch stood straight and took a step forward. "The deal was with her. She ain't here, we don't go in."

"That's my decision," Jeff snapped. "And they have the location of the other pack. We don't get that we're back to square one."

"We're close. Why else would they pick this dump to meet? We can figure it out from here."

"Or it could be across town," said Eddie. "Everybody has vehicles."

"Enough." Tasha snapped, then turned to Jeff. "In or out? We have work to do and no time to waste on this."

"I need to know the plan first."

"You make a distraction out back," Tasha said slowly and carefully, patience stretched she had to explain something so simple to this child. "Something that stops them letting loose with their hardware. I go in through the roof and release the hostages. With Jane in play, we attack from the rear and neutralize them."

"You say distraction like it's a straightforward thing. They got guns. We haven't."

"We bought replica guns," said Eddie.

"*Toys*," Abbie scoffed, and the pack stirred.

"Ever seen one?" Eddie sounded like he had taken enough being sneered at for the day. "The point is to make them think twice, and you ain't thought at all if you even considered we might give you the real thing." He took a moment and made a visible effort to calm down.

"We have a flash-bang to set off outside, to get their attention. I'll call it in that I'm investigating the noise to keep the rest of the cops off our backs. We also know where the power enters the building, and we can cut it there. They come out and find you already waiting for them. It'll be a standoff, but enough of them will go out back that Tasha can sneak in from the roof."

"Meanwhile they open up with their hardware as soon as they see us and rip us apart." Abbie sneered at Eddie, then at Tasha, before turning to face the pack. "They want to use you as cannon fodder. They want to line you up so these hyenas can use you for target practice while they sneak in the other side, snatch what they really want, and run away. We get left to take the pain, take the battering, and pay the blood"

"That's not the—" Eddie started.

"Shut up." Abbie whirled to face him and snarled. "This is pack business, cop. You don't have a say here." She turned away. "Replicas? Movie props? Who are they kidding, and what do they know? This should be done the old way, the pack way. We find where they are and we hunt them, drifting through the shadows, stalking, taking our time then attacking. We take them with tooth and claw, the right way, the honorable way. We are *wolf*."

A few of the pack had been nodding, and when she finished, two began to howl into the dusk.

"Shut the hell up," said Jeff, not shouting, but close. "Do you want to tell them, and everybody within a mile, where we are?"

He looked at Abbie, disgust plain on his face, then turned to the pack. "She is as full of shit as these two. What does it matter if we go up against this pack with replicas or teeth? They have real guns, lots of them. Yes, they're on our turf. Yes, they are violating the accords and hunting on our range. No, they have no honor and yes, they will get all of us into trouble if anybody starts to draw boundaries between our life and theirs. There's no argument they have to be dealt with. But we go in there thinking we can hunt them the old way and we end up dead. We can't just leave it either, so if we're going to do anything, our best hope is with some support." He hooked his thumb over his shoulder in the general direction of Eddie and Tasha.

"I don't want blood spilt on this if we don't have to, ours or theirs. If we can just get them to move along out of our territory, that works fine for me—and I'm alpha here, so that works for you too, unless you want out of this pack."

"This pack has two alphas, Jeff, and I am tired of us being led by a coward."

A profound silence fell, and everybody stared at Abbie like she'd announced she was an alien. Until a lumberjack-sized man took what looked like a reluctant step forward.

Jeff looked at him. "Over her? You want to fight me over her? Because this time it won't be playing pool, brother."

The challenger looked profoundly unhappy, his eyes switching from Jeff to Abbie and back again.

"Don't look like I have a choice."

"Wait." Tasha tried to keep herself from laughing. "You fools are telling me your about to go into a testosterone fueled dick-waving contest right now? Over *her*?"

Jeff looked apologetic. "Has to happen when it needs to."

"And even if you win, you still have that bitch to deal with?"

Jeff shrug, and gave her a small, sad smile. "That's about the measure of it."

"To hell with that. I challenge *her*."

The pack gave a collective gasp, followed by a round of uneasy laughter.

"You want to be careful, lady. I might just take you up on that."

"Come at me." Tasha held out her hand and curled her fingers in beckoning. "See what happens."

"She can't, and you can't. We can only resolve challenges in wolf form, and as you can't ..."

Something flew towards her and Tasha snatched it out of the air. "What is this?"

Jeff and Abbie looked for a moment, both open mouthed, then turned back to their pack.

"Who threw that?" Abbie screamed in fury. "Which of you filthy bitches threw that?"

But it seemed everybody else already knew, because a gap had opened up around one of the girls.

"I did." Her head was up, and she wasn't afraid. "I'm sick of this all the time. Alphas need to be mates, not enemies. There's no consensus, and I'm tired of you pissing over the rest of us."

There were a few murmurs, mostly from other females, but they soon fell silent.

"Will somebody tell me what this is?" Tasha demanded, holding up the pendant.

Jeff turned to her. "It's her wolf stone. Not stone, obviously. We get the urge to start carving them when we're kids. Then one day, when you feel it's finished, you go out somewhere quiet and put it on for the first time. That's your first change, and your life is never the same again."

The light was fading, so Tasha couldn't make out all the details, but she could see the medallion was about an inch and a half across and threaded on a leather cord.

"And I'm holding it because?"

"There's a legend that says we can gift the change to another who truly wants it. Just once. But it also says it can go wrong, and the person you gift it to stays as a wolf forever." He looked a little uncertain and rocked an outstretched hand back and forth. "Or you can never use the wolf stone again to change yourself. Ever." Once he said this, he looked very directly at the girl who had thrown Tasha the token.

Tasha raised her voice so they could all hear it, but she was speaking to the girl. "You're prepared to risk that?"

The girl shrugged. "I'm sick of her. She wins, I'm leaving the pack anyway. You get stuck, that's your risk."

"And if it works, my challenge is valid? She has to fight me?"

Jeff nodded, but Abbie looked like she was starting to panic.

"This is bullshit. It's just a legend."

But the rest of the pack, including Jeff, was backing away.

Tasha raised the loop of leather over her head.

"Well, let's find out."

Bitch Fight

T asha felt her vampire strength and abilities drain away, and with it a portion of her self. The whole world became fuzzy, and she felt her body dissolve into some elemental state from which it could become anything.

Forces molded her, rearranged her. It wasn't painful. In some ways it was sensual. It was precise, delicate, and yet incredibly swift. It took away things and put them who knew where—though she could tell they would still be there when she needed them back. Other things it added, until Tasha felt herself settling out, like ice forming, or jell-o setting.

When all was done, she stretched out and leant against her forelimbs. Her fur was white, or so pale a grey it didn't make a difference. She eased the kinks out of each of her hind legs then she shook, and found out why dogs always look so pleased with themselves when they finish. Most enjoyable.

Even more so were the new palette of senses. Scent and sound merged in an astonishing richness and detail. Her sight, conversely, was colorless and flat, though with astonishingly bright flickers of movement.

But she could see Abbie. She could smell her, radiating her fear and her anger. Tasha turned her to face her adversary and growled a challenge, deep in the throat, her upper lip curling back as she imagined her teeth ripping into Abbie's throat. Her head dropped low, and she stared.

"This is ridiculous. I am not fighting her. She's not one of us."

Jeff opened his arms and shrugged. "Challenge is issued and form taken. Looks legit to me."

"But she's not a wolf."

The girl who threw the amulet stepped forward. "She changed with my wolf stone. You saying I'm not a wolf?"

"I'm saying you're a pet, and that you enjoy wearing a collar and playing the little bitch for Sy whatever form you're in. "

"I'll take you right now," snapped the girl and surged forward. Tasha leaped in front of her, while hands from the pack reached out to hold her back. Then Tasha turned to face Abbie again, while from behind her the girl cried out, "Fight! Or are you afraid? Coward."

Tasha watched as Abbie looked for allies in the pack, anybody to back her up and stop the fight, but it looked like she was on her own.

"There is going to be such a reckoning after this," Abbie swore, still looking at her pack, then she took a few steps to put herself in clear space.

"First blood only," called Jeff, but both Abbie and Tasha shook their head.

"The old rules say to the death," and Abbie grinned as she said it. "And she didn't say any different."

And before anybody else could argue the point, Abbie shifted.

Tasha wondered if this had been such a good idea. Abbie was bigger than her, not by much, but maybe by enough. And she had done this before. She knew the tactics, and she knew a wolf's body better than Tasha did. Tasha did what she could to clear her mind, to let the body she now wore do what it knew, rather than putting herself too much in control.

The rest of the pack spread out. She and Abbie circled each other, growling, snarling. She was trying to keep closer to the vehicles, where she might find some kind of cover if she needed it, but Abbie was pushing her out into open space.

When the attack came it was so fast Tasha didn't have time to react. Abbie's teeth clamped on her shoulder, biting hard. Her neck wedged so hard against Tasha's head that Tasha couldn't twist around to bite back. The pain was excruciating, and she yelped over and again, until she figured the only counter was to drop her head. It made her shoulder hurt more, but she could get under Abbie's neck and clamp her jaw around Abbie foreleg. She ground her teeth against the bone as hard as she could, until with a scream, Abbie let go and backed away.

They circled again, both limping. Tasha was worse. She tried to switch direction, to put her good side towards Abbie. Surprisingly, the alpha let her. They circled again, twice, then Abbie darted in closer. Tasha flinched back, put all her weight on her bad shoulder, and yelped as she almost went down—just as Abbie planned.

The alpha backed off without striking, circling then darting in again. Once more Tasha flinched back, stumbling but managing to stifle another cry of pain. Around the circle they danced, and Abbie darted forward again. It made sense; Abbie wanted Tasha to keep straining the muscles around her wound. Wise to the trick now, she didn't react.

Except Abbie kept coming. Taken off guard, and with her weight on all the wrong paws, Tasha tried to duck under the charge. Abbie missed the throat hold she had been aiming for, but got her teeth into Tasha's ruff. As she scrambled over Tasha's lowered shoulders, she rolled Tasha onto her back.

The ruff was of no tactical use to Abbie. Tasha tried to protect where the bitch might strike next, but there were so many vulnerable places while she was rolled onto her side. Abbie shifted her bite, and ground her teeth onto Tasha's hind leg, stabbing sharp canines into flesh and tearing muscles.

The best Tasha could do was twist and wriggle, which made the tearing worse. She nipped and bit at the skin along Abbie's back, but it was too tight to get a hold of. Eventually she turned herself far enough to get a grip on Abbie's ear. She clamped her teeth as hard as she could and pulled. Blood flooded into her mouth, hot and sweet, stirring a monster deep inside her. Abbie pulled herself free, leaving a sliver of her ear in Tasha's mouth.

They broke apart. Tasha waited until everybody could see, then spat out the chunk she had bitten from Abbie's ear. The alpha circled again, blood pouring down the side of her face, while Tasha hobbled on the spot, lame now on both sides. Had she made a mistake, and overestimated her abilities? Abbie had the upper hand in body mass and wolf tactics.

But was this all about being a wolf? Might Abbie be so absorbed by her lupine self that she would ignore basic *human* traits? If what Tasha thought of backfired, things would go horribly wrong, for her and for Jane. But without something new to try, things were going south anyway.

Hobbling, Tasha closed the distance between them until she was too tempting a target. Abbie charged. Tasha rolled over on her back, the common canine posture of submission and defeat. A collective gasp rose from the pack, and she heard Eddie shouting for someone to break things up, that they had gone too far.

But she was betting that Abbie wouldn't listen. She was betting that Abbie would want the kill, and that she would want to relish it. The alpha straddled Tasha's prone form, glaring down at her, saliva dripping from her teeth and tongue, savoring the moment and making sure the completeness of Tasha's defeat had fully sunk in. Tasha wriggled and squirmed, begging for mercy, then Abbie struck.

Except that Tasha struck first. The squirming shifted herself just far enough down the alpha's body that she had a clearer path to Abbie's neck than Abbie had to hers. Abbie's killing snarl was Tasha's trigger. Pushing up with her shoulder and back muscles, Tasha clamped her teeth around Abbie's throat and bit down.

Abbie howled and screamed, clawing with her feet but not daring to twist her head too far lest Tasha's teeth rip out her throat. And that wasn't what the vampire wanted anyway. The grip she had tried for, and that seemed to be working, was how a lion strangled its prey, squeezing its throat to suffocate it. Except she didn't mean to take it that far.

Abbie fell on top of her, mewling, wheezing, but Tasha held the grip. Even when Abbie went limp and they rolled sideways, Tasha kept her teeth clamped on Abbie's neck until every twitch had faded. Only then did she let go and lurch, unsteady, to her feet.

One by one the women of the pack shifted, until a half dozen more wolves faced her. She had taken down one of their own, and they were going to kill her. Tasha didn't have the strength to fight. She wouldn't go down without a struggle, but she had nothing left to run with.

The bitches formed a phalanx. Tasha expected them to flank

her, to attack from all sides, but they held formation. And then, as the lead bitch took a last step forward, she ducked her head and rubbed gently under Tasha's chin before softly licking her mouth and moving aside so the next could pay obeisance. And then Tasha realized what she had done. *She* was their new alpha. The pack was hers. Despite the pain and the wounds, Tasha raised her muzzle to the sky and howled, low and bell-like.

Her heart soared. So this was what it was to belong. This was family. No, *more* than family. This was *pack.* Who could want anything else, for there could be nothing finer? They should run, they should hunt.

But people were standing before her and her sisters, speaking to them softly in half understood words, cajoling her sisters to lose their true forms, to diminish themselves. Two humans stood before her particularly. She recognized the shape of both, but the scent of neither.

"Make her change back. Take that amulet thing off her."

"Can't. When she changed, the wolfstone became part of her."

"How the hell do we get her back then?'

'We don't. The decision is hers, and she must chose to return."

"She'll need a hospital."

"Hospital won't matter if she doesn't change back. First change is the best, and the most dangerous. If she runs, she'll never come back. She'll become more and more wolf until she forgets she was ever a person."

Well that sounded like a fine thing. Pain she could ignore, and the wounds would heal over time. Or they wouldn't. Such things were no fit concern for a wolf.

270

And yet, one of the tall things was making a sound that seemed to steal her attention.

"Nat? Nat? You have to come back. We need you. Your friend, Jane. Remember her? Short, feisty, braids. She's going to die, and I can't save her on my own."

Jane? The sound struck a chord deep in her heart. Pack? But different pack. *More* than pack? What could be more than pack? But there was something. Something even beyond friendship.

But oh, to step away from such wonder, such joy. To be a wolf was perfection of form and motion and thought. How could she turn her back on this?

Yet, deep in the bottom of the frightened residuum of her soul, so far down that in her human form she had not heard it, something thrummed to a slow, steady beat. Something that reached away from her through an unknowable medium, connecting her to something that felt warm and familiar, and alive.

Making the hardest decision in her life, she chose to become her old self.

Tasha staggered and would have fallen if Eddie hadn't grabbed her arm and steadied her. A second later, the strength she had stolen from the narcotics cop flooded back through her like a cocaine rush. It repelled her, disgusted her, but then she felt the strength and the intelligence, infinitely more than these creatures surrounding her, and it was delicious. She turned to tell Eddie to get everybody moving, but somebody shouted, "Look out!"

Tasha spun around. Abbie, still in wolf form, galloped towards her, face a snarling hate mask. Tasha watched her, immobile, until Abbie leapt. Then her arm shot out, flat-handing Abbie in the breastbone with the force of a battering ram. Tasha didn't move an inch, but everybody heard the sickening crunch. Abbie flew back twenty feet before landing with a yelp and scraping along the hard top.

By the time she scrambled to her feet, now in her human form, Jeff was standing beside Tasha, and on her other side was the lumberjack. Eyes desperate, Abbie looked from one to the other of her pack mates, and each one turned away from her, or stood with Tasha.

"You broke the rules," said Jeff. "You attacked someone in human form while wolf, and you attacked them from behind."

"She cheated first. We were supposed to fight to the death."

"She spared you," snapped Jeff. "And I'm doing the same thing. Walk away, Abbie. You're not alpha anymore. In fact, you're not pack. You are expelled." He looked around the rest of the people standing here. "Anybody wants to go with her is free to leave, with my blessings and love."

Nobody moved. Abbie curled her lip, trying for disdain and contempt, but just looking scared.

"Losers. I'm better off without any of you."

Three of the women took a step forward, and Abbie ran into the night.

Once her footsteps had faded into the darkness, the pack turned to Tasha.

"So," said Jeff. "You were telling us about this plan?"

Tasha looked at her pack, and realized something had changed, something inside her. She took Jeff by the arm and led him a few steps away from the rest of them. Her new plan would not sit well with the pack.

"Time to be a true alpha, Jeff," she murmured.

Excuses

"What's wrong with her?"

"I don't know. She passed out just after I started drawing the second unit."

The words were jumbled, out of sequence in time and space. It felt like I was flying, or maybe this was what tripping felt like.

"Is she sick?"

"Her pulse, BP, and blood oxygen are all where I would expect them. Her temp is down, but only a degree or so. I've pricked her with a needle and got no response. Should we take the collar off her?"

"No!" Panicked, urgent. "Never *ever* take that off her unless you've cut her open to make sure her heart's not beating."

"So what should I do with her? How will we feed her?"

"We can put a tube up her nose if we have to. He's seen her now. No need to keep her here in the executive suite. I think he's going to drain her anyway."

"I hate doing that."

"Stop whining. I'll send help for you to get her down to the cells. You can hook her up to a monitor, right?"

"Ye—es." Drawn out, dubious.

"Then make sure you don't let her die."

It was dark blue and peaceful at the bottom of my lake. I wanted to ignore everything and stay right where I was. All I needed to do was keep plucking at the string, though it was harder work than it seemed. I ached deep in my bones, and breathing felt like it got harder each time my ribs moved. I was hungry like I'd not eaten for a week. But these problems were outside, above the surface, and I had slammed the door on them.

A flock of names, all mine, started to buzz around me, more and more of them until their drone became impossible to ignore. They flew closer, like wasps and flies droning in my ears. Jane. Jane. JanejanejanejanejaneJANE."

One came too close, and I swatted at it—and my beautiful, peaceful lake vanished like a soap bubble popping. I opened my eyes to glare at all the people shouting at me and saw just one. The only person I didn't want to see. Ever again. Not for my whole life.

Miller.

I closed my eyes and squeezed them tight, hoping he would get the point and leave me alone. I would have traded another unit of blood for enough control of my body to tell him to piss off forever. That I couldn't speak, and that it was his fault I had been made a prisoner in my own body, started my emotional soup boiling again. Even the absurd expression the lack of eyebrows gave him didn't make me feel any better.

"Thank goodness. You've not opened your eyes for hours."

A row of windows along the top of the wall showed only darkness. What light there was came from behind me and flickered like a strip light with an old tube. Something started an electronic whine behind me.

"It's your vitals monitor," said Miller. "Someone will

274

come."

The room fell silent until the muted beeping of a keypad and the harsh buzz of a lock announced a visitor had arrived. It was Tracy, looking bed-tousled and wearing a Hello Kitty onesie.

"*Now* you decide to wake up," she muttered, almost under her breath. "They'll be kicking me for hours. Probably make me sleep on the outside." She fiddled with the monitor. The whining stopped, replaced by the soft tap of fake key clicks. "At least I know you aren't in a coma or something. There. I changed the limits now that I know you're OK." She backed up until she could look at me, and I was certain I could see pity in her eyes. I hated her for it. If she felt that much for me, she should be helping me, not empathizing with me.

"He should leave a message by morning. I know you must be hungry. Maybe we can set you up with an NG tube and get some food in you."

But I heard the clear implication that she may not need to, if the decision went the other way. I didn't like the idea of being fed through a tube stuffed up my nose, but it was better than dying. She looked at me a moment longer. All I could do was stare at her. She turned away and left both the cell and the room.

"They think my mouth is still covered." Miller spoke again a few minutes after it was certain Tracy had left. I wished his mouth *was* still taped shut.

"This is Hawke. He pulled the tape from my mouth, but he can't free me from the chair."

A shape loomed out of the darkness and pressed against the bars two cages away. He was so far away from the light that I couldn't make out all the details, but he looked cadaverously thin, and clumps of his lank hair had fallen out.

His cheekbones were so prominent I could have used them to pop the cap off a beer.

"So you're the other half of this rescue?"

"She cannot speak," Miller reminded him.

"That's right. Some idiot put a collar and leash on her, then handed himself in to the very people he was trying to save me from."

Seemed like a little deprivation hadn't made Hawke any less of an entitled asshole. I wasn't surprised. But I had to admit I agreed with him. Miller was an idiot.

"You had best hope they kill you," Hawke ranted on, doing nothing to improve my opinion of him. "You are finished if we ever get out of this. My sire will hear every last detail of this shambles and will strip you of your titles before he throws you into the pit and watches the changelings rip you apart as they drain you dry."

"Oh, shut up, you pretentious, posturing parasite on your sire's good nature." Miller sounded as if he had already heard enough from Hawke. "He wanted you recovered because you are an embarrassment to him, because you cause him shame every hour of your existence. He is looking to groom a successor, while you play with your food and prance about like a little boy playing at being a prince. My brief was to terminate you if I couldn't recover you."

Which was as much news to me as it probably was to Hawke. And so different to the game Miller had been playing so far, I wondered if it were true, or if he was just trying to shut the annoying little creep up. If so, it worked. The bars of the cage rang softly as Hawke pounded his fist against them, then he stormed off somewhere out of my sight line. I didn't feel the loss.

"This is not what was supposed to happen, Jane. I swear."

How was that supposed to make me feel better?

"After I recovered Hawke, I was going to storm the building with an army of vampires, to rescue you." He paused. "I have spent most of the day contemplating how I could have made such a catastrophic error of both tactics and judgement." Another pause. "But I am truly sorry."

He expected that to make a difference? Make me feel sorry for the pressure he was under that made him screw up? I was supposed to excuse someone I had come to think of as a friend from using me like a poker chip, like a party favor? For all he knew, they could have decided to drain me there and then, and it wouldn't have mattered if he had bought the entire vampire nation to rescue me.

I was still going to die. Everything else was just a matter of when.

"Did you hear something?" said Miller. "I thought I heard—"

The lights went out and the unheard sounds of a living building became noticeable by their absence. Radios squawked and cracked, and faint footsteps thumped through the concrete floor.

Then lightning flashed through the windows, and the building resounded to a sharp *thump*.

Assault

Tasha and the pack crept along the back of the building in the next lot, while Eddie snuck along the side of 2806 itself. Jeff stood beside her as they peered around the corner. One mercury lamp, high on the wall, cast a greenish light across the lot, ruining their night vision enough to mask anything buried in the shadows of the loading bay.

"Do you see them?"

Jeff peered into the darkness and shook his head. A wolf's eyes might be good at spotting movement, but they were no good for night vision. Unlike a vampire's.

"Either side of the loading bay, right at the back. Armed human on the left, animal form on the right. You happy with the plan."

"No, I'm *not* happy with it." Jeff sighed. "But I remember it."

"Then we just have to wait for—"

As if he had been listening for a cue, Eddie killed the building power and the mercury light faded to a red ember.

"Wait for my signal."

Tasha ran out into the black. She kept to the darkest of shadows, in case the hyenas were as good at spotting movement as the wolves. The fire exit wound down the side of the building into the back lot. She had to get there quickly, and without being seen.

Once there, she flattened herself to the wall and waited to see how the occupants would respond to the power outage. Sounds from inside, on both floors, but nothing directed at her. She ghosted up the fire escape, then turned back to face Jeff. Taking out her phone, she unlocked the screen then turned it to towards the wolves.

Which was the moment events took an unexpected left term. Tasha remembered that someone, somewhen, said something like 'No battle plan survives first encounter with the enemy.' As if to the make the point, LED emergency lights came on over the loading bay, sharp and blue-white. To add to the confusion, an alarm sounded inside the building. It didn't have the insistence of a fire alarm, but Tasha was still in an exposed location.

In all the commotion, her timing went to hell. Eddie was going to throw the flash-bang, but they planned for her to be on the roof by now. As she scanned the wall around her for a safe ledge or hiding spot, the pyro caught her unprepared. At least her back was to the light, but the sound made her ears ring, and now she couldn't hear if anyone was coming through the door. She had to get out of there.

The fire escape had a handrail, right around to the wall. Tasha climbed on to it, kept her balance with one arm against the side of the building, then looked up. Still buzzing with confidence and arrogance, she bent her knees and leapt. As she did, the wound Abbie had ripped in her thigh—partially healed though it was—flared with pain. The jump was short, and she drifted to the side. If she missed the roof, she would fall all the way to the ground.

She rose a single joint above the lip around the edge of the roof, but that was all she needed. Her fingers flexed to hold her in place, then the muscles in her biceps and shoulders clenched to pull her up and onto the roof. Behind her, the fire escape door crashed open and feet pattered down the metal stairs.

She crouched to her knees and looked down over the back yard. The wolves had arranged themselves near whatever cover they could find. Apart from Jeff. The guy was braver than he looked. He stood out in the open, hands wide and conspicuously empty.

"Pack to pack," he shouted. "I challenge your alpha."

Three people stepped forward from the loading dock: an unarmed woman and two very obviously armed men, behind and on either side.

"Challenge me to what?"

"This is our range. You can't hunt here."

"And your little rag-tag dog pack is going to stop me?"

Jeff settled his feet, but his head didn't move. "We are. We know the city, and we will pick you off one by one if we have to. It will be a long, nasty war with blood and death on both sides."

"Sounds like fun."

"Maybe for you. It won't be you doing the dying." He pointed over her shoulder towards the loading bay where, if things were going according to plan, most of the hyenas would have congregated. "It'll be them." He raised his voice further. "Doing their dying for you. That's not the mark of a true leader, or a true alpha."

"Then what is?"

"I challenge you. Single combat." He hesitated for just a

second, long enough for Tasha to hold her breath in case his nerve failed. "To the death. Loser's pack is banished and leaves the city."

The woman said nothing, standing motionless for a half minute. "You're serious."

Jeff nodded.

"Well, why not." The woman was already shifting and Jeff quickly did the same. Tasha swore. The hyena was a quarter bigger than the wolf and outweighed him by the same. Jeff was going to get ripped apart if she didn't move.

Now.

Covert Penetration

Tasha revised her plan. A quick look across the roof had shown no other way in. Besides, the alarms and subsequent evacuation had opened up a new, simpler opportunity. She ran back to the side of the roof over the fire escape and dropped back down to the platform. The door was still open. She eased inside, drawing it closed behind her. No point inviting any surprises from the rear.

Emergency lights shone over most of the doors, leaving bright white pools in the darkness. Tasha hadn't a clue where she was going. She would have to search room by room, and that was going to take time she, and Jeff, and Jane did not have. She let her stolen strength push her muscles to their delicious limit.

Five minutes covered the upstairs. Empty. She pattered down a flight of stairs and started on the lower floor. The first door she opened was almost the last, and she reacted, rather than acted. A metal tray made a passable frisbee, which she spun into the head of the only person holding a gun in the room. He dropped to the floor, blood pouring from a gash above his eyes. There were three more to deal with, all pouring buckets of chemicals down a pair of industrial sinks. It was a futile task. They had so much manufactured product, and so many raw materials, it would take a couple of hours to get rid of them all and clean everything.

But they were not going down without a fight. A short woman kept pouring stuff into the drain while the men split up to take Tasha out. One drew an eight-inch blade and the other picked up a metal pipe and started banging it into the steel workbenches.

Tasha grinned. Idiots. They had no idea what they were up against, or what she was capable of. Drawing deeply on her stolen strength, Tasha leapt at the one holding the metal bar. He still had it raised over his head when her foot smashed into his face. They went down in a tumble, but Tasha was rolling to a crouch before he finished bouncing off the ground. She smashed him across the jaw again for good measure, picked up his bar, and turned toward the other man.

It looked like the second guy was reconsidering his options now that he was the only one left fighting. He was making for the door, but Tasha couldn't allow him to leave. The bar flew from her hands, but towards his legs, not his head. She didn't want to kill him. Not because she cared, but because she knew others would make her life unbearable about it if she did. A bone cracked in sharp accompaniment to the flat, bell-like note of the bar as it struck. The man went down, screaming. Tasha ripped the knife from his hand, then clamped her hand over his face and fed. He was limp in a second and Tasha let go almost as fast. His aura was vile, and she wanted no more of it.

That left the girl. She had stopped pouring the chemicals and was cowering beside the sink. Tasha marched over to her, grabbed her by the front of her filthy lab coat, and hauled her to her feet. "Take me to the prisoners, or I'll kill you here and now.

The girl nodded, terrified. Tasha let her down onto her feet, and the girl tore off the lab coat to reveal cleaner, almost wholesome scrubs. "This way."

She led Tasha out the way she had come in, down a corridor that led deeper into the building, then another that branched off to the right. There were doors every thirty feet or so, and it was the very last one they stopped at. The woman tapped at the keypad, but nothing happened.

"Open it."

"I can't. The lock must not be on the emergency power."

Tasha pushed the woman aside so hard she fell to the ground and skidded along the floor. The door was metal, and so was the frame it. She didn't have time to search for keys, but Tasha would need to knock the entire frame out of the wall to get in.

She tapped at the wall. It sounded like ordinary cinder block. Could she? She sneered. Hell, she could do *anything*. She took a step back, spun on her heel, and kicked the wall.

The shock ran up her leg and rocked her to the core, but the wall cracked. Tasha settled herself and did it again. Her heel and hip screamed at her, but a Tetris block of four bricks all slid an inch back from their siblings. Tasha took a deep breath and battered the wall again. Tasha kicked out enough for them to crawl through and shoved the cowering woman through first. She was weak, human, and couldn't hurt Tasha even if she had the guts to try. Inside was a prison; a row of five cages made of welded steel rebar. Three of the cells held vampires in varying degrees of emaciation. Miller, strapped to a wheelchair, occupied the fourth and an immobile form on a gurney lay in the fifth.

"Keys," Tasha growled, snapping her fingers. "Now."

The woman in scrubs ran toward the door. For a moment Tasha thought she was trying to escape and shifted her weight to run after her, then she saw a bunch of keys hanging beside the exit. The woman ran back, holding the keys out in front of her. Tasha reached out, but rather than taking the keys, she grabbed the woman's wrist.

Tasha fed, deep and fast. This one was sweet, not like the last one. Her terror was a subtle overtone, lightly seasoning the compassion that made up most of her soul. She would be a fine feast, ripe to drain slowly, letting the knowledge of her death grow in her until that final sweet moment.

Tasha snarled and threw the hand away from her, stepping back and shaking her head. What was she doing? What was she *thinking*? She stretched down and, with trembling fingers, took the keys from the woman's prostrate body.

"Release me first," shouted Miller. "I can help."

Two of the three vamps were leaning against their doors, watching her. She ignored all of them and made for Jane. It was Jane she needed. Tasha needed a compass, a guide, and Jane was it. The door opened with the third key and she rushed inside.

Jane was awake. She blinked, but that was all.

"What's the matter with her?"

"Let me out and I'll come see," said Miller. Tasha almost moved to do it, but either instinct or memory took over. She couldn't trust him. Despite anything he might have said earlier, he worked for bloodsuckers and that made him as bad as them. She turned back to Jane and spotted the collar she had overlooked as jewelry.

"What's this around her neck?"

Tasha ran her fingers around the circlet. It felt cold, even to her, but she could find no sign of a clasp.

"Release me and I'll tell you. Or I'll leave her to die with the rest of us."

Tasha turned to face him. "Scum, just like them. Just like I knew you were." She turned back to Jane.

"You'll just hurt her if you try to force it open." The desperation in Miller's voice was music to her ears. Anything was right by her if it hurt him.

Tasha ran her fingers around it again, inside and out, probing for the most insignificant irregularity. She leaned close and turned it twice, looking for inconsistencies in the pattern. Nothing.

Outside, an animal screamed in pain. A mob cheered, too close and too loud to be the wolves. She was running out of time. She couldn't just pull it, the collar would crush Jane's throat, and for the same reason she couldn't twist it. But then she remembered, way back in her teens, snapping a wire hanger to replace the broken antenna of a car radio. She ran her fingers underneath the circle again. She had enough space for that. Barely.

It was stiff, but she was stronger, and driven by her feeding frenzy. The metal creaked, then screeched, and burned Tasha's fingers as she deformed it. She shifted her grip to bend it the other way and bore down with all the strength she could drive into her wrists and thumbs.

"Stop it," shouted Miller. "That thing is priceless, and there's no knowing what it will do if you break it open. It's incredibly powerful. Please. I'll tell you."

But the fact that Miller valued the thing made Tasha all the more determined to destroy it. The tendons in her wrists creaked, but the circle bent back the other way. Slowly, reluctantly, but it bent. Back to where it had been before, and past.

Tasha let go, panting, flapping her hands and wriggling her thumbs to clear the cramp, then she took the circlet again and bent it back for a third time.

It snapped. The sound was no more than a tiny metallic *tink*, but the flash of blue light burned at her eyes and a powerful jolt of a power like electricity coursed through her arms and across her chest. She flew back across the cell and bounced her head off the iron bars.

Tasha had no time for pain, nor the spots dancing in front of her eyes. The room could spin around her as fast as it wished, but she hadn't the luxury to react to it. She forced herself to her feet, stumbled over to the gurney, and stared into Jane's face. Her eyes were rolled back in her head. Tasha called her name, shook her shoulders, but she wouldn't move. Catching her bottom lip between her teeth, she drew back her hand and slapped Jane's face.

The eyes didn't change, but a hand swept up and slapped her in return. Jane's back arched off the gurney as she took in a huge breath, and when she sank back down her eyes were open. She was confused but awake.

"Who did this to you. The hyenas?"

Jane shook her head and tried to speak. Nothing came out. Tasha saw her work her tongue around the inside of her mouth and across her lips. Then she whispered.

"Miller."

Tasha strode out of Jane's cell, stood in front of Miller's, and ripped the door free from its lock with a brief shriek of tortured metal.

"Wait. Miss Campbell, please. I have a—"

She walked behind Miller's wheelchair and kicked it towards the door. A wheel struck the doorframe as it passed, sending the wheelchair spinning on its side across the floor. It smashed into the opposite wall, and enough of it broke off to allow Miller one free hand. As Tasha closed on him, Miller ripped desperately at the tape holding his other arm to the chair.

Tasha ran the last three steps and aimed a savage kick at Miller's throat. Had it connected, it might have ripped his head from his shoulders. But crossed wrists rose towards his face while his head bent back. He deflected Tasha's boot just far enough that it passed over his head and connected with the wall rather than smashing his windpipe. Miller continued the motion, ramming Tasha's leg up and throwing her backwards—giving him enough time to undo the strap around his legs. He rolled free of the wreck of the wheelchair just as Tasha leapt to her feet.

She was fast and strong, but he was skilled—and perhaps there was an edge of something else, too. No human should have been able to take on a vampire hand to hand, and certainly not one as empowered as she. But Miller did. Just. He could defend himself but had nothing extra to take an attack to her. She screamed in frustration and threw herself forward in a flurry of punches and kicks, and again he managed to hold her back, though this time he ended up sliding away from the fight on his backside. Tasha ran after him, intending to stamp on the rat while she had it on the floor, but the air in front of her turned thick and held her back.

"Enough." Jane's voice was weak, but they both turned to look at her. She was sitting on the edge of the gurney, and it horrified Tasha to see their skin was about the same shade of dead. "What the hell is going on? Can I hear a dog fight out

288

there?"

"The wolves are making a diversion for me while I rescue you."

"And you leave them to that while you settle a private score with him?" Jane shook her head. "Throw him the keys."

"What?"

"Do it."

"They're by your door. He can fetch them himself as he passes."

Jane saw where Tasha was looking and hopped down off the gurney. She wobbled, and Tasha almost ran to her. She saw Miller's hand reach out, too. Jane took a moment, walked over to the keys, and held onto the cell door for balance as she kicked them over to Miller.

"Take these, take your vampires, and get out. I never want to see you again."

"Jane, I—"

She gestured and his words stuck in his throat. Literally, from the way he was working his mouth and trying to swallow. "I don't care. Get out of here, or I'll kill you myself."

Miller looked at her for a long moment. He looked sad, or pretended to, then nodded and rose to his feet. While he freed the vampires, Jane waved Tasha over and leaned on her while she got back onto the gurney.

"Now, what the hell kind of mess are we in?"

Is that a...

Tasha outlined the plan and I listened with half an ear, while I watched with half an eye as Miller gathered his charges from their cells and ushered them toward the door. Once they were all through he paused, looking back at me. "You're not up to this fight. Come with me. I can get you both clear."

"I don't leave my friends." I was too tired, too weak, for an extended argument. "Get out of my sight."

The wall I built to stop them fighting had taken so much from me that I didn't have. My head was spinning and all I wanted to do was sleep, because the damned collar Miller had stuck on me wouldn't let me do that either. Nor had I been able to get back into that trance. Miller's offer was more attractive than he knew.

He left, and I turned my full attention back to Tasha.

"So what was the plan to get clear?"

Tasha looked blank for a moment, then two spots of color appeared on her cheeks.

"You didn't think of that? Jeff is out there, fighting for his life, and you have no exit plan?"

She shook her head and I groaned. "Get me to a window. Anywhere I can see what's going on."

The windows were too high to see out from where we were, so we had to get out and find somewhere else. As we left, I saw a huddled form not far from the door. It was the girl, Tracy, who had been taking the blood from me.

"Did you kill her?"

Tasha wouldn't meet my eyes, but she looked defiant. "No. Not quite."

With Tasha's arm under my shoulders, we left the room. I didn't know how I felt about Tracy. What she did was monstrous, but she had tried to take care of me. How much of that was for me, and how much was to make me last longer, I didn't know. I think I was more worried about Tasha. She seemed wired, edgy, and I worried she had been feeding on people to take them out. For her, that was playing Russian roulette without knowing how many rounds were in the gun.

A fire escape at the far end of the corridor opened at the bottom of a flight of metal stairs, off the side of the building. We crept up to the corner and peered around. Jeff, somehow, was winning. He was bloodied up around his face, but his limbs looked in one piece. The hyena was limping, with one hind leg dragging so badly it was useless, and a gash in its shoulder. They were circling each other, and both groups were howling encouragement.

I don't know what made me look. Perhaps I was getting a little smarter, and a little better at my job. Perhaps I was learning that the main event was often not the most important event. Maybe I realized that while we were distracting them, we were also distracting ourselves.

Whatever the reason, I looked up along the building, trying to see how many of them there were, where they were, and how we might be able to get loose from this mess without everybody getting killed. And that was when I saw it. It lined up with the edge of a row of vents that ran just under the eaves of the roof. Then it moved just a bit too far and a reflection from one of the safety lights glinted along it. The long, thin line of a rifle barrel sticking out of a window.

"Tasha." I pointed. "Up there. What do you see?"

"I'm on it."

Before I could argue, she was a blur up the fire escape. It was frightening how fast she could move when she wanted to. I turned my eyes back to the rifle and tried to gather enough strength to do something. But what, I had no idea.

...rifle?

asha had already looked into every room on the second floor, and was now confused. They had all been empty. And they had all had big windows. What she had seen the rifle poking through wasn't that big, wasn't a window, and a row of them ran just under the roof. She ran to the far end of the building and checked again. She was right; the place had no other stairs, no hidden third level. What had she missed?

There, right next to the fire exit. She had been in such a hurry to get in, both times, that she had run past it. A maintenance door, and it was ajar. She pulled the door open. Inside was a service riser, full of pipes and cables, and a ladder bolted to the wall.

Tasha climbed, quickly but quietly, up into the roof space. A floored track ran to the other end of the building, but as soon as she turned onto it, Tasha saw a shape lumping out of the shadows at the far end, right up against the wall. She would be in full view of whoever was there, and it was an even bet that if they had a rifle, they had a sidearm too.

The rest of the roof was steel rafters, four feet apart. An uncomfortable stretch to walk across, but the only other option. Her boots had high grip soles. She would be fine. Tasha moved to the front side of the building and began to hop from rafter to rafter.

It was harder than she expected. Her boots didn't hold that well, and she fought for balance each time she landed. The lack of progress frustrated her. She burned for action, for combat, and the subtlety of what she had to do gnawed at her. She picked up the pace, found a rhythm, and made progress.

Until the rifle barked. Until an animal howled in pain and a roar rolled up from below, all mixed anger and approval.

The subtle approach became old news. The unmistakable sound of a bolt being pulled back, pushed forward, and locked reached her. She had to get to the shooter before they could fire again.

She let out a battle cry and ran straight towards the shape in the corner. The shape let out a startled curse then rolled over, trying to get to its knees while it scrabbled at its hip. Tasha was quick, but the uncertain footing stopped her from using her true speed. That gave the shooter time to get off one hurried shot.

Fire seared across Tasha's hip, the same one that Abbie had already done such a number on. The energies swirling around her body had done much to repair the damage, but the fresh injury was too much. The leg started to give out as her weight landed on it. She could either make use of the change of motion, or fall flat on her face. Tasha let her knee dip lower, making it look like she was hit bad, but she rolled her weight forward, over the knee, until she could push off. It hurt like hell, but the low jump caught the shooter off guard. The second shot went high, but close enough Tasha heard it whine as it passed over her head.

The shooter panicked. She might be good with a rifle, but

she wasn't used to shooting at a rapidly moving target. Instead of unloading the mag at Tasha, she fell back, landing on her rump then using her feet to scrabble backwards, away from the black outline moving impossibly fast towards her.

"Stop," called Tasha, trying to halt herself. "I won't hurt you."

But the shooter wasn't listening and was facing away from the looming disaster Tasha had already seen. She kept backing up, straight through the open window. Her arms flailed for a second as her balance, and her life, hung on the edge of the sill. Tasha leapt forward, hand outstretched, but her fingertips only brushed the sole of the woman's boot before she fell, screaming.

Catch

The best I could think of, with what strength I had, was a trivial little whirlwind. I knelt down, put my hands to the earth, and drew what I could to me. Then I looked up, twirling a wisp of air into a tight little zephyr and sending it up in front of the rifle. Not touching it, in case the shooter felt the disturbance, but an inch in front. Then I thickened it up as much as I could. It wouldn't stop anything, but it might deflect it.

The gun cracked. Jeff howled as he got thrown to the floor. A howl of outrage rose from the wolves, matched by jeers and catcalls from the hyenas. I saw weapons being raised on both sides. This was going to end in bloodshed.

Then Jeff got back to his feet—or his paws—raised his muzzle and howled so loud it sounded like a siren. He was OK. Well, relatively. A lot of blood ran from a head wound by his ear, but he was stable and was moving with menace. His pack answered, their own eerie screams echoing into the night. The hyena he was fighting cowered and started to back away. Nobody lowered their weapons, and it seemed neither side was as honorable as they said they were.

But over all of it, I heard Tasha shout. I couldn't make out what she said, but it sounded urgent, and I looked up to where

I had last seen the rifle. The gun was missing, but as I watched a shape slid backwards through the vent and fell.

I raced a few steps closer then dove forward, my arms held out to catch though I was yards away. But the pillow of air I summoned billowed up under the falling figure. She still hit hard, but not enough to break anything, and only then did I realize it wasn't Tasha. Damn and blast, I had just burned through the last of my energy—my personal, internal energy—saving a stranger. And one of them. I slumped, if it's possible to slump when you're already lying face down.

There was a champagne fizz of magic real close to me. Someone grabbed the back of my jacket and hauled me to my feet, then something cold and hard pressed against my throat. A voice next to my ear shouted so loud it hurt. "Nobody move." It was Gina.

Jeff changed too. "So this is your definition of honor?"

"Oh, shut up. What do you think this is? Disney? Or Camelot? Cover them all."

They raised weapons on both sides.

"Uh, Boss?"

"What?" Gina didn't look around to see who had spoken.

"You're lit up, Boss. Whoever threw Hanna out the window has a spot on your back with her gun."

"So what? With that cannon, he shoots me, he kills her too."

"But what about the rest of them, Gina?" I spoke loud enough they could all hear me. "And it's a she. The spot's to make a point, so they can all see it. To let them know the first one that runs, the first one that tries to take a shot, gets their head blown off."

Tasha, bless her, must have heard me threatening them, because the rifle cracked and a round skipped off the ground somewhere behind me. It started out as bluff, but I felt something, and it was from Gina. I felt her magic. It was weird, and not something she could control. I guessed I might feel the same thing from Jeff, if I ever got this close to him. It reached out like a net to all of the hyenas, and gave me an idea. I took the terror I had stored in the Magni ring and trickled it into their net. Slowly at first. I wanted to start with a sense of unease.

She's behind you. She'll shoot if you move. I whispered the fear out towards them.

"Down on your knees." I shouted, and leaked more fear into their net.

Gina didn't take it well. The knife dug tighter into my throat and she started to drag me backwards, towards the edge of the building. "Shut the hell up," she hissed in my ear, then shouted. "Don't listen to her. She's using magic on you."

I didn't say anything, but I pushed more of Freddie's fear into the air.

"I will *end* you, bitch," snarled Gina, but then she stumbled against something.

"That's witch," snarled Eddie. "And this thirty-eight will mush your brain first." Then came the wonderful triple click of a hammer being pulled. "Now drop the damned knife."

As I dumped the rest of Freddie's terror into the hyena pack, I felt it hit Gina. For a moment of my own fear, I thought she was still going to slit my throat, but her hand opened and the knife clattered to the floor. As I staggered forward, I looked over my shoulder to see Eddie pushing Gina down onto her knees.

When I caught Jeff's eye and nodded, he waved his arm over his head. The wolf pack surged forward, kicking guns away from hyenas and strap-cuffing their hands behind their backs. I turned to Eddie and gave him a grin.

"Excellent timing."

He grinned back, still in the process of cuffing Gina. "Serve and protect, Miss. Happy to be of service. Cavalry will be here in a few minutes."

"What?" Tasha was at the top of the fire escape. "What have you done?"

"Miller's gone; situation's contained. I called it in."

"You *idiot*."

Units on Scene

L ook, I was down three pints of blood, maybe more, and drained to my bones, which didn't leave me on my best game. Which was why I looked on, open mouthed, as Tasha ripped off her ski mask, ran down the fire escape at full speed, then on out into the yard. She waved her hands over her head at the wolves and shouted.

"Run. Get out of here. Take everything and *go*."

That they all immediately did exactly what she said came as something of a surprise. They disappeared in seconds, leaving the hyenas looking at each other as confused as I was. Tasha stomped back across the yard towards us, thunder on her face. I walked out to meet her and heard Eddie a step or two behind me.

"That wasn't the plan. You *promised*."

"I don't see the problem," Eddie grumbled, as up the street roared two black SUVs and a van.

"*This* is the problem," Tasha snapped, pointing. "Who did you think would get here first? What do you think they will do to our people if they catch any of them?"

Tasha put her Glock and a knife on the floor, turned her back to the vans, and dropped to her knees with her hands behind her head. "That's two guns you owe me, Weston. I don't buy weapons so you can just give them away. Jane, get down. Quickly."

I got a glimpse of special forces or SWAT or something nasty pouring out of the cavalcade and did as Tasha said. There was lots of shouting, and from the corner of my eye I could see the hyenas being rounded up. But there were boots crunching towards us, too. Weren't these guys supposed to be on our side?

The boot between my shoulders said not; a nasty kick that would have driven my face into the dirt if I hadn't made myself a little cushion to land on. I saw Tasha take it on her elbows, which must have hurt like hell. Only then did somebody yell, "Face down, arms out". Nasty little timing tactic for bullies, but it gave me the opportunity to put my hands directly to the Earth. I was too weak to draw much, but I could feel the contact restoring my reserves.

There were more footsteps. One person, walking around us, stopping next to Eddie. I turned my head so I could see what happening, and got a boot pressing between my shoulders as a warning.

"You stupid *bastard*."

The trash talk came as no surprise, but the kick he landed into the side of Eddie's gut was. It wasn't just mean, it was nasty. Dangerous, too, and delivered without caring about what it might do. Who was this guy? Tall, dark hair and beard cut into a fuzz. Didn't wear a helmet or a mask like the others, so he wasn't afraid of anybody knowing who he was. He *wanted* people to know who he was. He wanted the fame.

"Palmer, I—"

Ye gods, this creep was a *cop*? He stamped on Eddie's back and put weight on his foot until Eddie couldn't talk any more.

"Go on. Move. Struggle. Just give my boys an excuse. Blue on blue, unidentified plain clothes officer, mistaken for a perp trying to escape."

Eddie made like a statue, but I could see his ribs fighting for air. Palmer held him for more than a minute, then briefly stamped his foot down harder before lifting it with a disgusted snarl. "Coward. Should have taken the easy way out."

Sirens were getting closer.

"You are finished." Palmer delivered another kick in the ribs. I ached to do something, but with my face in the dirt I wasn't sure what I could do without the risk of making things worse. Lights flashed and bounced as units pulled into the yard.

"Damn. I told them this was ours. You useless old shit. I will take your job, your pension, and break every part of your miserable life for this."

"Lieutenant, what do—hey, watch who you're pointing those things at."

"Get lost. How many times do you uniform cretins have to be told? Never approach within thirty yards of a Narco unit without permission. Get out of here. Secure the perimeter and don't bother me."

The footsteps receded, and now I was scared. Bad. This guy was bat-crap crazy, and his stormtroopers had to be just as bad to follow somebody so nuts. Without warning, he kicked Eddie in the ribs again. Something cracked and Eddie howled.

"Same goes for you bitches." He walked around us and stood with his feet either side of my head. More units were turning up, but they were staying well back. I was going to have to do something soon, but I was still coming up empty as to what.

"I don't know you and I don't care. Both of you are going

302

to lose your PI licenses. Hell, I'm even going to have them take away your driver's license, your money, your car, your damned *home*. I will *ruin* you for screwing this up for me."

My ears perked up, and I wondered if the others had heard that, but then his foot turned on its heel and the front of his boot came over the top of my right hand. His weight came down on my fingers and he twisted. I screamed, and started begging him not to do it again, but I had managed to put an air-cushion over my hand, just enough so his boot slid across it, rather than crushed and ripped it. Minor victories were all I could manage for the moment.

Another engine, but no siren, revved hard as it come closer. Palmer moved to Tasha, no words this time, same position. "And you better learn to write left-handed," As the approaching car slid to a halt Palmer raised his foot, not to grind, but to stamp and crush. He had no fear.

"Palmer, what the hell are you going. All of you, stand down. This is a police officer."

"Was. Step away, captain. This is none of your business."

His heel was still poised over Tasha's hand. I didn't know how much I could protect her from a deliberate stamp, but I built what I could over her, drawing frantically on the trickle of energy I could summon from the all-mother.

"You are certifiable. Get away from these people."

"Bad time to find a spine, Garibaldi."

"I'm your commander."

Palmer laughed and stepped back. I groaned and let the now wasted structure over Tasha's hand drain back to the source. "Now who is certifiable? Run along and play with your uniforms, Garibaldi."

"I can't hush this up, dammit. There are too many units

here, and they are all watching every stupid thing you are doing. How many do you think have cellphones taking photos and videos of what you're doing?"

Maybe it was the little strength I had managed to draw from the all-mother, but I realized I *did* have a little something left. There was just a trace of Freddie's terror left in the Magni ring. I slid my left hand a fraction closer to him and released it, twirling it up and around his leg on its way to his head. He stepped back, away from Tasha.

"Damn things. I told you to stop them carrying personal phones."

"Like that's going to happen. Get your dogs off these people before somebody sends something to the press."

"This conversation is not over, Garibaldi." He tapped Tasha's arm with his boot. "And I'm not finished with the three of you, either." He marched away, and several more pairs of boots followed him. I rolled over, half expecting to see another gun in my face, but it was a hand, held out to help me up. I ignored it. Next to me, Eddie had let out a deep groan. Tasha hurried around to his other side.

I looked up at the captain. "If you want to help, find me a paramedic, or at least a stretcher."

The hand drew back slowly, and I didn't know if I'd offended the guy. Didn't care, to be honest. He looked like he was in a daze about something, but he reached into his pocket and pulled out a radio. I turned back to Eddie.

"Dispatch? Garibaldi. I want a paramedic to my twenty, sixty seconds ago, officer down. Any unit with a stretcher or a body board, to me, now. Repeat to all units."

The radio warbled a nasty two-tone howl that would cut through anything. "All units, all units. Priority, priority.

Officer down, officer down, rear of ..."

It wasn't easy, but I filtered it out. Tasha was feeling Eddie's spine and gently probing his ribs. "What does he have?" I asked.

"Two, maybe three broken ribs. Noting spinal, but the ribs could be distracting him."

"He kicked Eddie hard in the side, just above his hip," I said.

"So we have to add possible liver lac and ruptured spleen." She shook her head. "I don't dare move him or turn him, but he's not breathing well."

A new siren screamed its way closer. Tasha lowered her mouth to Eddie's ear, and I heard her murmur "Trust me."

She pulled off a glove and took a grip on Eddie's wrist. I felt her magic and saw her face scrunch in on herself, like something was too much. Her eyes opened, and they looked wild.

"Tasha. Tasha. Let go."

She ignored me, and I reached over to pull her hand away. She snatched it from me and raised it like she was going to smack me, but I held her eyes and she lowered the hand.

"You can't do this," I said. "I don't know why, but I can see it. Let me try."

I'd no idea how, but I had been able to help Freddie. Wouldn't this be the same? I grabbed Eddie's other wrist and opened myself. It was the same, and it wasn't. I gasped and fell forward, catching myself on my free hand. Damn, he was hurting *bad*.

Again, I found a way to separate myself from the sensations pouring into me, to bottle them up and hide them away in the Magni ring. This was flying by the seat of my pants and I probably could have done it better. I certainly wasn't doing as good a job as Tasha would have, but I could feel his heartbeat steady and his lungs breathe a little easier. I stuck to it until the paramedics arrived. Tasha held them off until she had briefed them, and only let them loose on him when she was sure they knew what they needed to do. Then she took my hand away from his wrist, she picked me up, and carried me over to the ambulance as well.

She set me down with my back against the wheel. I pulled my knees up and wrapped my arms around them while I shuddered, the echoes of Eddie's pain still flushing from my mind. Someone pulled a blanket around my shoulders, but I didn't know who.

I was just starting to get warm when I heard Tasha's voice, raised and angry, and realized I had more to do. Using the side of the paramedic's truck to help me up, I threw the blanket in the back and hurried to find her.

"Then I'll make an official complaint." She was nose to nose with the Captain.

"Don't," said Garibaldi "I can't stop you, Campbell, but he'll have ten witnesses, with photographs, proving he never attended the scene. He'll have other witnesses saying you were involved in the organization. If you're lucky you'll just come out of it looking stupid. You could come out of it with a record and a stretch in County"

"There have to be fifty cops here. You're here."

"They have wives, kids, girlfriends. So do I. We all want to stay alive and keep our jobs, Campbell."

"You're a gutless bastard, Garibaldi."

"I do what I have to do. We all do. You don't know this guy. His suit is Teflon, and he's connected. Do yourself a favor. Go home. Better still, think about leaving the city. You've made a dangerous enemy tonight."

Tasha drew breath and raised an accusing finger, but I stepped in between them. "The captain has a point. Eddie's on his way to the ER. Let's get out of here before anything else happens."

She raised her finger again, but I took hold of it and forced it down to her side, then pulled on her wrist until she followed me. I had my phone in my other hand and made a call to Jeff. By the time we were outside the police cordon, his pickup was driving up the road to meet us.

The New Queen

"**A**re you OK?"

Tasha felt Jane's hand on her arm, as she asked the very same question Tasha had been asking herself. And the answer was clearly that she was not. Looking back over the past three or four hours, Tasha had not been OK since she had almost killed the narcotics officer outside her apartment. She shuddered as she remembered how close she had come to taking his life, and that of the girl in scrubs. That ultimate act that would have taken her life too. Jane must have felt something, because she squeezed Tasha's hand tighter as the dreadful thought occurred to her. Tasha put her other hand over Jane's to let her know she had been heard.

But what was it that disgusting reprobate of a mentor had said to Tasha? When she told him she was an abstainer?

For now. You all lose in the end.

Was that her life now? Afraid to feed, because every time might be the time she lost control? She raged at the injustice of it all, the anger boiling up inside her, until she realized it wasn't directed at anything. It wasn't even rage. It was energy, dark and bubbling within her. She was overloaded and overloading.

She needed to burn the energy off, and away from anybody

she might hurt.

"Will you do me a favor, Jane?"

"Of course."

"Go keep an eye on Eddie? At the hospital? I don't trust Palmer not to go behind Garibaldi's back and arrange an accident."

"I'll keep him safe." A hundred questions sparkled behind Jane's eyes, and Tasha loved her all the more for not asking any of them.

"Jeff?" His eyes met hers in the rear-view mirror. "Change of plan. Mercy first, then the farm."

"The farm?"

"Please. And I need you to make a call."

"To?"

"The ladies of the pack. Anybody who fancies their chances at being your new alpha."

"Oh, crap. Now? Tonight? You ain't starting a fight, are you? I still ache all over and I don't want to—"

"No fight, Jeff. I promise. But it will be better than shooting pool."

He gave her a guilty look in the mirror and made the call.

Jane hugged Tasha when they got to the hospital, holding on as if she was reluctant to let go, and kissing Tasha's cheek before she dropped her arms. Tasha looked out the back window as they drove away. Jane looked small on the sidewalk, and her wave was forlorn. Tasha waved back but couldn't tell if Jane saw it. Perhaps, she thought, Jane saw something of the struggle going on inside her. She hoped not. The idea of putting that burden onto another disgusted her. But she couldn't help taking a little comfort from the possibility that someone else might understand.

She put her head back against the rest, closing her eyes, and hoping Jeff would take the hint.

The entire pack was there when they arrived, and four of the women stood apart from the rest. The girl who loaned Tasha her wolfstone was among the contenders, which didn't surprise her. She got out of the SUV and stood in front of the hopefuls, grateful for the presence of Jeff. He stood close but not in the way, supporting her without knowing what she was about to do. How had she managed to earn that level of trust? All she had done was use him and his people.

"It is not right that I am your alpha," Tasha began, feeling awkward, but heard a murmur of assent, and even approval. "But I'm not stepping aside."

Now you could have heard a pin drop.

"There will be no pool tournament to auction off my right." That got a muted chuckle and a few smiles. "But I will not tolerate any bloodshed."

She took off the wolfstone the girl had loaned her and returned it to its rightful owner.

"The new alpha will be the one who can catch me, in their wolf form, in a wild run."

She heard laughter again, but it died away when they realized she wasn't joking. "How much head start do you want?" somebody called, and it was her turn to smile.

"Absolutely none," she said, and set off. Behind her, the pack howled their challenge into the night as she hurdled the six-foot fence around the yard without a missed step. She wondered if she still held on to something from her time as a wolf, because the sound made her ears ring and her heart sing. The air was cool and silent, and a half moon threw down just enough light. Tasha leapt high into the air, screamed her own challenge into the night, and *ran*.

Safe and Sound

I really didn't want to get out of the pickup. Something was very wrong with Tasha, and it hurt a little that she couldn't tell me what it was. I had this nasty feeling she was going to do something rash, something dangerous. But Jeff was with her, and he had a level head. Still, I couldn't turn away until the pickup was out of sight.

I walked up to the desk in ER, said who I was, and asked to see Eddie. He wasn't there. It took some digging to find that he had already been through triage, scanned, and taken to a room. Either they were absurdly efficient here, or something was going on. I got his room number, then went up to the fifth floor.

I checked in with the nurses' station.

"He's in 527, but if you're not on the list, you won't get in."

"What list?"

"Well it ain't our list, hon. Straight along the hall, on the right."

Bemused, I ambled down the hall.

My heart sank. Outside Eddie's room were two stormtroopers, wearing grey camouflage pants and black combat tops. They weren't wearing masks, or helmets, but they were both armed and both standing up. In front of the door was a table, and on the table was a clipboard. They were already looking at me, and it made my skin crawl.

"Close enough, ma'am." One held up his hand when I was about ten feet way. The other, on the other side of the table, had his hand on his sidearm. "May I ask your name and the purpose of your visit here?"

Professional and courteous, which made me suspect they weren't part of Palmer's crew. I couldn't see a reason not to cooperate. Yet.

"My name is Jane Doe. I'm a friend, just checking up on him."

He picked up the clipboard and put a finger on the page, I assumed to run down the list to find me. Except his finger didn't move. His eyebrows did. He put the clipboard back on the table and snapped to attention. His colleague looked surprised for a second, then did the same.

"Thank you for your time, Miss Doe. Go right in."

I stepped closer, edged passed him, and moved into the room. But I turned in the doorway.

"Are you guys hospital security?"

"No ma'am."

"Police?"

"Definitely not, ma'am."

"And you aren't going to tell me, are you."

He didn't answer, but I got the faintest lift from the corner of his mouth. Then I got an idea. I reached under my top and pulled the Duke's Tongue out, letting it dangle in front of me.

"You boys know what this is?"

Eyes went wide as saucers and they strained into even more rigid attention, if that was even possible.

"Yes, ma'am," they both snapped. So the vampires were

313

looking after Eddie. I smelt Miller.

"Relax gentlemen. We are all on the same side. By chance, do either of you know *what* I am?"

Two hesitant nods.

"Then I want half an hour of peace and quiet with that door closed. I'm going to make your jobs easier and build some wards into that doorframe. Can't protect him if he's outside the room, but I can stop anybody who wants to hurt him from getting in."

"That's most helpful of you, ma'am. We'll make sure you're not disturbed."

I smiled and closed the door. Half an hour was way more than I needed to weave the wards, but I did need a good fifteen minutes of meditation to draw in enough strength. I still felt lightheaded, like I wasn't quite connected to everything, and it was interfering with my magic. First, though, I had to check on Eddie.

He had no tubes down his throat, which I supposed was a good thing, but they made up for it with tubes in his arms. From the bag of watery blood hanging below the side-rail, I guessed he had a tube between a couple of his ribs, too. The face mask had slipped up to his forehead, so I eased it back to where it should be. He shifted and moaned. I put my hand on his, just to let him know somebody was there, and his fingers closed around mine.

Well that was a little awkward. I mean, I didn't know the guy, and to be honest I didn't have a great opinion of him. But he saved my life, so I owed him. I hitched myself up onto the bed beside him. I had time.

The room felt huge and empty. Physically, it wasn't, but emotionally it was a deserted warehouse. The monitors were all silent, so the loudest sound in the room was us both breathing. Where were his family? Perhaps not a wife, but a girlfriend, or his mom? Or maybe there were more people like me in the world than I wanted to think. Solitary sounded good, kind of dramatic and noble, but it wasn't. It was lonely. I couldn't be the only orphaned soul out there. Eddie groaned again, and his fingers released mine. I took my hand away and pulled in a deep breath. I had work to do.

Which for the moment consisted of me sitting in the guest chair and relaxing. Trust me, it can be harder than it sounds, and being so far above the ground made it much slower to draw in the strength I needed. I set a fifteen minute timer on my phone, switched it to vibrate, and closed my eyes.

It worked, and better than I expected. The building reverberated with healing, and perhaps that was what I needed more than strength. At least I felt up to the work now. I eased up on the door so as not to startle it, and ran my hand around the frame, just so it could get to know me. Every doorway is a portal. Some, like ones into a home, take their job more seriously than others which have nothing to protect. I just needed to explain to this one that she had been promoted.

The Grumpy Old Man had made me study wards and protections from the day he had stepped in as my mentor. He made a good case for it; I had inherited a set of mighty potent protections around *my* home, and they had saved my life before I even knew they were there. I owed it to Tamsin, the witch who gave her life to find me, to understand them and nurture them, and I was getting pretty good at it now. This one was tricky, though. Lots of people needed to come in and out. I just needed to put up an intercession—one of the Grumpy Old Man's big words—that would make it next to impossible for anybody who harbored ill will toward Eddie to enter the room.

But I thought about that. I would never get the chance to come back and dismantle the ward. It seemed a shame to leave it there with nothing to do, so I tweaked it. Not only could it take a little energy from any person of good will who entered the room, but the ward would protect *any* patient brought in here. Well, I didn't want it to get bored and mischievous.

I picked up my coat and purse and opened the door. The two vampires outside snapped to attention. I explained what I had done, and they promised to pass it on to their reliefs. I turned to close the door and take a last look at Eddie. Again, he seemed to look very small in a very big room.

"On second thoughts, can you guys organize a coffee, and sandwich and a bear claw? I think I'll stay with him a little longer."

Back in the room, I put my coat and purse on the foot of the bed and slid the chair closer. He didn't know I was there, but I had nowhere else I needed to be. I could get a free meal on his health insurance and soak up some more of those healing vibes, and that was pretty much the only reason I was hanging around.

And don't you dare tell anyone anything different.

An Unexpected Invitation

The text from Miller was not welcome and I couldn't believe he had the balls to try to talk to me. I thought we had made our positions clear the night he ran out on us, in the Battle of Mulberry Drive. No, I was sure I had. My finger hovered over the delete button for a good fifteen seconds.

But I opened it. A ridiculous amount of money—and I'm talking six figures here—had already arrived in my account. Part of me wanted to send it back, but when I tried to find out how, my bank got all defensive, then finally admitted they weren't sure how. Something to do with a protected access offshore bank. So I shunted it into a new savings account and tried to forget about it. I opened the message to see if he had anything to say about it, and maybe demand they take it back.

Ms. Doe. There are a number of issues outstanding following the successful conclusion of your engagement with the Citadel. I am instructed to request your presence, and that of Ms. Campbell, at 6103 Douglas Av. The event is scheduled for 10:30am, Wednesday morning. Please arrive no later than 1000 and follow the instructions of the guide meeting you. The event will occur with or without your attendance, but the Citadel feels you may be interested to see it in person rather than on the news.

Miller

Cold, formal, unapologetic. So typically Miller. I let the idea rattle around in my head for a couple of hours, but still couldn't make up my mind what I should do. So I did what I usually did and called Tasha.

"I meant to call you. Eddie is being sent home Thursday."

"Well that's good." Except I had already heard something in Tasha's voice to suggest it wasn't.

"Perhaps. Not if his private army doesn't go with him. Did you hear how many people they turned away?"

Apart from that day I had sat with him for a while, I hadn't been to see Eddie, so I hadn't spoken to the guards. He wasn't really a friend, so the idea seemed awkward.

"They said eight people tried to get into his room," said Tasha. "Eight! And four of them would have made it if it hadn't been for your wards. I can't thank you enough for doing that."

Even though she couldn't see me do it, I shrugged. "I needed the practice."

"Good. Now I don't feel so bad asking if you could maybe do the same for his apartment? Before he gets cut loose."

"Of course. Did you get this crazy text from Miller?"

She hadn't and I sent it to her to save a lot of explaining. The phone went quiet longer than it took to read the message.

"Are you going?" Tasha's voice was neutral.

"Still trying to make my mind up."

"Over what? The creep used you as a bargaining chip and almost got you killed."

"Something about the way it's written. It's him, but it's like he's writing something he's been told to. What can you think of that's unfinished business?"

"Nothing." Tasha's reply was instant and absolute, but I

had doubts I couldn't shake.

"How about we go see what he wants, then go over to Eddie's place and I can set some wards up?"

"That's cheating."

"A little. Please? I don't want to go on my own, but I can't shake the feeling there's something important hanging in the air."

"Are you predicting the future now?"

"Gods forbid." I shuddered. "Can't think of anything I would want to do less." Then I waited, trying not to let the silence from the other end of the call get to me.

"Very well. But if he is just trying to ingratiate himself, we leave."

"Works for me."

6103 Douglas Avenue was in a manicured, affluent suburb to the north of the city. Realtors would brag about the freeway access and the fine schools. The house had a big drive out front and looked like it had four or five bedrooms. As we pulled up on the street, a figure appeared from the side of the house and waved us onto the drive. He looked like a typical agent, with a bug in his ear and a bulge under his jacket; the guy could have been CIA, NSA, or Mr. Smith. They all looked the same.

We got out of the car to a curt, "Follow me, please." He led us down the side of the property and across the lawn at the back. Someone had lifted a panel out of the fence across the bottom, and we stepped through into another plot on the next street over. Another agent waved us across an equally pampered expanse of grass and in through a kitchen door.

In the living room, Miller stood next to a mobile flatscreen at least 60-inches wide. He looked stiff, and his face showed nothing. On a coffee table in front of the TV were two envelopes and a box, about the size of a medium pizza but thicker. The agent who showed us in left without a word.

"Please, take a seat."

"You brought us here to watch TV?" Tasha didn't sound pleased, but I was more curious than annoyed. This was a lot of drama and organization. I hoped the punchline was worth it.

"I would prefer to have you watching directly through a window, but I have been firmly advised that it could adversely impact the operation."

"What operation?" I know; he left a hook dangling and I had just pulled on it.

His hands, which until now had been behind his back, came around front and in one he had a radio, which he lifted to his face.

"Unit commander from Emissary."

"Command aye."

"Now, commander."

He lowered the radio, but we could still hear it.

"All units, all units. Strike, strike, strike."

Miller pointed to the TV. "Across the street is the dwelling of one Gregory Palmer, lately commander of the city's Narcotics Strike Force. The Citadel considers this man to be a dangerous menace. Rather than working to remove the narcotics threat from the city, he has, in fact, been running a racket to protect it. The Citadel has brought details of a number of his activities to a range of authorities, who have chosen to act."

There were no sirens, but three blacked out SUVs pulled up in front of the house and vomited operatives onto the street. In seconds, they had made entry and vanished into the house.

More vans arrived and set up forensic tents across the front of the garage as they unloaded cabinets of equipment to take inside.

"That's DEA," said Tasha, peering at the screen.

"Indeed. Mister Palmer will be found guilty of possession of raw materials, paraphernalia to manufacture, and finished product. There will be images on his laptop, or equivalent, to further incriminate him. Four other members of his team, deemed unacceptably dangerous, will also go to prison, and the rest of his unit will almost certainly be dishonorably dismissed."

"You're framing him?" How was I supposed to feel about that? The idea was outrageous, but it had a certain justice to it. And I had been wondering how long it would be before Palmer and his charming boys decided to pay one of us a visit. This solved that problem, too.

"Not at all. We are bringing forward evidence of activities he and his team have been involved in or have chosen not to impede."

"Did anybody just—?" I was sure I had heard something, like a door closing a little too hard. Tasha and Miller were arguing too hard to hear me.

"You can't do that." Tasha repeated.

"Ms. Campbell, I am doing nothing. The Citadel has conversed with a number of authorities in the government and is assisting them with existing and new cases. I have no personal involvement in any of this. In fact, I have been warned that my remit is to speak the words of the Citadel, but that I am not to take any initiatives myself while I, also, am subject to a review."

That caught my attention. Somebody was less than pleased

with him, and the only person that could reprimand him was the duke himself. Andrea could possibly tell him off, but only at a personal level. Miller had pissed off Ladislav and now he was paying for it. Interesting.

But not as interesting as the radio.

"Strike leader to Emissary. Urgent."

"Emissary."

"Target not acquired. Repeat, not acquired."

"Then where the hell is he?"

There was a loud *phut* and the radio, still held to Miller's face, exploded into shards.

An Uninvited Guest

"Anybody moves, everybody gets a bullet in the head. Ah, who am I kidding. You're all dead anyway."

Miller had fallen to his knees. His hands and the side of his face were so messed up with blood I couldn't see how bad his wounds were, but he slumped back against the wall and his hand dragged the cable for the TV out of its socket. The screen went blank.

"How?" Miller groaned. I thought he was dead.

"How? You're about to die and you want to know how?" Palmer chuckled. "Control freak to the end."

It sounded like he had relaxed, almost as though he had perched on the arm of a chair to chat, but when I saw his refection in the now black screen of the TV, he was holding a gun in a rock-steady two-handed grip that could turn on any one of us in a split instant. Had Miller pulled the power on purpose, as he had gone down? To give us a view of our attacker? I was still mad at him, so I decided it was a lucky accident.

"Your team was sloppy. Poor reconnaissance. Letting me see the idiots who live here shuffling out of their house at six in the morning with the kids and overnight bags. Excited faces, not sad, so no sudden family situation. Midweek. Work day. School day. I was out the back door and circled around before the surveillance crew arrived. I've been hiding in the garage here, waiting for whatever it was to go down. And here we all are. Apart from the dumb-ass detective. Which isn't a problem. I hear he's coming out of the hospital tomorrow. Or maybe I'll wait and take him while he's grieving at your funerals."

A decision rang in his voice, and in the dark mirror of the flatscreen his eyes locked onto Tasha. I took a breath of air, hardened it onto a brick, and smashed it against his wrist. The gun went *phut*, louder this time, as it swung right and down, and a puff of plaster erupted from the wall.

Tasha flipped the couch. I got no warning at all and squealed as I rolled untidily over the back. My arms and legs got tangled up, and I couldn't do a thing as Palmer turned his gun towards me. Tasha was still rolling backwards, more elegantly than me and very in control. She kept her body straight and her legs long, and kicked at Palmer as she rolled up onto her hands. She missed his head, but her other leg smashed down onto his arm. The bullet chewed a hole in the carpet a foot in front of my head. This guy was dangerous. It wasn't enough we stop him from killing us, we couldn't let him get away either.

He had pushed Tasha away before she could knock him to the floor, and now his gun was swinging to line up with her. That was my limit. I'd had enough of this jackass hurting people I cared about or worked with. I thickened a handful of air into the size and weight of a baseball and pitched it at him. His head snapped back as it whacked him right between the eyes. Then I whistled up a battering ram and threw it at his chest. It drove into him like a flying kick and slammed him against a wall.

What I wanted to do was burn him alive, but that might raise to many questions. I had to stay with wind. But he was tough. Though I'd thrown him into the wall hard enough to crack the sheetrock with the back of his head, he kept his feet. His eyes were blurry, and he didn't seem able to focus on us, but he was bringing up that damned gun again.

Tasha got to him first, grabbing his gun hand and twisting him around over her outstretched leg. He fell like a log but kept fighting her for the gun. It went off again, just missing her and making a hole in the ceiling. We had to put this guy down.

So I jumped on him. He almost bucked me off, but I didn't need much of a grip. Somehow, I got my hand to his neck and, at the last minute, remembered I shouldn't kill him. Without thinking about it, or planning it, I dumped the contents of the Magni ring into him. He screamed, then screamed again as the pain he had inflicted on Eddie flooded through his neck and into his head. It twisted around his jaw and across his teeth, then boiled up through his eyes. His body twitched and spasmed like he was on the nasty end of a taser, but I didn't stop until I'd give him everything he'd inflicted on Eddie. By the time the Magni was empty, Palmer's eyes were rolled back in his head and he was out for the count.

I *got* the bastard.

But that didn't seem enough for Tasha. She rolled to her knees and ripped his gun from his fingers. Shoving me aside, she jammed it up under his jaw. I didn't argue, though I knew Eddie's pain was still washing around Palmer's body and would keep him out for a while. Tasha had a wild look, muscles twitching along her jaw and eyes bugged wide open—something I didn't want to get involved with, at least not yet.

Using the back of the chair to clamber to my feet, I stumbled over to the front door. After I opened it I called, "Hey," a couple of times, but nobody from the other side of the street paid any notice. I put my fingers to my lips, twisted in a little magic, and let out a shriek so loud they all covered their ears.

"You geniuses might have missed something over here. Bring guns. And a medic."

They all froze in a moment of confusion, then someone with a brain took over and they went all SWAT, a bunch of guys coming out of nowhere with assault rifles, body armor and helmets. They saw Tasha on the floor with Palmer and gathered around them, rifles raised.

"We'll take it from here, ma'am." But Tasha ignored them. I could see her arm was as steady as a rock, but her finger was trembling on the trigger. Only I could have noticed it. She wasn't having a problem holding the gun, she was having to focus everything she had to stop herself firing it.

"Stand down, lady."

A hand reached out to pull her away by the shoulder. I stepped forward and slapped it away. "Pull on her shoulder and she'll not only kill him, but two of you before you can put her down."

I knelt in front of her, next to Palmer's head.

"Tasha? You have to stop now. Help is here. Tasha?"

Something had happened to my friend, and I had no idea what. She hadn't been acting like herself for days. It was like she was fighting something she couldn't tell me about. I raised my hand, palm open towards her, and put it into her line of sight—not so far in that it would block her view of Palmer or the muzzle she held under his jaw, but enough that she couldn't ignore it. Her finger lifted off the trigger, then moved out to rest along the top of the trigger guard. I breathed out and put my hand around the barrel, twisting the gun until she let me take it from her.

After I waved the damned piece around for what felt like a half hour, somebody finally took it from me and I could help Tasha to her feet. I guided her to a chair that hadn't been shot up or overturned and made her sit. By the time I turned back, Palmer had been cuffed and hauled to his feet, and was being marched out of the house. I figured a thank you might have been in order, seeing as how we had not only managed to not get ourselves killed, but had managed to catch the very person they were trying to arrest. Seemed they didn't consider us worth their time. Perhaps they were embarrassed by how badly they had messed up. Besides, the medics were pushing their way in now, and I didn't want to get under their feet.

Miller let them fuss over him for a while, which told me he was either hurt or rattled. Once they wiped some of the blood from his face, it was obvious most of the damage was to his hand. They bullied him onto a gurney, but he insisted on sitting up, and he wouldn't let them leave until he had called me over.

"Miss Doe. Once again it seems I have put you in harm's way. My apologies. I fear my already tattered reputation with my employer will be taking another knock."

The mention of his employer reminded me of something. I still had the Duke's Tongue, and since I had no intention of having anything else to do with this man, I should give it back. As soon as he realized what I was doing, Miller held up his hastily bandaged hand.

"That was one of the things I had instructions to discuss

today. My employer has expressed a wish that you retain the token, and the authority. His exact words were 'I need someone out there who is not a cretin.' If you still wish to return the token, please discuss it with the Lady Andrea."

"We need to go, sir," said a paramedic. Miller raised his hand to brush them away and winced.

"One last thing. Take the box and the envelopes with you when you leave. They are tokens my employer believes will be of interest to you, but I would suggest that neither of you open them alone."

He settled back on the gurney and they wheeled him out, while I looked at what he left on the table like it was a rattlesnake.

Last Supper

I made Tasha give me her car keys and I drove us back to my house. The ride was eerie; silent and uncomfortable. Tasha stared out of the windshield the entire trip, not moving or looking from side to side. I had to touch her arm to get her attention once I'd pulled up. She jolted like I had sparked her with static, then looked around like it surprised her we had arrived.

"You have to come in," I said. "I'm not letting you drive while you're like this."

She looked like she was giving some thought to arguing, then nodded and reached for the door. She could have objected all she liked, but I was not handing the keys over until I was sure she was safe to drive. I got out, opened the rear door to fetch the box and the envelopes, then blipped the key to lock the car. As I tuned to go into the house, I caught a flash of movement above me. Another damned curtain twitch. I swear, if I hadn't had more important things to do, Amanda would have been getting her final notice to quit.

But I did have more important things on my mind, so I hurried to catch up with Tasha and unlock the door for her. I steered her to the kitchen, dropped the stuff Miller had left us on the table, and turned away to make coffee. I changed my mind. The situation called for something stronger.

"Are you going to tell me what's messing with you?"

There was a long silence, and when I turned to look, Tasha was gazing out of the kitchen window. I left her to it until the chocolate was ready, then broke her focus by putting a mug in front of her.

I tried again. "Want to share?"

She looked hard at me for a moment, like she was weighing me, and I almost resented it. What could she need from me she wasn't sure I could give?

"Not really, but I think I have to. Partly, anyway."

"Tell me."

"I did something stupid. Remember I told you I could never take a life by feeding, or I would finish turning?"

I nodded, suddenly terrified.

"I got too close. Way too close. It's like I took an overdose. I'm doing things I shouldn't. I'm being tempted."

Crap. What was I supposed to say to that? "How can I help?"

"Time?" She shrugged. "Space? I'm not sure. There are some people I need to find, people who can help me. Hopefully."

"Let me come with you."

She didn't answer and wouldn't look at me. She tapped the box on the table as distraction. "We should open these."

I tried to look into her eyes, but she wouldn't take them from the box, so I slid it across toward me and opened it. And frowned. Why did Miller think I wanted the blood the hyenas had stolen from me? Tasha seemed to think it was a big thing.

"Thank goodness. Is it all here? How will you destroy so much?"

"What?"

330

Now she did look at me, confused, surprised. "It's your blood."

"I know that."

"So is it all there?"

I wasn't sure. I remembered Tracy drawing off three bags, but I didn't know how many small vials she had taken. Then I remembered another bag, a small one. The vamp they had offered my blood to, who had seen Miller but not been seen by him. He had asked for a sample.

"No. I don't think so."

Tasha looked deeply concerned and, though I had no idea why, I started to feel worried too. "I thought you magic folk were paranoid about blood and hair and stuff getting into the wrong hands. That's why I took everything from Doc and burned it."

"Do you know why?"

Tasha shook her head. "I think you need a conversation with that disgusting gnome who teaches you."

I agreed, but I didn't say anything. Tasha seemed to have enough on her plate without worrying about me. "I'll speak to him soon," I promised, and pushed the envelope with her name on towards her. "Your turn."

Tasha slid a finger under the flap and opened the envelope. Inside was a single folded sheet of white paper, and I could make out a single line of type in the middle of the page.

"This I cannot deal with right now." She tossed the paper onto the table and wouldn't look at it. I reached toward it but waited until I saw the barest nod of her head before I picked it up. My hand shook, and I had to read it a second time.

"The person responsible for your kidnap and torture after your rebirth was not working under the auspices of the Citadel,

331

but of agencies unknown. His name is Victor Corvax."

My mind was screaming at me so loud I couldn't make sense of either voice. Corvax had tried to use Tasha as well as me? And what did they mean *is*? I killed him.

Didn't I?

"This is huge, Tasha."

"I said I can't deal with it. Not now. I can't deal with anything but finding the help I need, and I don't want you to get involved. You need to keep yourself safe. You have to do that for me, and you have to look after the business while I'm gone."

"You mean you're going *away* away? How long for?"

"As long as it takes. Will you do that for me?"

"I'd rather help."

"And this will. I need to know you'll be safe."

I didn't want to agree, but it was what she needed, and that was more important. How safe I was going to be able to keep myself might not be something I had a lot of control over, but I could try. I got a smile, a grateful one, and missed her already. She slid the other envelope towards me.

"Your turn."

I tore the flap open and reached inside. My paper wasn't pristine photocopier like hers. It was battered and folded a hundred times, and smelled musty. I unfolded it, turned it right side up and froze. I couldn't breathe, or move, or even blink. Tasha reached over the table, turned the paper to face her, then looked up at me with wide eyes after she read the top line.

"Adoption papers? Whose?"

Good question. Almost all the information had been struck through, redacted with thick black lines. It left me wondering if somebody thought they were helping me or were taunting me.

Tasha glanced at me, but looked away, and I could see the conflict in her face. I spoke the hardest words to ever pass my lips.

"Go. I've got this. Both of them, even."

Her eyes came back to mine, uncertain, still full of guilt. "Are you sure?"

I nodded. "Whatever this is, it's past. Whatever you need to do, you need to do it now, and that makes it more important. I got your back. Just make sure you come home."

Who am I again?

J immy's was quieter than I had ever seen it, but I was rarely there on a weekday. It was still better than half full. A troll on stage was doing a passable Adele sound-alike. Really didn't help me that he mostly sang angsty heart-rippers off the '19' album.

A jack-on-the-rocks sat on the table to my right, an empty espresso of Jimmy's special blend to my left, and that damned adoption document directly in front of me. A week had passed since Tasha left, and I had no purpose. The only thing I could do at the office was tell people I couldn't help them, so I put a sign in the door and closed up that morning. How long for I couldn't guess. I couldn't settle at home either, so I took my motorcycle down to the Dark and we roared recklessly around for a couple of hours.

I was stupid, taking absurd risks and almost losing her twice going too fast into corners. After the second, I admitted I was out of control and went to the only place I thought I might get help. Jimmy wasn't there, but it felt better just being in the place.

I'd been there an hour, and was on my second round, when I heard Jimmy bellowing out back, ordering people out of his way with an urgency I'd never heard him use before. The

334

door to the kitchen slammed open just as I turned to look at it. Jimmy burst forth, worried face and eyes searching back and forth across the room. I twitched when he saw me, and I realized I was what he was looking for. The chair beside me creaked as he dropped into it.

"I got here as soon as I could."

Confusing. "I didn't—"

"The wards felt you come in. They summoned me. I think they like you."

Somehow, that made me feel gushy and a little tearful. But then, I did say hello and goodbye to them each time I visited.

"I'm fine," I lied, and Jimmy gave me a face that said he knew I wasn't.

"How can you be, with Tasha leaving?"

It hadn't helped, and I missed her like crazy, but that wasn't it. Hadn't planned on sharing the details, but my head shook 'no'.

"Then what?"

I used my eyes to point at the paper on the table. Jimmy looked but didn't touch. "Yours?"

"I've no idea. I think the Citadel sent it, like some kind of bonus. Tasha got something too."

Jimmy was still studying it. "Not very helpful."

"No," I agreed.

"Have you tried anything?"

"Thaumaturgy isn't my strong point. I'm better at blowing things up. I tried Winston's *Revelations*, but all I heard was someone laughing in my head."

He pulled a sour face. "I don't trust contemporary wizards. Did you try La Sirvienta's *Desenmascarar*?"

My eyes opened wide. "Way beyond my grade. Peterson told

335

me to stay clear of the Galician Magi." And how did Jimmy know about Magi most people had never heard of?

He grunted but didn't elaborate. "What is the worst that could happen if you try it? You remember it?"

I did, but I didn't have an answer to what could go wrong if I screwed it up. Setting the paper on fire, maybe? And what was with all the advice from Jimmy? But what the hell. If I did destroy it, at least it wouldn't be on my mind anymore. I opened my hands and held them over the paper, then constructed a virtual circle. All thamaturgic magic needs a circle to contain and control it, but the spells don't actually need to be written down on anything. I simply imagined it—easy after the Grumpy Old Man made me practice for two hours a day, every day, for a month.

Anyway, in the circle I built the pentagram, and into three of the points of the pentagram I dropped the sigils that went with the spell—like over-complicated runes. Then all I had to do was feed power into the circle and speak the invocation.

As I drew breath to speak, the energy wobbled, a sigil cracked, and the whole thing unwove like dried noodles in water. I cussed.

"Try again." Jimmy changed chairs so he was sitting opposite me. I wanted to beg off, but I didn't want to disappoint Jimmy. I drew it all again, the circle, the pentacle, and the sigils. Then, just as I let my energy flow into the construct, I felt Jimmy's hands touch the back of mine.

I've no idea what it was, but something else flowed down into my virtual working. It felt old, and like nothing I'd ever touched in this world, but when it hit the circle it became visible, glowing like silver thread on the table.

I almost lost my focus, but whatever Jimmy was doing held

the circle firm until I could get my concentration back. Then I whispered the invocation.

"*Desenmascarar lo que está oculto.*"

The paper fought back, or something on it did. It wasn't just thick lines of black ink. Something arcane on the page resisted me too. But I didn't go into combat mode. That was always my first response to any situation. Fight back. More power, hotter flame. Overwhelm resistance with greater force.

But I didn't. Today, in this moment, I simply held firm. The spell was every part it needed to be. This was a battle of wills, mine against whoever didn't want this information revealed.

Time was meaningless, but it felt like I had been holding the *Desenmascarar* for hours. I was getting tired, but my focus was still rock solid. So I was crushed when the damned thing unraveled itself in front of me, disappearing into fairy dust that evaporated up from the table.

I was too tired to be angry. I let my hands drop to the table and muttered, "Aw, shit," when I saw the bold lines of redaction were still all over the page.

"Hold it up."

"Huh?" Was as much as I could manage at that moment.

"Hold it up to a light."

It's difficult to say no to Jimmy, and he had been trying to help, so I humored him. The light over our head made my back ache as I tried to lift the paper, so I lined up on one of the wall lights.

"What am I looking for, Jimmy?"

"Give it a moment."

My arm was aching, but I shifted the paper to my other hand and stared at it again. The paper didn't change, but what I could see did. The black lines didn't disappear, but I could read what was beneath them. Some of it was still impenetrable, but some I could make out.

A date of birth that matched what I now knew was mine. The names of the birth parents were missing, blank, but someone had written a name and address in the space marked 'Person(s) offering child named below for adoption:'

And below that was 'Child's Name(s): Pauline'.

I looked at Jimmy. His face was full of compassion, like he had known all along, but he had his finger held to his lips. I didn't know if I was to keep silent about the paper, or about him doing magic with me. I looked around and nobody was taking any interest in what we were doing. Knowing the crowd in here, that seemed unlikely. Jimmy reached across the table and cupped my cheek in his hand for a moment.

"Better?"

I thought about it. Now I knew a secret about Jimmy, and I knew who's the adoption papers were. All I had to do was find the person who put me up for adoption, assuming they were still alive. I had a question or two I needed to ask, and first of those would be 'Why?'.

I nodded to Jimmy. "Better."

I've always hated lying to my friends.

oOo

Hi.

Jane here. Again.

So you stuck it through two books. Good for you. Maybe there's something to what Marr says and people really do want to hear about my daily disasters. So, could you leave a review? You can go to bit.ly/Bloodfire. Help a girl out and get the author off my back. Robin keeps going on about how important these are.

If you thought this one was interesting, wait till you read the next one: Demon's Promise. Check out the author's web site for info – robinmarr.com . You can sign up to the mailing list too, and get all the gossip automatically.

And there goes the phone again. Telling all these callers we're closed is breaking my heart. Where *is* Tasha?

Jane xx

Printed in Great Britain
by Amazon

62943841R00206